WHITHER, UTOPIA'

WHITHER, UTOPIA

ERIK DECKERS

4 Horsemen
Publications, Inc.

4 Horsemen
Publications, Inc.

Published By: 4 Horsemen Publications, Inc.

4 Horsemen Publications, Inc.
PO Box 417
Sylva, NC 28779
4horsemenpublications.com
info@4horsemenpublications.com

Cover & Typesetting by Autumn Skye
Edited by Jen Paquette

Library of Congress Control Number: 2024952054

Paperback ISBN-13: 979-8-8232-0783-6
Hardcover ISBN-13: 979-8-8232-0784-3
Audiobook ISBN-13: 979-8-8232-0786-7
Ebook ISBN-13: 979-8-8232-0785-0

DEDICATION

For Toni. I couldn't do this without you.
For Maddie, Emma, and Ben. I love you all.
For Declan. I hope you read this someday.

CONTENTS

Introduction ix

Chapter 1 1
Chapter 2 18
Chapter 3 28
Chapter 4 42
Chapter 5 54
Chapter 6 73
Chapter 7 84
Chapter 8 89
Chapter 9 102
Chapter 10 112
Chapter 11. 125
Chapter 12 138
Chapter 13 152
Chapter 14 162
Chapter 15 169
Chapter 16 182
Chapter 17 197
Chapter 18 221
Chapter 19 233

Chapter 20 246
Chapter 21 259

Book Club Questions 265
Author Bio 267

INTRODUCTION

THE CONSERVATIVES WERE DEAD. LITERALLY.
Well, most of them, anyway.

The conservatives were dead, and the liberals were not exactly happy about it because they were liberals, and one does not cheer the death of another. But they weren't unhappy about it either.

Half the world died in the summer of 2038 after a deadly virus burned around the world, striking most of them down. The nationalists in every country were gone. The separatists, the extremists, the fundamentalists. All gone. They had spent a few glorious months scoffing and deriding the liberals and leftists and ignored the scientists who were sounding the alarm, accusing them of "fake news" and being woke liberal elites.

So they were more than a little surprised when they died off.

The disease originally started in Tasmania after a pharmaceutical research administrator, Richard Schiffler, was bitten by an infected Tasmanian Devil and was unknowingly infected. The disease, called the Dunor Virus, spread when he flew from Tasmania to Australia, then to a five-day layover in Los Angeles, and finally on to New York City, where he dropped dead three days later from what his employer's PR department called a "low-grade flu."

Schiffler had attended three Republican fundraisers in LA and New York, where he had infected several different state and local Republican leaders, many of whom were also leaders in their churches, fraternal organizations, and business communities.

Faint memories of the COVID-19 pandemic eighteen years earlier bubbled up in the people who were old enough to remember as public health experts began to sound the alarm. The experts were shouted down with cries of "Okay, Zoomer" and "Elites!" by the general populace, who were suspicious of anyone who sounded smarter than them.

The media ran stories featuring doctors and nurses who had lived through the original pandemic. They told tear-jerking stories about what had happened to family, friends, and colleagues, and the media ate it up.

No one cared.

Instead, the Republican president followed the playbook of a former president (and his father), whom historians agreed was the worst US president in history. The president first claimed there were only a few cases, and it wasn't a big deal. Then he blamed Tasmania. Then he blamed his Democratic predecessor. And then he fired his entire pandemic response team, all on the day Richard Schiffler died.

Next, he fired the head of the CDC, who had been a young doctor in 2020, and replaced him with an insurance company CEO who had helped write their latest Medicare bill. That bill helped insurance companies get reimbursed double the amount of every Dunor claim it was forced to pay.

Then, proclaiming they had beaten the virus, the President, who was the dumbest of his five siblings, held a series of Mission Accomplished rallies around the country where he would shout to his thousands of supporters, "It's a Democratic hoax!" He boasted that he knew more about this virus than all the scientists. His supporters sprayed angry spittle as they gave full-throated, open-mouthed support to the man who told them what they wanted to hear.

"Fake news! Fake news!" they chanted, just as their parents and grandparents had done three decades earlier. The President pursed his worm-like lips and crossed his arms in homage to his hero, Benito Mussolini.

"Lock her up! Lock her up!" they chanted, waving their middle fingers at the news drones hovering overhead. No one really knew who "she" was or what "she" had done, but it was now something they chanted at every rally unless one of the president's female aides or appointees was in legal trouble that week.

"These so-called scientists want us to practice," the President made air quotes "'social distancing,' which is just their way of saying they can't get a date." The crowds roared, even though he told this joke at every rally, sometimes twice.

In order to "own the libs," many supporters started the practice of whale spouting, which involved taking large gulps of water, drawn from nearby rivers, and spraying a vertical spit take.

It was their way of giving the finger to the world's scientists and liberal elites and showing their contempt for their hoax virus.

"Own the libs! Own the libs!" they chanted after yet another impromptu whale spouting by several hundred rally attendees.

Many of the attendees went to work the next day, ignoring the CDC's pleas to stay at home.

The liberals did as they were asked, and the conservatives did not, which summed up the world's response to the new pandemic.

"We have to support our economy, even if a few people die," said the workers, who refused to wear masks or keep their distance.

"Would you rather go through a few days of discomfort or a few months of a recession?" said the conservative TV pundits. "We can't let the libs drive this country into the toilet just because they hate America."

Many conservative churches continued to meet, saying no one could infringe on their right to assemble, and that Jesus was more powerful than some tiny virus no one could actually see. The atheists responded that Jesus must not be real since none of them had ever seen him either.

The churchgoers gathered each Sunday, shook hands, embraced, stood closely to speak, and packed together as tightly as they could to sing to the Lord. They gathered to pray for strength for the country's leaders, as well as "Brother Jacob's mother who has come down with a minor cold. Also, Brother Jacob's wife. And also Brother Jacob, now deceased."

Many people refused to wash their hands because scientists had said they should. They posted "pee, then eat" challenge videos where they, well, peed, and then ate various finger foods.

Many restaurants had shut down but offered carry-out and delivery business. Many others refused to shut down or let their servers wear masks. A mobile app developer became an overnight billionaire when he created the Eat Red, Eat Blue app. It showed users which restaurants were completely open for business and banned masks (Red) and which ones required employees to wash their hands and wear gloves and masks, and only served takeout or delivery (Blue).

Liberals, of course, avoided the Red restaurants while conservatives refused to eat at Blue restaurants. Most of the Blue restaurants began to falter and fail after just a few weeks of limited income while the Red restaurants thrived and grew rich, at least until the waitstaff began to die, along with their families and patrons.

The survivalists and doomsday preppers didn't fare well either, which is a shame, since this is what they had been preparing for their whole lives. Their survival food kits had all been contaminated by workers who had previously attended the president's rallies and been whale spouted several times.

When it was over, the right half of the political spectrum had died off in four months.

Conservative media outlets shut down, not only because of a lack of viewers but because the on-air talent and the crew had died.

The pandemic ended almost as quickly as it began with only a few conservatives surviving: the Senators, Congressmen, the President, and their staffers who, despite urging their constituents to ignore scientists, had taken every precaution they could, including experimental vaccines.

With half the voters dead and the economy in shambles, Election Day was termed by some pundits as "the worst slaughter since Custer's Last Stand."

The President, who had spent months claiming the virus was a hoax, was not only voted out of office (107 million to 12,376), he was banished from the country and spent his remaining years living in a compound in the New Republic of Texas.

The liberals had finally won and achieved everything they had ever dreamed of. No more racism, no more sexism, no more homophobia. They could cut military spending, increase educational spending, and devote more time and money to the arts.

They had achieved the utopia they had wished for.

Except they fucked it all up.

CHAPTER 1

"**N**O CHANGE, NO PEACE! NO CHANGE, NO PEACE!"
The protest chants had been going on for nearly three hours, and Sara Cooper's head felt like someone was hammering a nail between her eyes. She was also sure some of the students were chanting "Know change, know peace" just to be assholes.

"Alright, alright!" she shouted, but no one heard her over the chanting.

"No change, no—OWW!" howled the crowd of protestors.

Sara released the siren button on her bullhorn and smiled at the sudden silence. *Now* that *is real power*, she thought. She gazed out over the group of students seated around the lobby of the W. S. McIntosh administration building on the campus of Appleseed College. Her brown eyes watered as she was buffeted by the smells of the three P's of college life —pizza, pot, patchouli—not to mention the ripe B.O. of sixty-seven students who hadn't showered for two days. She had been with them since 8:00 a.m. the day before—Friday—and was mostly used to it, but she got blasted with a fresh burst whenever someone opened the entrance doors.

Sara was tall and slender with light brown skin, black hair that hung to her shoulders, and shiny brown eyes. She often wore it tied in a ponytail, like today, and was generally a happy, pleasant person who loved student activism and social justice.

The students, who were a mix of races, ages, genders, nationalities, and sexual orientations, were seated on the floor inside taped-off areas that created a walking path for foot traffic. Administrators and students walked respectfully through the gathered throng as if they were used to this sort of thing.

Appleseed College Of The Arts was located in Appleseed, Ohio (population: 67,850), the county seat of Chapman County, about ninety minutes north of Cincinnati, Ohio. The school's mascot was the Fighting Summer Tanagers, a change that had been made from the previous mascot twenty-five years earlier. It happened because students felt the team name, the Lumberjacks, was inherently sexist and exploited people who performed manual labor for their living.

Students and alumni rallied and protested, both for and against the name change, and nearly every student on campus felt they had a dog in the fight.

Most students wanted to change the name to something artistic like Potters, Metalsmiths, or Writers, but this upset the performing artists, and they insisted they be represented as well. This united the two opposing groups who all agreed that the Appleseed Fighting Modern Dancers sounded idiotic.

As a compromise, they selected the Fighting Summer Tanagers before defending against another complaint that the "fighting" part glorified violence. That group was told to shut the fuck up, and everyone else agreed that Fighting Summer Tanagers was as good as it was going to get.

Not that it mattered since the school only had a collegiate co-ed Ultimate Frisbee team, plus a soccer team and skateboarding team. Still, the name change launched a long-standing tradition of protest, social activism, and advocacy at the school until it became part of the curriculum at the school.

"Okay, I think we've made our point with the chanting," said Sara. "What's next?"

Kyle consulted his tablet. "Next we're supposed to break off into discussion groups and come up with a mission statement."

"Oh, fuck," said Sara. "Can we just do more chanting?"

"No, Professor Barker was very clear. Chant for at least two hours—we've done three—followed by the mission statement." Kyle Shehadi was a serious-looking young man, dark-complected, tall, and lanky with unruly black hair he was constantly raking out of his eyes, only for it to fall back again. He looked like he might be the captain of the Appleseed co-ed Ultimate Frisbee team, which he was.

"Finally," he continued, "we need an in-depth discussion about why we want to bring about the proposed change."

"To change the name of our residence hall!" shouted someone from the back.

"No shit, Sherlock," someone else called. "But why?"

"Because the namesake was a bad man," someone else offered.

"We have to be more specific, Griffin," said Kyle.

"Because President William McKinley was specifically a bad man," said Griffin MacKenna, a pale young man with long red hair tied back into a bun.

"Well, yeah, but I think he meant—"

"Because when William McKinley was President of the United States, he annexed Hawaii in 1898 and led us into the Spanish-American War," said Callie Wong, another classmate. She frequently gave answers in class without waiting to be called on; Sara disliked her intensely. "We believe he should be condemned for those two acts and that the school should change the name of the residence and dining hall to Natalie Clifford Barney Hall, an Ohio playwright and early LGBTQQIP2SA activist from the 20th century."

"Right, Callie, but for now we need to focus on writing a mission statement," said Sara.

"Oh, I already wrote that up while we were chanting," said Callie. She tapped her personal display terminal twice and said, "Beam Mission Statement eight-five-three to Sara Cooper-Wright." There was a quiet blip that only Sara and Callie could hear, and a dialog box appeared in Sara's field of vision.

The personal display terminal, or PDT, looked like a regular pair of glasses but with a processing unit that had more power than the biggest mobile phones of thirty years ago. The user could read the internet, emails, text messages, and even make voice calls. Video calls were pointless with a PDT, however, since all the callers could see were the other person's eye.

"Accept," said Sara. She nodded her head sharply once, twice as she scrolled Callie's mission statement on her own PDT.

"Okay, this is a good starting point, but we're really supposed to do this as a group," said Sara. "Professor Barker wants us to work together to come up with our mission statement, our rationale, and a list of demands."

"Hard pass. We can't even agree on a lunch order," retorted Callie.

"No chicken, no pizza!" someone chanted, and the rest of the crowd joined in. "No chicken, no pizza! No chicken, no pizza! No—OWW!"

Sara released the siren button. "How about this? Let's break up into six collaborative facilitation clusters. Each cluster will come up with a mission statement, and then we'll vote on the one we like best."

"How many people to a group?" asked Griffin.

"Ah-ah. Collaborative facilitation cluster," corrected Sara. "We should have no more than ten."

"Anyone who wants to work in my CFC, come over here!" shouted Callie, shooting her hand up. The overeager type-A students had already been sitting close to Callie, their spiritual leader, and quickly snapped to her side like someone had flicked on an electromagnet.

As the remaining students slowly shambled their way into loose CFCs, a man and woman appeared behind Sara.

The woman cleared her throat. "Excuse me, Sara," she said.

Sara turned around, startled. "Professor Sartoris, Professor Welch, what are you doing here?"

Katie Sartoris, Ph.D. in Educational Psychology, was the faculty advisor to Sara's protest group, as dictated by Section 22 of the Student Handbook: "In order for protests to count for class credit, all student protest groups must have at least one (1) faculty advisor, preferably two (2). Professors teaching SocJust 319 may not serve as faculty advisors."

Dr. Sartoris ("Katie, please. We're all adults, and I don't believe in superior-superordinate labels") had agreed to Sara's request when Sara first enrolled in George Barker's Principles of Organizing Grassroots Communication course.

Katie's paramour, Dr. Bert Welch ("Dr. Welch, if you don't mind. I spent six years earning my Ph.D.") was the other faculty advisor, at Katie's request. The two had been semi-romantically connected for six years because Bert "didn't want to put a label on anything."

"We just wanted to check in and see how the protest was progressing," said Katie. "We were listening on the campus radio station, and you seemed to be getting plenty of coverage. What's your KNCLD score?"

KNCLD was the social media app that calculated a person's social acceptability score and determined whether they should be canceled—"KNCLD"— by the online community at large.

The higher your score, the more acceptable you were. Post an uplifting story or photo, and the KNCLD algorithm would not only calculate your score based on the engagement by your peers, it would also factor in their own KNCLD scores to determine how valuable their attention was. If someone with a high KNCLD score amplified your post, it carried a lot more weight than if ten people with a low score did the same.

But if you posted something the algorithm deemed inappropriate or potentially hurtful to another group, your score could take a hit. Any score above 50 was very good, and anything above 80 was damn near sainthood. Anything below 20, and you had to take a government-mandated inclusivity seminar, which meant watching twenty hours' worth of videos. If you didn't attend the "completely voluntary" course, you could lose your job, access to banks and credit cards, and even be denied the ability to take out a loan or rent a home. It was the modern version of "your permanent record" that has hung over every school child's head since time immemorial.

Sara tapped the side of her PDT. "I'm at 68," she said. "And the group's aggregate is 62."

"Excellent! You're doing so well," said Katie, smiling proudly. She loved this group and had been proud when they asked her to be their faculty advisor.

"Yes, very well done," agreed Bert, looking around the room. He wrinkled his nose at the smells and brushed imaginary dust particles from his vintage tweed jacket. He was less enthusiastic about being an advisor and only did it because Katie would have made him attend a lecture on teaching methodologies of 18th-century agricultural societies.

As they talked, an older man approached them. "Ah, Katie, Bert, good to see you. Hello, Ms. Cooper-Wright. Excellent turnout, I see. I've been able to hear you from the office. Very robust and fervent chanting!"

President Caden Grogan wore a white suit in homage to 20th-century author Thomas Wolfe. He was tall, thin, slightly stooped, and had lost most of his hair except for a white fringe around his head that hung nearly to his collar. The few strands on top of his head waved under the air conditioning in their own protest against a cruel universe that had taken so many of their brethren.

"Hello, President Grogan," said Sara, tearing her eyes away from the wispy protest on President Grogan's skull.

"Oh, hi Caden," said Katie. The two moved in for a brief hug.

"Hello, President Grogan," said Bert, extending his hand. President Grogan stepped in for a hug and looked taken aback when Bert's hand poked him in the belly. He shook it and tried not to make a face at Bert's limp, lifeless grip.

"Do you have a moment?" asked President Grogan. "Excuse us, please, Sara."

He turned and picked his way through the gathered protestors, greeting them warmly and calling many of them by name. Katie and Bert followed, Katie shaking hands and hugging those she could reach; Bert merely smiled and nodded at random people, holding his hands up near his chest as if he was afraid of getting patchouli cooties.

As the three were seated at the small conference table in Dr. Grogan's spacious office, he asked Katie, "How's the protest going? I've heard some great chanting, and I think you even sang a few verses of 'We Shall Overcome.' I haven't heard that in years." President Grogan rubbed his hands together and beamed. He was a jovial, smiling man with deep crows-feet around his eyes from years of being pleased with everyone and everything.

"In fact," he said, "I've been so pleased that I called an emergency meeting with the board of trustees, and we've agreed to accede to the group's demands and change the name of the McKinley Hall dormitory to one of a more acceptable historic figure."

"Wonderful," said Bert. "That frees up our weekend. Now we can attend that lecture on musical influences on neoclassical industrial architecture."

"No! You can't do that," blurted Katie.

"What do you mean we 'can't'?" said President Grogan. "This is what the entire protest was about, and I thought they did it very well, so we unanimously agreed to accede. And in only 37 hours. That's got to be some kind of school record."

"Katie, I was really looking forward to that lecture," said Bert.

Katie ignored him. "I understand, Caden, but many of them are trying to meet their Social Justice hours. Some of these kids—excuse me, 'pre-adults'—are seniors and need at least 20 hours of protesting to meet their graduation eligibility. If you capitulate too soon, several of them will be at least 12 hours short, and there are no approved protests coming up soon."

"It's not capitulation," said President Grogan, who looked as if Katie had just sworn in his preferred house of worship.

"It's prudently exercising leadership in the face of growing political pressure."

"Call it what you want. They're still 12 hours short of their graduation requirement."

"What about Professor Cooksey's Cut The Athletic budget protest next week?" asked President Grogan.

"It's already full, and they've got a waiting list a mile long," said Katie.

"How? It's going to be held on the Ultimate Frisbee field, isn't it? That's plenty large enough to handle a few thousand protestors. Remember, we expanded the field's footprint after the entire student body participated in the Eliminate D's and F's protest and collapsed several of the bleachers. Then we expanded it even farther, right after the protest about buying replacement bleachers with ethically sourced recycled aluminum."

"Even so, they won't be able to take up the whole field for the protest," said Katie. "They've got the regional tournament coming up."

Ultimate Frisbee had become the major collegiate sport after football had been banned in 2041 owing partly to the increasing number of concussions among players every year as the athletes grew larger, stronger, and faster. Even though helmet technology had improved to the point where players wore a helmet-and-harness system that could keep their heads immobile, there were still three or four concussions each game, not to mention a compound fracture or two. Teams had to expand to 120 players just to reach the end of a season with a barely full complement.

The National Collegiate Athletic Association and the larger college athletic conferences had been on the brink of insolvency after more than 700 former players filed a class-action lawsuit, having been concussed so many times that many of them could not even brush their teeth without getting a headache.

So the NCAA banned college football altogether, elevating other less violent sports to "flagship" status. As a result, Ultimate Frisbee was now considered one of the premier sports, along with soccer, lacrosse, and skateboarding.

"The Frisbee team did agree to let Professor Cooksey's group use the sidelines for the protest," said Bert.

"Well, that was very generous of them."

"But that means that there's not very much room since there are already 120 students signed up for that protest," said Katie. "Ange told me there won't be any extra room since there will also be a counter-protest by the opposition group."

"Oh, that's right, that's right," said President Grogan. "Who's advising that group?"

"That's also Ange Cooksey's group," said Katie. "They're each capped at 120 students per side, plus campus security will need to be on hand. And the Ultimate Frisbee team will join the counter-protest in an unofficial capacity."

"Wow, that's impressive. Ange always gets such interest in her protest groups."

"So back to my original point, Caden. You can't capit—er, accede just yet. The kids need at least 12 more hours. Plus I know one or two of them are hoping to run this until Monday at least for their grad school applications."

President Grogan gazed out the window at Golden Delicious Quad. A light rain had begun, and students were racing to get out of the rain. "I'm sorry," he said. "The board wants us to move ahead on this because they want Mayor Windsong to dedicate the new name on Tuesday morning."

"Why Tuesday?"

"That's the only day she has free on her schedule."

"Are you going to be able to get the new sign made in time?" asked Bert, irritatingly practical about such matters. "Doesn't that take time?"

"Oh, no, not at all. We installed a new sign base that uses electromagnets to hold the letters in place, which makes replacing them a breeze. We just flick off the electromagnet, and they can change sign names in minutes. Next year, we're replacing all in-ground building signs with this new magnet system, which should save us $250,000 a year in protest-related name changes alone."

"Seriously?" asked Bert. "How?"

"Last year, we renamed the student center three times during Homecoming Weekend alone. We had already installed the new magnetic sign, and our maintenance staff were able to change each new name in about 20 minutes, just in time for the next protest group to show up. It used to cost $20,000 just to change a single sign; now it's only $100 for the hour."

"Well, shit," said Katie. "I don't know how these kids are going to make up their social justice requirements in time for graduation."

"Maybe they should have thought about that instead of waiting until the last minute," said Bert. Sometimes, Bert could be an insensitive asshole, Katie reflected, not for the first time.

"I'm sorry, Katie. We have to get moving on this if we want to meet Mayor Windsong's schedule. Maybe you can schedule another protest next week about the lack of diverse protests on campus."

"I suppose," murmured Katie.

"If that's all, Katie, I have an appointment across campus," said Bert. "Can you tell Sara and the patchouli patrol? Thank you, President Grogan. 'Bye, Katie." He squeezed Katie's shoulder in a respectful, non-possessive manner and left before she could say anything else.

"OK, all in favor of Group 6's mission statement, 'We are a dedicated collective of community activists who seek to bring about much-needed change to Appleseed's campus and the surrounding area'?"

Several hands shot up, and Sara counted them. "That's eight. It looks like CFC One's statement—'We are a committed group of campus activists who desire to effect a much-needed change to Appleseed's community and the immediate area'—wins with 12 votes. So, that's our new mission statement," said Sara as the different groups applauded graciously. Callie and her Type A troupe pumped their fists.

"Point of order," said one person, raising their hand, "can we say we're a committed and diverse group of campus activists?"

"And do we have to be 'campus activists'? That limits us from protesting in the city," said another.

"Or even the state. What if we wanted to protest in Toledo or Cleveland?" added Griffin.

"Do you really think you're going to protest in Toledo or Cleveland, Griffin?" asked Callie.

Griffin hung his head. "Well, no," he said. "But maybe this protest will get national attention. You already said our KNCLD score was 62, and the campus radio station has been reporting about us all morning."

"To an audience of sixty, Griffin. Their digital audience metrics show an audience of sixty."

"So?"

"So how many of you in here have been listening to the coverage on your PDT today?"

Everyone raised their hands.

"Exactly, and there are 60 of us. And our KNCLD score has not moved off a 62, either up or down, since we got here."

"So what are you saying, Sara?"

Sara looked out at the crowd of students, still clustered in their CFCs. "Nothing, I guess. I—just let's not put so much effort into the mission statement. That's not what's going to effect change; it's our actions. Our protest should be bigger than just changing the name of some old white dude who died 160 years ago."

"Don't you think this is important?" challenged Callie Wong.

"Of course I do. But don't you feel like there's more to it?"

"Uh, Sara, can I have a quick word?" Katie appeared at Sara's shoulder again.

"Jesus, Professor!" *What is she, a ninja?* wondered Sara. "Uh, I mean, sure Katie."

Kyle joined Sara as Katie spoke in hushed tones about President Grogan's decision and what it meant for students like Sara and several others. Students near the trio strained to hear what was being said. Callie was loading a lip reading app on her PDT when Sara shouted, "But I needed 12 more hours!"

The group began to murmur as Katie hugged Sara and quickly walked out of the building.

"Well, shit," Sara said to her classmates.

"Did the administration say no?" shouted Griffin. "That's bullshit! We'll stay longer. We'll chant louder. We'll write another mission statement! I'm so mad I could write a strongly worded email!"

"No, it's not that," Sara said into her bullhorn. "The administration capitulated. We get our name change."

The crowd roared its approval and quickly began to disperse, heading back to their dorms, including the newly minted Natalie Clifford Barney Hall, whose new sign was nearly complete when they arrived in time for dinner. A small crowd of bystanders applauded when the new sign was clicked back on, and the electromagnet hummed once again.

"It's alright, Sara," said Kyle, putting his feet on Sara's coffee table. The two had returned to Sara's apartment, along with Griffin, Callie, and a few other students to rehash the day's protests.

"No, it's not, Kyle!" Sara took a big slug from the celebratory margaritas Griffin and Callie had made. "What the hell are we even doing?"

"Celebrating our victory," said Callie. "We worked hard on it, and we got the administration to cave in 17 hours. That's got to be a new record."

"If you don't count the triple name change at Homecoming last year," said Griffin.

"Yes, but they had alumni dollars fueling that protest," said Callie. "Plus, the first two groups were not very selective about their name change. Rutherford B. Hayes Student Center? Come on, even a freshperson could see that one was problematic."

"Seriously, you guys—" said Sara.

"Ah-ah," said Callie.

"Oh, give it a rest, Callie," said Sara. "'Guys' has been an acceptable gender-inclusive group pronoun since the 2032 Gender Inclusivity Council of San Francisco."

Griffin raised a finger. "Well, actually—"

"I swear to CHiP, Griffin!" Sara shouted.

CHiP stood for Chosen HIgher Power or Choice of HIgher Power, depending on who you asked. The President's Council

On Shared Inclusivity and Tolerance, not realizing the acronym spelled PC-O-SHIT, launched a national campaign encouraging everyone to avoid using religiously exclusionary language like "I swear to God" or "Jesus Christ" as exclamatory phrases and to instead use more neutral language like "I swear to the Universe" or to actually name their own chosen higher power.

This—along with the name of the council—was so roundly mocked on social media, even by the most outspoken and obnoxious of liberals, that they began to use the phrase "I swear to CHiP." It was used ironically by most people, although the Unitarians embraced it wholeheartedly. It eventually entered the lexicon and was used as a throwaway exclamation or whenever people didn't feel like saying, "I swear to God."

Of course, literally, nobody ever said, "I swear to the Universe," including the members of PC-O-SHIT, who were so ashamed of their involvement in the committee that they never even put it on their résumés.

Sara set her margarita down and began pacing. "My point is we're not actually accomplishing anything. I don't even care about my social justice credits right now. We can always protest the food service's use of genetically modified potatoes in the tater tots and knock that out in a weekend.

"What I'm saying is that we're not doing anything of substance. I mean, when our parents protested, they got shit done. I've been learning about protests in my Recent Modern History class, like Occupy Wall Street and Black Lives Matter, that our parents and grandparents were involved in. Even before that, there were the Vietnam War protests in the 1970s that our great-grandparents were doing. But all we're doing is canceling some guy because he annexed some islands 160 years ago?"

"So you're saying we should turn a blind eye to those atrocities?" said Callie. "Are you pro-colonialism now, Sara?"

"Holy fuck, give it a fucking rest, Callie! I'm just saying we didn't actually accomplish much. If we didn't get the name changed, someone would have changed it anyway. If it wasn't our class, Dr. Barker had another SocJust 319 group that would have stepped up and done it. We just submitted the forms first."

Kyle drained his margarita and got up to pour another. "So what are you saying, Sara?"

"I'm saying we come from a long line of protestors and activists who achieved some great things. They toppled city governments and disrupted police departments and banking systems. They made great societal changes that made a huge difference in how society treated everyone. But after The Takening, there has been nothing left to protest. Hell, we could have written a group email to President Grogan, and he would have changed McKinley Hall's name."

"Barney Hall," said Griffin. "Er, sorry," he said as Sara glared daggers into his soul.

"My point is we didn't do anything. Instead, we held a protest to change something they were going to change anyway."

"So what are we supposed to do about it?" asked Kyle.

"We need a real challenge. We need a real fight. We need to organize and fight for something that's going to take some real blood, sweat, and tears, like our parents and grandparents. We need a lost cause that we may not win. Maybe even one that puts us in a little danger. "

"Uhhh—" said Griffin.

"And we need to do it in a way where the outcome is not only unknown, it isn't spoon-fed to us by our professors."

"Are you saying what I think you're saying?" asked Callie, shooting to her feet.

"Yes, I am," said Sara, stepping up onto her coffee table, hands on her hips, looking off toward the future. "We need to become alt-right activists!"

"That's not what I thought you were going to say," said Callie.

Kyle tapped Sara on the knee. "Dude, you're standing in the hummus."

CHAPTER 2

SHEILA WINDSONG WAS HAVING AN EXCELLENT DAY. As the mayor of Appleseed, Ohio, Sheila often had excellent days. But not many of them involved receiving a white silk blouse from her wife Fallyn for her birthday this past weekend. And they certainly didn't involve solving her city's trash problem while embezzling several million dollars.

That made today extra special.

Sheila hummed to herself as she cruised into her office, large soy latte in one hand, synthetic leather briefcase in the other. She glanced at Roy Burkhart-Lanning, a lobbyist with Braun McLaren Energy who was going to make today extra special, sitting outside her office.

Sheila was white in her mid-50s, soft and curvy with tightly curled brown hair that hung down to her shoulders, brushing against her new blouse. Her brown eyes took in every detail about her surroundings, including her administrative assistant, Tiffani. Sheila walked quickly, taking as big a step as her slate gray skirt would allow.

"Roy, come with me," said Sheila. "Tiffani, please hold my calls," she said to the grandmotherly woman sitting at the desk outside her office.

Roy followed her. "And close the door, please, Tiffani," Sheila said over her shoulder.

"Computer, close the door," Tiffani hollered. The door closed automatically, a fact Sheila seemed to ignore, no matter how often Tiffani reminded her of it.

Sheila sat behind her desk and gestured for him to sit down. Roy unbuttoned his suit jacket, which had been tailored to fit his slim-but-muscular torso, and sat down across from her.

Sheila pulled a tablet computer out of her briefcase and tapped it a few times, looking at the screen and then around her office.

"Good morn—" said Roy. Sheila held up one finger at him and then put it to her lips.

Next, she picked up a small device that looked like an old smartphone that was sitting in a charging cradle on her desk. She tapped it a few times and held it up, aiming it at different parts of the room. Satisfied with the results, she put the device back into the cradle, folded her hands in front of her, and smiled.

"Good morning, Roy. Thank you for coming in so early."

"Uh, you're welcome," said Roy. "What was that about?"

"Security measures. I sweep my office for bugs and wireless cameras at least once a day. You can never be too careful."

"Careful of what?"

Sheila looked at him as if she frequently gave this speech. "As the mayor of Appleseed, I hold a very powerful position. My political enemies would love to find out what happens here in the most powerful room in the city and use it against me."

There wasn't actually much that happened in the city, but it made Sheila feel important to think that she had enemies who would want to spy on her. In her eight years of scanning, she had never once found a listening device, although they'd had a bit of a scare last winter when Tiffani's retro clock radio had set off a false alarm.

"Seriously?" said Roy. "I've known you for years. I can't imagine you would do anything wrong in here."

Sheila smiled at Roy's word choice, not sure if he meant it intentionally. "Of course not! But they would love to take something I say out of context and use it to hurt me politically."

"So we just need to make sure not to do or say anything wrong?"

"No, we just need to make sure to sweep the office for bugs."

Roy chuckled, showing his perfectly straight, white teeth. "Excellent."

He ran his fingers lightly through his dark hair, which was cut short on the sides, longer on top, and gray at the temples. Roy spent a lot of his time running and working out in the gym of whichever city he was visiting. He had his colorful suits tailor-made in London, and his shoes were the finest in Swiss craftsmanship, now that most of Italy's finest fashion design factories were underwater. The Italians had all fled to Switzerland for higher ground and re-established the normally stolid and precise country into one of passionate flair and high fashion.

"So what is this new job of yours? Last time we talked, you were a lobbyist for that waste management company in Old New York, and now you're working for Braun McLaren Energy? That's a big step away from waste management, isn't it?"

"It's closer than you think," said Roy. "We convert a city's trash to energy to power their utilities."

"You said something about that in your email. What did you call it? Plasmic gas?"

"Plasma gasification. It's a technology that was introduced at the turn of the century, and it basically uses plasma energy to turn waste into a syngas."

"Sin gas?"

"Synthetic gas. Basically, we can turn organic waste, like food scraps, into a combustible gas that can be used to create electricity. We can also use it to 'incinerate,'" Roy used air quotes around the word, "medical waste and other hazardous waste without toxic byproducts or a lot of off-gassing. And we can use it to 'incinerate,'" air quotes again; Sheila was getting annoyed, "electronic waste and then extract precious metals like gold and platinum out of the syngas to make more electronics."

"Seriously? Why haven't we been doing it already? Why didn't they start using this at the turn of the century?"

"Well, the technology wasn't that advanced. We could 'incinerate'—"

"Please stop doing air quotes."

"Sorry, force of habit. Anyway, we could incinerate waste, but the energy conversion was not great. We actually operated at a net loss of consumption versus creation. But the government has been putting a lot more money into alternative energy since The Takening. Now, we can create nearly double the amount of energy used to run the system.

"That energy has to go somewhere, so we feed it into a city's power plant and power the city. It's not completely renewable, like solar and wind, but it cleans up existing landfills. Based on the estimates my civil engineers did, if we were to use your county landfills as fuel, we could run for about ten years until we eliminated all waste in the county."

"What happens when we run out of garbage?" Sheila asked, taking a sip from her latte and leaning forward. She was interested. Sheila had been an advocate for the environment but never could figure out how to eliminate Chapman County's old landfills.

"Again, based on our civil engineers' estimates, Appleseed creates enough waste to operate the gasification plant to run four months out of the year, or at one-third production throughout the whole year."

"So what do we do with the rest of the capacity?"

"Bring in garbage from surrounding counties and communities?"

"How much is that going to cost us?"

"Nothing," said Roy, leaning back and smiling.

"Nothing? How do you figure?"

"Because you're going to be helping those communities get rid of their own garbage. They'd pay you a disposal fee to get rid of their waste instead of dumping it. You could even help them clear out their own landfills, a service they would also pay for. You would charge each of them $25,000 per month for waste disposal, which puts $3 million in the city's coffers, per city. And the best part? They're paying you to produce your own energy."

"No shit? That's brilliant! So how much is this going to cost us to install the system?"

"Well, it would normally cost $150 million to install it, but Braun McLaren would cover $100 million of the cost."

"And how the hell do we come up with the other $50 million?"

"Bond issue. You can issue municipal bonds and use that to fund the remaining amount."

"Easier said than done. So what do you get out of it?"

"This would be a public-private partnership. Basically, Braun McLaren would take over the management of the city's energy utility, and we would be paid by people paying their electricity bill. We wouldn't even have to raise the rates."

"And I suppose your engineers know how much that is?"

"We would make back our initial investment in less than ten years, and we would manage the utility for thirty. After that, our successors will negotiate a new contract and give the city the option to either buy the plant from us, or we can dismantle it, and you return to full solar and wind production, with slowly filling landfills."

Sheila clasped her hands together and pinched her upper lip between her index fingers, deep in thought. Roy knew better than to say anything; he just watched the wheels turn. Finally, Sheila said, "I'll need to run it by the city council, but I'm pretty sure I can get them on board."

"Just pretty sure?"

"Well, there are five of them. I may run the day-to-day operations of the city, but they set the policy. I think I can get Chase Maitland and Caitlyn Dhillon to vote for it."

"You can definitely get Chase to vote for it."

"How do you know?"

"Because we just hired his out-of-work uncle to work as an 'input monitoring supervisor,'" *More fucking air quotes*, thought Sheila, "in our solar plant in Macon, Georgia. He just has to sit there and keep an eye on some dials and make sure they don't get into the red zone."

"Why? What happens if they get into the red zone?"

"It means the panels are taking in more sunlight than the system can hold. He's supposed to hit a button to pivot the panels 12 degrees."

"Why wouldn't you just build a system that could handle that much sunlight?"

"We did," said Roy, tapping the side of his nose. "He just sits and reads and glances at the dials every few minutes. It's a make-work job. Besides, we've already automated the system to rotate the panels to follow the sunlight. If it was actually possible to get too much sunlight, they would just rotate the other way.

"So that's two votes," continued Roy. "What about the other three?

"Cody Asher will say no because that little fucker opposes everything I propose," said Sheila. "I beat him for mayor eight years ago, and he's never forgotten it. He figures that by opposing me enough, he'll make me look like an idiot, and he can run against me in four years."

"Why not this year?"

"Because I'm better at my job than he is at his. He hasn't been able to trip me up or find any weakness."

"And Naomi Saito?"

"Naomi goes along with everything Cody says, and I've never seen her vote against him for anything. I think they're in a relationship."

"That leaves Zack Windless."

"He's the unknown. He actually votes his conscience, which is what makes him so dangerous. He could be persuaded that a $50 million bond isn't worth what we're saving, or he could be persuaded that this will help clean up our local landfills. You'd have to persuade him somehow."

"We could always make a donation to his re-election campaign."

"He's actually running unopposed like I am. His opponent dropped dead from a heart attack six months ago, and the Reformed Democrats haven't even bothered fielding a candidate."

"That's alright. He's still running for election. And thanks to the Denton-Dietz Act of 2045, corporations like ours can donate up to $500,000 for a political campaign."

"Sounds like we've got our three votes."

"Assuming you can actually deliver them."

"Oh, I can deliver them. If you help with Windless, I'll deliver the other two. Who knows? I might even be able to persuade Naomi Saito. She's always complaining about the number of landfills in Appleseed and wants the feds to remediate the sites."

Sheila leaned back in her chair and put her hands behind her head. "Now then, what do I get out of it?"

There it was. The question Roy had been waiting for. Every politician he had ever worked with, from the greenest Democrat to the purest Republican, asked The Question. It didn't matter how much it helped their citizens; they were more concerned with their political future or, more likely, their financial future. Every project, no matter how many jobs it created, no matter how much money he could save them, no matter how many problems it solved, they all asked The Question.

Even before The Takening, he was asked every variation of The Question. It didn't matter how cleverly they disguised their intentions; he always knew this was foremost on their minds.

"Well, we would need to put the PG plant somewhere that's not too close to the city, but still has straight-line access to the actual power plant."

"Which affects me how?"

"Your family farm is nearly two miles as the crow flies to the Appleseed Power and Light generators, which we could reach with high-tension wire. We would pay a $650,000 per year leasing fee to turn the farm into our PG plant."

"$900,000 per year. That farm has been in my family for generations."

"$775,000. Your father bought it in 2017 because he thought the government was going to legalize marijuana."

"$775,000 plus an $8 million 'consulting fee,'" this time Sheila made the air quotes, "to be paid for each term I'm the mayor."

"$8 million? Your mayorship could end at any time. This year is an election year. Why wouldn't we just wait and see who the next mayor is?"

"Because there's no one to run against me. Appleseed has always leaned left, but ever since The Takening and thanks to the Appleseed College Of The Arts, I can always rely on the artists' vote. No one has ever even considered running more than a token candidate in the last three elections—I mean as a political token, not a racial token, so don't 'at' me—and this year, the Reformed Democrats aren't even putting up a candidate. Even Cody fucking Asher doesn't want to risk a run. So, my guess is you'll have me for at least 12 more years until I decide to retire. So, sure, you can wait and see who *might* be the mayor in four years, but oh look, it's still me, and so now my fee is $10 million per term."

"How do you know we won't go anywhere else?" said Roy. "There are plenty of other cities your size."

"Yes, but not many cities have the lax bureaucracy and rubber stamp city council that we do. Whatever I propose, my people go along with it. Not to mention, I'm the only mayor who's got so large a property so conveniently adjacent to the utility company."

Sheila leaned forward and lowered her voice. "You see, I have my own engineers who tell me what's going on, and they told me that you've only got a few other options that are anywhere close to Appleseed's. Florida is half underwater;

Bemidji, Minnesota solved their garbage problem years ago; and Bangor, Maine gets so much snow, you couldn't deliver the garbage for three or four months out of the year."

Roy thought for a moment, then stood up and stuck out his hand. "Madame Mayor, I'm going to enjoy working with you."

Mayor Sheila Windsong stood up and shook Roy's hand. "Thank you, I am, too."

It was indeed an excellent day.

CHAPTER 3

"Excuse me, Professor Gant."

Will Gant peered over his thirty-inch 64K computer monitor to find four students standing at his office door. "Yes, can I help you?"

"My name is Sara Cooper-Wright, and these are my friends: Kyle Shehadi, Griffin MacKenna, and Callie Wong. We're in Professor Barker's Social Justice 319 class, and we just did the name change for Barney Hall."

"Oh, yes, I saw that on my way into the office this morning," said Will. "Congratulations. What can I do for you?"

It was Monday morning, and Will was preparing for his first class of the day, History 373, The Political Landscape of 20th Century America. It was an in-depth look at the previous century's, well, political landscape and the different social movements that all led to societal upheaval around the country, from the GI Bill that allowed World War II veterans to go to college to the Beatniks and hippies, the Civil Rights

Act, the abortion fight, and various liberal and conservative politicians.

Will's course, like Will himself, took a centrist, balanced, unbiased look at both sides of history, which often earned him the ire of Appleseed College's student body for teaching the "bad parts" of American history. Still, there was enough support from the rich alumni of the school that Professor Gant stayed in his position, and he refused to mask the history, saying "If you don't know where you came from, you'll never know where you are."

"My friends and I want to find out how to become alt-right activists," said Sara. "You're the furthest right person we have on campus, so I wanted to see if you could help us."

Will stood up. He was Black, fairly tall, muscular like he worked out regularly, and his hair was closely cut. "Why would you want to be alt-right? And are you sure you want me to help you?"

"Of course. Why would you even ask that?"

"Well, look at you. Look at me."

"So?" said Kyle.

"The alt-right were white nationalists from the early 21st century. Don't you think a Black man helping an Arab-American and Asian-American student to be white nationalists is a little weird?"

"Oh, holy shit! No, we don't want that!" said Sara, holding her hand out toward Will to reassure him. "No, CHiP! I'm sorry. That's not what we want."

"But that's what you asked for."

"We're just tired of participating in school-approved protests and being activists for meaningless victories. This stupid Barney Hall name change didn't mean anything. We had to do it for a course requirement, and the thing didn't even last the full four days, so we didn't get course credit. There's nothing to protest against anymore because all the real protests were done a long time ago. Now, the only changes we can bring about are stupid name changes no one actually cares about—now is not the time, Callie."

Callie lowered her finger and closed her mouth.

"Yes, but being alt-right is absolutely not the way to go about it. Those people were terribly racist and sexist and homophobic, and they all died in The Takening."

"We certainly don't want to be that," said Kyle.

"Or to die," said Griffin.

"So what do you want?" asked Will.

"When our parents and grandparents protested with Occupy Wall Street and Black Lives Matter, they had a common enemy. They had someone to push against. We don't have that. We could push against the school administration, but they're our biggest supporters. We're just protesting things that could have been changed with a gently worded email, and it's boring."

"What's wrong with boring? The world is finally the way liberals have wanted it. It's free of hatred and violence. We eliminated war. We increased education and arts funding. It's utopia."

"And it's boring as fuck," said Callie. "We got everything we wanted, and now there's nothing to do."

"Spoken like a child who got everything she wanted," said Kyle. "Check your privilege."

"Check your own fucking privilege, Kyle."

"Knock it off, you two," said Sara. "This isn't helping us with Professor Gant."

"I don't know if I can help you anyway. What are you actually asking me to do?"

"Teach us how to be the opposition," said Sara. "Show us how to be more on, uh, you know, the other side."

"Do you mean right-wing? Do you want to be more conservative?"

"Right-wing! That's the word we were looking for," said Griffin.

"Yes, right-wing," said Sara. "We want to be more right-wing. And you're the most right-wing person on campus."

"What makes you say that?" asked Will.

"Well, that's what some of the students say."

"The same students who thought right-wing meant alt-right?"

"I'm not going to live that one down, am I?" said Sara.

"No," said Will and Kyle simultaneously.

"Jinx," said Kyle. Will ignored him.

"I mean, we've talked amongst ourselves and in a couple of our classes, and they said you were the furthest right professor on campus."

"Well, technically that's true," said Will. "Although before The Takening, I was a moderate Democrat. Afterward, when all the conservatives and Republicans were gone, the political spectrum was more or less cut in half. Everyone on the right was gone, and everyone in the center became the furthest right on the spectrum by process of elimination.

"What does it even mean to be moderate?"

"Basically, to be moderate meant you didn't go overboard in all your beliefs. For example—and I'm grossly oversimplifying this—a conservative might want twenty percent of the government's spending to go for the military, but a liberal might want to eliminate nearly all military spending and instead spend that money on education. In that case, a moderate might agree to a more equitable ratio of twelve percent on the military and eight percent on education."

"Why only eight percent?" asked Callie. "Don't you think education is worthy of greater spending?"

"That's not the point," said Will. "I'm using those numbers as an illustration."

"Yeah, but why only eight per—"

"Callie, shut up," said Sara. "It was a hypothetical."

Callie folded her arms and huffed. "You're hypothetical," she muttered. Sara ignored her.

"Now that the far-right is gone," continued Will, "the liberals still want to cut military spending and give most of that money to education, and the moderate still wants to spend twelve percent. But since the far-right war hawks are gone, the moderates are now the *de facto* war hawks. Do you see?"

"That makes sense," said Kyle. "So, you're not really conservative. You're just the most conservative relative to what's left—er, remaining."

"Right—er, correct, even though I'm really just a moderate."

"So how do we go beyond that?" asked Sara. "How can we be more right-wing than you so we can actually get people riled up and get emotional about the changes we want to make?"

Will sighed and sat back down in his chair. "Well, that's the big question, isn't it? At its simplest, almost simplistic, foundation, conservatives and liberals—Republicans and Democrats—were nearly always automatically opposed to whatever the other stood for. It's normally hard to define yourself by what you don't believe in, but both sides managed to do that for each other. They defined their adversaries by their opposition."

"How so?" asked Griffin.

"Let's take education versus military spending again. If Republicans wanted a big military budget, but the Democrats didn't, the Republicans would call the Democrats weak-willed peaceniks. Meanwhile, the Democrats would call the Republicans saber-rattling warmongers.

"For many of them, the argument wasn't about smart budgeting or having the right size of military. It was a fight over 'we want the best military in the world' versus 'we don't need a military that big.' They saw it as a binary, black-and-white issue. You were either for their side, or you hated everything they stood for."

"And how did that work for education?" asked Callie. Her lifelong dream was to be a teacher because if she could get drafted out of college by even a second-tier school system, she could easily earn a six-figure salary in her first year as a middle school math teacher.

"Pretty much the same way," said Will. "The Democrats wanted to increase education spending, and the Republicans saw it as a luxury. Again, it wasn't about smart budgeting or spending the right amount on education; it was more like 'we want the best educational system in the world' versus 'we don't need to spend that much.'"

"Surely it wasn't just that," said Kyle.

"No, no, I'm boiling it down to its barest essence. There were nuances to the argument, and in the end, both sides had to compromise in order for each of them to get a portion of what they wanted. So, for example, the Democrats might agree to spend only twenty percent of the budget on the military if the Republicans would agree to spend ten percent on education."

"Bleah, that sounds terrible," said Sara. "Nobody got what they wanted."

"Exactly. Compromise is never a great way to negotiate because nobody is happy. But at least everyone is equally unhappy, and in politics, that was sometimes the best you could hope for. That you weren't miserable because you completely lost what you wanted."

"So how do we use this for ourselves?"

"I don't know if I should help you," said Will. "Things got pretty terrible before The Takening. You would have all only been babies when it happened, so you probably don't remember the ugliness of it all."

"My parents told me a little about it," said Kyle.

"My parents kept me pretty sheltered when I was a kid," said Callie.

"Me too," said Sara.

"I don't remember much of anything before I was four," said Griffin.

"I don't have a lot of time to explain right now because I have a class in five minutes, but I'll let you borrow a few of my books, and you can see for yourself."

"Wait, are those real books?" said Kyle. "I've only seen them in videos."

"My parents had a few books," said Sara. "I wasn't supposed to touch them though. They thought I would be too rough with them, so I just read on my tablet or my PDT."

"Tell you what," said Will. "How about I loan you this one, *Beyond The Messy Truth*, about the 2016 presidential campaign, and this one, *Fall of The American Empire*, which discusses the 2048 presidential campaign between Eric Trump and Chelsea Clinton, which nearly led to a second American Civil War? If it hadn't been for The Takening, it might have happened."

"Does this mean you'll help us?" asked Sara.

"Well..." said Will.

"All we want to do is become a protest group," said Sara. "We don't want to overthrow anything, we don't want radical change, and I certainly don't want to go back to what there was before The Takening. I just want to fight for something and have a risk of losing."

"Think of it as an educational experience, Professor Gant," said Kyle. "We can form a student activities group, and you can be our faculty advisor."

"Sure!" said Sara. "We can be the Students For a Conservative Future."

"With no racism?" asked Will.

"None at all!" said Sara. "Fuck, were there ever any Conservatives who weren't terrible?"

"Well, you really need to go back to the 1970s and 1980s for that. They were still racist, but they kept it hidden. The Republican Party in the late 20th century believed in smaller government, lower taxes, and reduced social spending and education in favor of a strong military."

"Our military is currently 27th in the world, right behind Portugal and France, so we could always ask for a bigger military," said Kyle.

"Yeah, but The Takening happened in other countries too, so we don't need to actually fight anyone," said Callie.

"I don't think we should reduce education," said Callie.

"How about if we just advocate for smaller government and lower taxes?" said Sara.

"Sure. The best place to do that is to get started locally and see it up close on a small scale," said Will. He pulled an old political science textbook from his shelf that looked like it was from the last century.

"That must be worth a couple thousand dollars," said Griffin. Most books had become outdated relics of the past now that people read books on their PDTs or tablets. Owning books was a luxury, similar to the vinyl record resurgence at the beginning of the century.

"Oh, probably," said Will, "but books are worthless if we can't use them or learn from them. Besides, I have a second copy at home. My father was a reader, and his father before him, and they were big believers in the power of books. But if it's all the same, don't eat or drink anything while you're reading it, please."

The next day found Kyle, Griffin, and Callie at Kyle's house, poring over Will's books. They occasionally took turns reading passages to each other and shaking their heads at what they heard. As Kyle read from the political science textbook, he took notes and began fleshing out their platform.

Kyle's PDT pinged, and he tapped one of the temples. "Sure, just come in," he said. "Jasper, unlock the front door."

"Very good, Mr. Shehadi," said a disembodied voice. Kyle's home assistant was programmed to sound and function like a British butler but without the actual snootiness.

"One of your ...*friends* has arrived," said Jasper. OK, without *most* of the actual snootiness.

The door unlocked, and Sara walked in and joined them at the kitchen table.

"Well, we're officially registered with the school as the Students for a Conservative Future," she told them. "I'm the president, Kyle is VP, and Callie is Secretary-Treasurer."

"What am I?" asked Griffin.

"Uh, they only had three slots we could fill."

"That sucks. Why couldn't I be Secretary-Treasurer?"

"Because you can barely manage your own money," said Callie.

"How about you be the Sergeant-at-Arms?" asked Sara.

"What does that mean?"

"I'm not sure. Maybe you get to handle security."

"Are we going to need to be armed? I don't know if I'm comfortable with that."

"Republicans loved guns," said Kyle. "I was just reading about how Republicans loved the Second Amendment and fought for their rights to bear any kind of gun, even when there were dozens of school shootings and mass shootings every year. Even when hundreds of kids were killed each year, they kept fighting for their rights to own guns, and they would buy more immediately after every school shooting."

"Fuck, that's terrible!" said Griffin.

"Yeah, but most of the guns are gone now," said Callie. "The rest are seriously regulated."

"True, plus I don't think we're going to need much security," said Sara. "I got a few raised eyebrows when I submitted the forms at the Student Activities office. And I just sent out a campus-wide email to invite everyone to our first meeting next Monday. We probably won't get a big turnout, so we won't need any actual security."

"I think we need some actual security," said Griffin. "There's at least two hundred angry protestors out there."

"Well, they're certainly getting their protest credits," said Sara.

It was Monday evening, and the Students for a Conservative Future were meeting in the Political Science building in one of the classrooms. There were fifteen students who had arrived early for the meeting. There had originally been twenty, but five of them had left when they learned there wasn't going to be any pizza.

"I thought reduced pork spending meant veggie pizza," groused one disappointed attendee, taking four friends with her.

The remaining students were interested in making waves, rebelling against their parents, and disrupting the status quo, as Sara's campus-wide announcement had promised.

The protestors outside were chanting, "Hey, ho, alt-right Nazis gotta go!" which wasn't terribly rhythmic, but they were making it work.

"Shit, what's this going to do to my KNCLD score?" lamented one of the new members, Grace Blasingame-Odoyo, a young woman dressed in a skirt and suit jacket with shoulder pads.

"Relax, it's not going to do anything. It takes a lot to drop a KNCLD score," said Kyle.

"Now it's a 64!" shouted Grace, tapping at her PDT.

"What was it?"

"Uh, 64.2," said Grace Blasingame-Odoyo.

"Like I said," said Kyle. "I don't think it will happen just because we held a meeting of Republicans."

"You'd better be right. I need a 58 or higher to get into grad school."

"OK, let's get this meeting started," said Sara, banging a makeshift gavel on the lectern. "The first-ever meeting of the Students for a Conservative Future is called to order."

"Point of order," said Trent Chang-Ramirez, another student wearing a wrinkled shirt and tie with suspenders. "I feel like banging the gavel is a violent gesture, and I gently request that we do away with it."

"Fuck your feelings!" shouted Callie.

"What?" Trent shrieked, unaccustomed to being shouted at in that manner.

"Sorry! I'm sorry. That was really mean," said Callie. "I was watching some old videos about the 2016 presidential race, and that's something the Republicans would shout at the Democrats. That was way out of line, and I apologize."

"I move to censure Callie for her violent and uncaring language," said Trent.

"Tell you what: let's put that down for later on the agenda," said Sara. "For now, let's just talk about our goals and how we want to move forward."

"Fine," said Trent, pointing at Callie. "But I won't forget it."

"Move to censure Trent for making a threatening phallic gesture," said Callie.

"Both of you, knock it off," said Sara. "It's been five minutes, and I'm already sick of politics." She looked around and made sure she had everyone's attention, wishing not for the first time that she had her bullhorn.

"The reason we formed the Students for a Conservative Future is because we're tired of all the protesting and activism that doesn't actually do anything. When I was growing up, my moms used to tell me stories about protests and parades they attended as they fought to bring about major societal changes. They had to fight for their very right to get married, and they had to keep fighting so that right wouldn't be taken away. And they had to fight to protect their identities and even themselves from people who hated them and would rather see them dead than happy.

"But what do we fight for? We fight to change names on residence halls from one minor political figure to another. Or we fight to create a separate Ultimate Frisbee team for nonbinary players. Our fights don't actually matter because there's no one to push against and the administration just goes along with whatever we want without a fuss.

"We want to fight against the establishment. Maybe we won't effect any changes, but we'll sure make a bigger impact and what we do will be louder and more dramatic than anything we're doing right now. So we want to adopt some of the platforms that the old-school conservatives had nearly a hundred years ago and fight for those principles."

"Do you mean we want to become racist and homophobic?" asked Branden Wilkins-Assad, a nonbinary student from the coastal city of Orlando, Florida.

"No, not at all," said Sara. "We still believe in the principles of humanity and compassion and treating everyone with dignity. But the conservatives from the 1970s and 1980s were all about smaller government, lower taxes, and fewer regulations on businesses. We can support those things without being bigots. So we want a platform of principles that model the economic and fiscal issues of last century. Then we'll be able to start a substantive fight to make some real changes."

"We'll need a mission statement. Can I help write a mission statement?" said Amity Withers, a young woman whose grandmother had once served as a senator for the breakaway nation of Mackinac Island 50 years earlier.

"We already have a mission statement prepared, and I can share that with you now." Sara pressed a button on her tablet computer, and the mission statement document was beamed to everyone's PDTs.

"Accept," murmured everyone quietly, and everyone read the brief statement.

"I have a few suggestions for the mission statement," said Amity.

"Tell you what: can you head up a committee to explore those changes and then report back to us?" said Sara.

"Ooh, I would love that," said Amity. Tales of her grandmother's love for mission statements was legendary among the Withers family, and she hoped to carry on her grandmother's legacy.

"Excellent, thank you. Anyone who would like to join Amity on the Mission Statement committee, see them when we break out into committees. Now, let's talk about our platform and its planks. I spoke with our faculty advisor, Professor Will Gant of the History department, and he suggested we focus on reducing government spending at the local level, lowering taxes on the wealthy, and raising or removing the profit caps on successful businesses. Let's start with the language on government spending. If you want to help with the platform, join me over here. If you want to be on Publicity and Social Media, go with Kyle. And anyone who wants to focus on the mission statement, please see Amity."

For the next two hours, the fifteen students—minus the five who abandoned their political futures over pizza—discussed, argued, and debated the merits of the language on the three planks before coming up with a cohesive platform they could all support.

The Publicity and Social Media Committee drafted a press release that would be shared with the school media outlet as well as local and regional news outlets about the new student organization and their desire to make major changes to the Appleseed city government.

And Amity sat by herself, making notes about the mission statement in a retro notebook with her grandmother's antique fountain pen from 2015, thinking, *Grammy would be so proud*.

CHAPTER 4

"ALL RISE FOR THE PLEDGE IF YOU ARE ABLE," said Carl Frostwhistle-Nguyen, the sergeant-at-arms.

It was the second Tuesday of the month, which meant the Appleseed City Council was meeting in the Toni Morrison Meeting Hall and Cafeteria. They met on the second and fourth Tuesday of every month, except for the fourth week in December between The-Holiday-Formerly-Known-As-Christmas (also called THoFKAC) and New Year's Day.

The five city council members sat at a long and stately table at the front of the room. The table was made with recycled lumber and had modesty panels in front so no one could see the council members' legs and feet. Mayor Sheila Windsong was seated in the middle with Chase Maitland, Caitlyn Dhillon, and Zack Windless immediately to her left. Cody Asher and Naomi Saito were seated to her right; Cody and Naomi were sitting a little closer than one would expect, and Sheila was sure they were playing footsies under the desk.

"I pledge allegiance to the symbol of the unity of our nation. And to the diverse individuals who stand if they are able, or kneel if they choose, one nation, under my personally Chosen Higher Power, with liberty and justice for all."

"This meeting of the Appleseed City Council is now called to order," said Sheila. As the mayor of Appleseed, Ohio, she led the meetings and ran the agenda.

"Point of order," said Tully Bascomb, one of the citizen watchdogs who attended every meeting and nearly always had something to complain about. Today was no different. Tully considered himself part of the "loyal opposition," meaning he objected to everything the council proposed, and he exercised his freedom as often as he could.

"I object to the phrasing in the pledge 'who stand if they are able.' I feel it's ableist and doesn't allow for personal choice."

"Jesus Christ, not this again," muttered Chase Maitland to Sheila. "Why do we keep letting this fucker in here?"

"Oh, he's harmless enough," whispered Sheila from behind a glass of water. "Mr. Bascomb, as you know, the pledge is one that was adopted by Congress after The Takening, so it's not up to us to amend it. As we've mentioned before, you can write to your local Congressperson and ask her to change it."

"I think we should amend it here on our own and not wait for the do-nothing Congress to actually pick up this important and worthy cause."

"We can't change it here though. We're just one small town in a nation of 53 states. Write to our Congressperson, but otherwise, we need to move on to actual, achievable city business."

"OK, first up on the agenda: the Arts Council. Naomi, as the chair of that committee, what do you have for us?"

"It's Councilwoman Saito," corrected Naomi, rolling her eyes. This was a common point of contention between Naomi and Sheila, and it played out the same way every time.

"Fine, whatever," said Sheila.

"Fine, whatever what?" said Naomi.

Sheila glared at Naomi and fantasized about smashing Naomi in the forehead with her gavel. "Fine, whatever, give your report," she said through gritted teeth. Her knuckles went white as she tightened her grip on the gavel and fought the urge to swing it.

Naomi stared daggers at Sheila but started her report. "The Arts Council met last week and completed this year's grant review. Every artist who applied has received a $17,000 grant, which can be used for art supplies, studio rental, and personal support. Additionally, all painters received ten hemp canvases, and the sculptors received ethically sourced hammers and chisels or welding equipment."

"What did the writers receive?"

Naomi checked her notes on her tablet. "They each received a box of pencils."

The room burst into laughter.

"Oh, and we found some extra funding, so all writers who want new laptops can apply, and they will be granted a new laptop with a supplemental forty-eight inch, 96K IMAX monitor. That's an upgrade from the computers we gave them last year."

"Excellent, thank you for that report, *Naomi*. Please pass the council's thank you to the Arts Council, *Naomi*," said Sheila. She consulted her agenda on her tablet. "Next, Deputy Mayor Enrique Medina has a report on the two-day educational seminars the city recently organized for our citizens as part of our Inclusivity Counseling Department. Enrique?"

A Latino man seated in the front row rose to his feet. He was tall, slender, dressed in a retro suit from the 2010s, faux leather shoes polished to a high sheen, and wearing something the council members recognized as a "necktie" from their history lessons in school. Enrique was known around Appleseed as a collector of vintage clothing, owning suits and ties from as far back as the 1990s. Rumor had it that he secretly owned a couple pairs of leather shoes, which had been banned by Congress in 2036.

Enrique pulled up his notes on his tablet and began to read. "As you recall, we began our voluntary two-day in-person educational seminars six months ago as a way to help Appleseedlings who have been heard to utter discriminatory, biased, or anti-equality ideas."

"Point of order. I thought we were called Appleseeds," said Tully, rising to his feet.

"I thought we were Appleseedians," said a voice from farther back in the room.

"Appleseedies," called another.

"I thought we were human beings first," said a third.

"Shut the fuck up with that bullshit," called another. The room erupted as people shouted, waved their fingers, and screamed their suggestions for the name that citizens of Appleseed, Ohio, should be called.

"Order! Order, goddammit," Sheila shouted, banging her gavel. She banged it several times until the room quieted down.

"I object to the banging of a gavel as a patriarchal act of violence left over from the days of the colonizer," said a woman, leaping to her feet. She had a wild mane of curly hair and wore a patchwork jacket with white painter pants and ethically sourced cork clogs.

"Not now, Melody," said Sheila, banging her gavel again.

"According to our town's Wikipedia page, we have been known as Appleseedlings since the founding of this city. And Appleseedlings we shall remain." She glared out over the audience until they returned to their seats.

"I still think it's violent," mumbled Melody. Everyone ignored her.

"Enrique, please continue."

Enrique rose to his feet, adjusted his tie, and cleared his throat. "As I was saying, we started our voluntary two-day educational in-person seminars six months ago. Citizens were strongly urged to attend by our peace force, the Appleseed Counseling and Enforcement Division, and several were escorted to the seminar. Those who refused to attend—"

"As is their right," said Naomi.

"As is their right," said Enrique, trying to keep his voice from sounding like a spoken eye roll. "Those who refused to attend, or left the seminar after one day, were then strongly urged to reconsider their stance and attend the next two-day event, which is to be held in three weeks. Those who still fail to voluntarily comply with our strongly worded suggestions will have a voluntary fine levied against them."

"Can I ask why we have a fine if this is a voluntary program?" said Naomi.

"We have found that people often refuse to do things that are actually good for them. Before Congress passed the tax increase on the consumption of murdered animals for food, many people refused to stop eating meat despite the health benefits. It didn't matter how many doctors' recommendations, government reports, or protests by animal rights groups there were. People continued to eat meat even though it was against their own best interests."

"And what does that have to do with these penalties and incarcerations?" asked Naomi.

"Ah-ah, *voluntary* fines and seminars," corrected Enrique. He was a close ally and occasional sexual partner to the mayor, so he knew Naomi could not actually do anything to him.

"Uh-huh," said Naomi. "This sounds like the same justifications the government made for putting my Japanese ancestors into internment camps in the 1940s."

"We are nothing like those monsters in the 1940s!" shouted Enrique.

"Order! There will be order in these chambers!" shouted Sheila, banging her gavel and wondering if she should get a heavier one. "Naomi, this is nothing like Japanese internment camps. We are doing this for people's own good. Not only does it help *Appleseedlings*," she glared out at the audience, "be better people, but our community KNCLD score increases, which can earn us some additional grant money from the government. Now, if you'll let Enrique finish his report, we can continue with this meeting."

"Thank you, Madame Mayor. As I was saying before I was interrupted," said Enrique, glancing pointedly at Naomi, "there was an increase in voluntary attendance thanks in large part to the strong urging by our peace force. And the threat—er, potential for voluntary fines, we saw an eighteen percent increase in overall attendance and a corresponding decrease in refusals and early departures."

"Can I make a suggestion?" asked Chase Maitland. "If you want to really make sure the lessons stick, could you have a four-day educational seminar? I know the facilities at the YMWNBCA camp—the Young Men's, Women's, Non-Binary Citizens Association—are available after the summer ends. Maybe you could work out an arrangement with them to start holding the seminars there."

Sheila sent a quick note from her tablet to Tiffani to prepare an executive order to that effect, and she would sign it the next morning.

"That's a great suggestion, Council Member Maitland," said Sheila, looking right at Naomi Saito. "Enrique, can you speak with the YMWNBCA and see what it would take to make that happen? Then report back to us at our next meeting."

"I was also thinking, Madame Mayor," said Caitlyn Dhillon, not wanting to be left out of Sheila's praise, "that we could institute a five-point KNCLD penalty against the people who refused to participate. If someone refuses the peace force escort, they could implement the five-point penalty right there. Then, don't remove it until the person has completed their voluntary training."

"Excellent idea, Council Member Dhillon," said Sheila. Caitlyn beamed and shot Naomi a look that said, "And that's how you play the game."

Sheila tapped another note to Tiffani to add that penalty to her executive order. *Fuck these city council bureaucrats*, Sheila thought. *Rome wasn't built by a fucking committee.*

The council covered several more items on the meeting agenda—passing a resolution congratulating the Appleseed College students on their recent residence hall name change; adding more buses and routes to the municipal bus schedule; approving additional funding for the youth Ultimate Frisbee league; denying a budget extension for the feral cat feeding program—until they reached the last item under the section on new business.

"Finally, I was approached by Braun McLaren Energy about installing a plasma gasification plant in Appleseed."

"What is plasma gasification?" asked Zack Windless.

"It's a process that basically uses plasma to incinerate and disintegrate all trash, breaking it into dust and separating its component parts out. So you could throw in a bunch of old computer monitors, and all the raw materials that went into making them like the plastic, silicon, and gold can be pulled out and reused. The Braun McLaren guy said we could go through so much of our own garbage that we'll run through our entire landfill in three years and then can start charging other communities to accept their garbage as well."

"Why are we just now hearing about this?" asked Cody Asher.

"Because I just met with Braun McLaren yesterday, Cody," said Sheila. "The guy literally came to my office 36 hours ago with a proposition."

"Then why is there already an impact statement available online?"

"The developers provided it, along with a budget, when I met with them."

"And why didn't you notify any of us about this proposal?"

"I'm notifying you now, Cody," said Sheila.

"That's not good enough. We need to be notified any time a major proposal like this comes across your desk," said Cody.

"That's bullshit, and you know it. I am not obligated to share anything of the kind until we meet on official city business."

"Something of this magnitude should be shared with the council as soon as it happens."

"Well, that's not going to happen. As long as I'm the mayor, this is how I'll operate. And until you're able to vote me out of office, we're going to continue to operate in this manner."

Cody glowered at Sheila but remained silent. Sheila had been re-elected mayor for the last two terms and showed no signs of being replaced any time soon. Cody had run against her in the last campaign three years ago and only received thirty percent of the total vote. His was the best showing in fifteen years, and it looked like no one was going to run against Sheila in this year's election at all, which was going to take place in four months.

"I suggest that we review all the materials and be prepared to vote on this in two weeks' time."

Zack Windless raised his hand. "Excuse me, Madame Mayor. I think we need to investigate this matter further and ask questions of the developers. I'd like to know more about how they gathered this information and reached these results. And I think we owe it to the citizens of Appleseed to get their input and feedback. We still function in a democracy, after all."

Sheila knew better than to pop off at Zack because he was the critical vote she needed to pass the plasma gasification plant in the first place. If she alienated him, she could kiss the plant and Braun McLaren's millions goodbye.

"Wise counsel, Council Member Windless," said Sheila, a saccharine smile cracking her face. "Let's ask for citizen feedback over the next three meetings, and I'll have someone from Braun McLaren on hand to answer everyone's questions. Unless anyone has anything else, can I have a motion to adjourn?"

There was a motion and second, Sheila banged her gavel, and everyone mingled and chatted as the meeting broke up.

Carmen Cowen, a reporter for the *Appleseed Mail-Journal*, tapped notes on the tiny keyboard that was connected to her PDT, putting the final notes on the story about tonight's meeting and sending it off to the *Mail-Journal's* editor.

```
Sparks flew at tonight's Appleseed
City Council meeting as dis-
agreements erupted between Mayor
Windsong and Council Member
Naomi Saito as well as between
Mayor Windsong and former may-
oral candidate Cody Asher.

Last on the agenda, but first
in importance, is the proposed
```

plasma gasification plant proposed by alternative energy giant
Braun McLaren. The proposed
plant can convert Appleseed's
trash—as well as the trash of
surrounding communities—to a
synthetic gas, which can then
be used to supply Appleseed's
power needs.

According to a report by Braun
McLaren, Appleseed can generate
$3 million in trash reclamation
fees alone, but the savings in
energy costs could be in the
millions of dollars.

The motion to investigate and
allow for community feedback for
the next six weeks was made as
council members will review the
Braun McLaren report before the
next city council meeting in two
weeks. At that time, a representative of Braun McLaren will
be available to answer citizens'
questions.

A copy of the Braun McLaren
report is available on the Mail-
Journal website.

"Mayor Windsong, a quick question?" Carmen leaped to her feet as Sheila made for the exit. "Can you tell us where the plasma gasification plant will be built?"

"Who are you?" asked Sheila.

"Carmen Cowen. I'm the new reporter for the *Mail-Journal*. I've got the local government beat." Carmen was of average height, around 5'8" with curly black hair and dark eyes. She wore a vintage concert t-shirt from the Rolling Stones' "Could Be the Last One" tour from 2043.

"Ah, that old rag. Any question you have for me needs to be submitted to our public information officer during regular office hours."

"But you're here right now. It's a simple question, Mayor Windsong."

"And I said you need to pass all questions through our public information officer during regular office hours."

"I'll be sure to mention that you appeared evasive and refused to answer questions in tomorrow's article."

"Listen, kid, I've been the mayor of this city since you were playing video games in your mother's basement, and I'll be mayor long after you're gone. But your failing rag is barely a blip on my radar. When I want to share news with the public, it comes straight from me on social media. We don't need you muckrakers spreading your fake news and upsetting the populace. Got me?"

"Whatever, Zoomer," said Carmen.

"What did you say?" demanded Sheila. She leaned in close and hissed, "You fucking Foundlings need to learn to respect your elders. I don't appreciate your ageist insults, and stereotyping an entire fucking generation based on a few people is inappropriate. I should report this on KNCLD and see what it does to your score."

"I don't imagine it will do much since your own KNCLD score is in the 40s."

Sheila was aghast. "How do you even know that? KNCLD scores are private unless the users want to share theirs!"

"Because your KNCLD score hasn't been private for the last two months. The last major update set everyone's scores to public, including yours. And that's why everyone can see you're hovering around 43."

"Fucking Foundling," Sheila hissed once more, spraying spittle onto Carmen's face.

Carmen calmly wiped her cheek and used her sleeve to wipe her glasses, leaving them on her face. "So is that a 'no comment' on the gasification plant location, or should I go with 'Fucking Foundling' instead?"

"Go fuck yourself," said Sheila. She stomped off toward the location, bellowing at Carl Frostwhistle-Nguyen. "You're the fucking sergeant-at-arms. You need to make sure the media rabble are kept away from me." Sheila slammed the door behind her, and everyone turned to stare at Carmen, who only smiled and tapped the temple of her PDT.

"Upload the video of that last conversation to the *Mail-Journal* website."

CHAPTER 5

THE MORNING AFTER THE COUNCIL MEETING, Kyle Shehadi hammered on Sara's apartment door.

"Come on, come on, come on," he muttered, waiting for her to answer, bouncing like a little kid who had to pee. He hammered on the door again.

"What?" Sara shouted, flinging her door open.

"Holy shit, did you see this?" Kyle shouted, barging inside, not even waiting for an invitation. He stopped in the middle of her apartment and whirled around. Sara's place looked like an art gallery, the walls covered with paintings given to her by her artist friends for her birthday, the holiday-formerly-known-as-Christmas, or whenever their own studios were too full thanks to a particularly generous arts benefactor or large arts grant. A glazed blue fruit bowl held pride of place on Sara's coffee table and currently housed her eight remotes to control all the different streaming devices plugged into her 64K TV.

"See what?"

"This!"

"You're staring right at me, so no, not since I looked in the mirror," said Sara. It had been twelve hours since Carmen Cowen had posted her story to the *Appleseed Mail-Journal* about the meeting, complete with Sheila Windsong's "Fucking Foundlings" remarks, and the comments section on the *Mail-Journal* was on fire with people demanding Sheila's resignation.

Of course, people demanded her resignation after every slight, misconstrued comment, and eye roll. ("I would think an elected official could better manage their emotions than to regularly commit violence with her micro-aggressions," said one commenter. "She needs to resign!")

Foundlings were the generation that came two generations after Generation Z, so named because of the number of children who had survived their parents' demise from The Takening. It was considered an insensitive label and any article that mentioned it often came with a trigger warning that the word was going to be mentioned. Some media outlets and blogs had begun offering trigger warnings to their trigger warnings, notifying people that the warnings themselves were going to mention "certain words some may find hurtful and insensitive." Some media outlets even provided a remote counseling service for a monthly fee to provide assistance to people who had been triggered by the word.

This had prompted a burgeoning movement of young Free Speech advocates who not only embraced the term Foundling as "our word," they had also begun eschewing trigger warnings, saying life itself was triggering.

"Sorry, I meant the story in the *Mail-Journal*," said Kyle.

"You still have to be more specific. There were a couple dozen stories in the *Mail-Journal*."

"Goddammit." Kyle tapped his PDT and said, "Send Fucking Foundling story to Sara Cooper-Wright." He waited as she scrolled through the story, nodding her head to advance the text.

"Holy shit," said Sara. "This is… this is what? What do we think about this?"

"I mean, it's pretty cool because it could help the environment."

"Fuuuuuck. I am so sick of hearing about the fucking environment. Everyone knows global warming is a hoax."

Kyle gasped. "What the hell are you saying?" He scanned the room for an old-time Victorian fainting couch, but finding none, he flailed for a chair and lowered himself gingerly into it.

"Sorry, I'm practicing my conservative talking points," said Sara. "The old Republicans used to be against anything that was beneficial to the environment. Man, they fucking hated the environment. Anytime the liberals wanted a pro-environment law passed, the Republicans fought it saying climate change was a hoax."

"You said global warming though."

"That's what they called it so they could pretend to be confused every winter. 'It's really cold outside. So much for global warming!'"

"Ah. Anyway, what do we think of this?"

"Well, we should probably talk to Will, but I think we could oppose it for some of the reasons the old Republicans would give. It's harmful to businesses—"

"Like who?"

"Waste management companies?"

"OK, go on."

"It's government interference and overreach."

"Ehhhhhh."

"It's going to use our hard-earned tax dollars to pay for something that will only benefit a few people."

"No, that's what they stood for."

"Well, it's going to use our hard-earned tax dollars that will take away from important social programs."

"It looks like there's actually going to be a net positive effect because we'll not only cut back on our power needs, but we'll actually make money as a community when other cities start shipping us their waste."

"Well, shit, how are we even supposed to oppose this?" Sara flopped down on the couch

"We could issue a statement about how we're offended by the way Mayor Windsong said—trigger warning—the f-word." He whispered the last part.

"Fuck?" said Sara. "Why would we care if she said fuck?" By this point in history, people had become so desensitized to the word "fuck" that it was considered about as bad as saying "darn" or "frigging." And since most of the people who pretended to be offended by that kind of language had died, society just embraced swearing and profanity as any other normal part of language.

"No, the other f-word."

"Foundling?"

"Sara, you're not supposed to say that!"

"Bullshit." As a new conservative, Sara was going to embrace the Free Speech movement and refuse to be triggered by the word.

"We should go ask Will about this," she said. "We can work up some talking points and write a press release by this afternoon."

Will Gant was in his office, flipping through one of his old textbooks and preparing for that morning's lecture. He looked only slightly surprised when Will and Sara burst through the door, out of breath.

"Professor Gant, have you seen this morning's *Mail-Journal*?"

"I glanced at it. I usually read it more thoroughly over lunch on my laptop."

"Did you see the story about the plasma gasification plant?" asked Sara.

"I did. What about it? Other than the 'Fucking, uh, F-word' comment?"

"We think we should be against the plant. As the Students for a Conservative Future, I mean."

"Why? I think it's a no-brainer," said Will. "It's good for the environment, it reduces waste, it reduces our utility costs, and we can even make money as a city."

"Sure, but what happens when other cities start getting their own PGPs? They'll stop exporting their trash to us, and we'll all be stuck with huge tax bills to pay for our free power."

"That's true. The plant is really only effective if it has a certain amount of waste being fed into it each day. OK, that's a good point."

"So how do we fight against it?" asked Will. "What should our stance be? We're going to have a hard time convincing people to fight against free power and less waste."

"Well, who benefits from owning the plant?"

"Don't we all?" asked Sara.

"Sure, but nobody builds a major public works project without somebody benefitting. The people who actually do the building can get rich off a single project, like a government building, widening a road, or installing EV car chargers. In this case, the PGP owner will benefit, and the land owner will, too. Where are they proposing to build this thing?"

"The story didn't actually say," said Kyle.

"Well," said Will, rubbing his chin with one hand, "one thing you could do is call the reporter who wrote the story. Ask a few questions and offer a statement about the SCF's opposition to the plan. Give her a couple basic talking points and start building a relationship. Having a relationship with a reporter will certainly help you promote your platform, and it never hurts to have someone you can share stories with. Plus they'll come to you whenever they need a quote or have questions. That's a good position for a politician to be in."

"Do it now?" Sara asked.

"No time like the present."

Sara tapped her glasses twice. "Call Carmen Cowen," she said to her glasses. "Hi, Carmen? This is Sara Cooper-Wright with the Students for a Conservative Future at Appleseed College. I had a question about your story on the proposed plasma gasification plant."

"Hi, Sara," Carmen responded. "What's the Students for a Conservative Future?"

"We're a new student organization that is seeking to disrupt the status quo and create the loyal opposition in the Appleseed community."

Kyle gave Sara a thumbs up.

"Really? I saw your press release yesterday. I thought one of the sportswriters was playing a joke on me."

"No, we're totally serious. We started the group because we wanted to fight the establishment. For too long, the liberals have run the entire playground, and they won't let anyone else play. The administration hands us student protestors meaningless victories without any real resistance, which makes it nearly impossible to effect any real, important social change."

"Are you opposed to the plasma gasification plant?" asked Carmen.

"We're still formulating our response, but initially, we're leaning away from it."

"Why? It makes good economic and environmental sense."

Sara had to refrain from shouting, "Global warming is bullshit." Instead, she said, "It smacks of government over-reach and interference. It could hurt small businesses and will spend taxpayer money but still only benefit a few people."

"That's very interesting," said Carmen, who was only a few years older than Sara. She remembered having that same drive and fire as the young conservative. She became a journalist after hearing stories from her grandparents and great-grandparents about coverage of the January 6th Insurrection Day as well as different political and sports scandals, and she decided she wanted to be a part of that. As a journalist, not a scandalous insurrectionist.

"What sort of support do you have for your stance in the city council?" Carmen asked.

"Uhh, nothing right now. If I'm being honest, we're still new at this. We just had our first meeting a few days ago, and we're still figuring things out."

Kyle slapped his forehead. Will said nothing.

"Don't you think you should find some allies on the city council? Maybe you should talk to Cody Asher and Naomi Saito. They didn't seem too keen on the idea when Mayor Windsong floated it. Call me afterward, and I'll see about interviewing you."

"That's a good idea. I'll do that." Sara thanked Carmen and hung up.

"She said there are two city council members who are opposed to the project: Cody Asher and Naomi Saito. Carmen seems to think we'd find support from them."

"I know Cody very well," said Will. "We're in the same book club, and we even went to college together. Let me see if he's available for lunch today."

A quick phone call and three hours later, the trio entered Vince's Vegan Venue, which many Appleseedlings affectionately called 'The Three 5s.'

"Will, over here," called a voice. They spotted Cody Asher standing and waving to get their attention. He and Naomi Saito were seated at an out-of-the-way table behind a short wall to hide from people walking past the restaurant or poking their heads inside. They shook hands all around, introducing themselves.

Cody was White, tall, and thin with thick brown hair and a prominent Adam's apple. His tan khakis and blue button-down shirt were pressed and starched to within an inch of their lives, and Sara wondered if she would hear any crackling when he sat back down.

Naomi was Japanese, a few inches over five feet, and had black hair pulled back into a bun. She was slender and wore an olive green blouse and black yoga pants.

The group made small talk until the server took their order, and once she left, Naomi dove right in with both feet.

"So you're the conservatives on campus?" she asked.

"Yes, we started a new group called Students for—"

"Oh, sure, we know all about you. Believe me, news like that doesn't escape the political powers that be in Appleseed, let alone Ohio. You've been the subject of discussion among many politicians in the area."

"Really? We just wanted to actually have a voice worth listening to. We're tired of making meaningless protests about no-brainer changes only to be placated by the administration like we're spoiled children. We want people to take us seriously."

"Trust me. We're taking you seriously. Everyone on the City Council takes you seriously. Some of them are a little more scared than others."

"But we don't want to be scary. I mean, we don't want to bring back the alt-right or anything like that. We don't want to bring back racism or homophobia or any of that other garbage."

"Yeah, we decided that right away. No alt-right bullshit," said Kyle.

Cody laughed. "No one is saying you are. But what you do represent to the establishment is smaller government, less government waste, and less spending on the arts and education. Ever since The Takening, the government has cut down on military spending and put it into education and the arts, which has created a leftist utopia. Artists can get lifetime grants, teachers get paid six-figure salaries, and competition for the best jobs is fierce. You represent a threat to all of that."

"We haven't actually talked about those parts of our platform yet. We just started last week and voted on our mission statement," said Sara. "We're still figuring out what we want to stand for, but right now, we're leaning toward lower taxes, supporting small business, and reducing government overreach."

"You finished your mission statement in a week?" said Cody, astonished at their efficiency. "Wow, you kids really are go-getters. Excuse me, you're not kids. That is, we recognize you as fully functioning adults with your own agency and decision-making capabilities. I apologize for infantilizing you."

"No need," said Sara. "I still think of us as kids sometimes. I'm only twenty-one."

"So, not old enough to run for mayor yet," said Naomi.

"Mayor? No! I mean, I just wanted to start—I couldn't—that is, I wouldn't even know—"

"Relax, Sara," said Will. "I think she's just teasing you. You have to be twenty-eight to run for mayor in Appleseed. But you could be on the city council..." He left that statement hanging.

"I'm only 20," Kyle offered helpfully. No one paid him any attention.

As their food arrived, they talked about the plasma gasification plant and brainstormed several reasons the SCF could oppose the installation that aligned with their nascent platform, not least of which that it would encourage more consumption and waste just to keep the PGP running.

"That will definitely benefit all the food producers and grocers. They'll be able to dispose of the waste and then use the disposal costs as tax write-offs. Restaurants could throw away more food instead of trying to be judicious with their food usage, which could have an impact on the amount of food donations. And recycling could drop off, which could require more things made from virgin plastic and paper, rather than recycled materials."

Will pulled out a small notebook made with real paper, a throwback to older technology. Seven years earlier, almost everyone had switched from using paper to using their mobile devices or tablets that recognized handwriting. Paper was still available—all recycled, of course—but it was a vintage luxury embraced by Generation Z much in the same way their Millennial parents had embraced vinyl records and typewriters.

"So who's going to spearhead the opposition?" asked Naomi.

"We thought you were," said Sara. "I mean, we can raise a lot of noise on campus, but we won't have the same impact that you can on the city council."

"True, but there are only two of us on the council who oppose it. Chase Maitland and Caitlyn Dhillon will vote for whatever the mayor wants. Chase because he's a brown-nosing yes man and Caitlyn because she and Sheila have been best friends ever since they were junior aides in our Congressperson's office thirty years ago. Zack Windless is the lone swing vote."

"But no one really pays attention to the city council, so we'll hold public hearings about the plant, but we'll get about thirty people to show up, the same people who show up at all of our meetings. You would think in a city with sixty thousand people, we'd get more at our city council meetings. Hell, that's why we were so excited about the SCF: because there were people taking an interest in local politics finally."

"Does that mean you're also conservatives?"

"Not at all," said Cody. "Our parents and grandparents would kill us. I was just eight years old when the alt-right emerged during He Who Must Not Be Named's presidency. They fought tooth and nail against everything they stood for, so they would be so upset if we switched to that party, even if it was the same one their own parents had supported in the 1980s."

"So who is going to be the public face of the opposition? Don't we need someone to speak to the public, do press conferences, and things like that?"

"Like a party leader?"

"Well, sure, like that," said Cody.

"We haven't really selected a leader yet. I mean, I'm the president of the SCF because I'm the one who signed up the group."

"I'm the vice president," said Kyle.

"And I guess I ran the last meeting. But I envisioned us as more of a leaderless collective where everyone got to be a leader of their own committees and part of the group."

"That's lefty talk," said Naomi. "Not that there's anything wrong with it, but conservatives don't think that way. They like hierarchy and power. You have to want to be the leader, even if it's only the appearance of leadership. It doesn't mean you have to be a dictator, but you do need to be the face of the party."

"But there's no reason for the media to keep talking to me. Don't we need someone who has a reason to be in the news every day?"

"You mean like a political candidate?" asked Naomi, her eyes twinkling. The mood around the table shifted imperceptibly.

"Uhh…" said Will.

"Yes, exactly," said Sara.

"Like a mayoral candidate," said Cody.

"Yes, exactly. But I'm not old enough to run for mayor."

"Neither am I," Kyle added, still helpfully. They still ignored him.

"Uhh…" Will said again.

"Can you do it?" Sara asked Cody.

"I actually ran against Sheila eight years ago. She beat me so badly that no one would agree to run four years later. I was barely able to hold onto my city council seat, but I've been fortunate to stay locked in since then. My last opponent actually died from a heart attack six months before the election, and I'm running unopposed in the upcoming election. That has been one of the upsides of The Takening. We're all shoo-ins for our offices."

"Cody, that's a little insensitive," chided Naomi.

"Yes, dear—er, dearplorable. That is, yes, it's deplorable what I just said," said Cody, badly covering his slip of the tongue. Will rolled his eyes at Appleseed's worst-kept secret in local politics. "Regardless, I can't risk another run, Naomi has no desire to, and you're both too young. That only leaves one of us."

"Uhh…" Will said a third time. The other four turned and looked at him. "No. No, absolutely not!" he blurted. "I refuse. I refuse. I just … refuse."

"Oh, come on, buddy! We need you," said Cody.

Will closed his eyes and shook his head. "Nope. Won't do it."

"The city needs you."

"No, they don't. The city has been just fine without me."

"Ohio needs you!" Cody felt patriotic pride swell within his heart and wished there was a brass band playing "America the Beautiful" behind him as an American flag fluttered in a strong, wholesome Midwestern breeze.

Will said nothing. He just crossed his arms and clamped his mouth shut.

"*Democracy* needs you!" Cody said, arms outstretched, the imaginary band swelling to its grand finale.

"Goddammit." Will hung his head. "I hate you," he mumbled into his chest.

"This is so exciting!" exclaimed Sara as they returned to Will's office. "I can't believe you're going to run for mayor! Can we work on your campaign? What's your platform going to be? We'll need fliers. Old-fashioned paper fliers! Ooh, and campaign buttons. We can frame you as the old-school politician who wants to return to old-school values."

Will tried not to dwell on the fact that, to Sara, "old-school" meant anything more than twenty-five years ago.

"Whoa, whoa," he said. "I'm still not entirely sure I want to do this. I mean, it's one thing to be a moderate in this community. People tend to leave me alone because of academic freedom. But once I out myself as anything but a Democrat, they'll roast me alive."

"Surely not," said Kyle, hoping they wouldn't ignore him now. "I mean, society is so much more accepting and willing to embrace diverse ideas nowadays, right?"

Will stared blankly at Kyle.

"Right?" Kyle repeated.

"Well, there will be the usual political battles, but if we're right, people will see the need for a loyal opposition and at least support our right to our ideas," said Sara.

Kyle looked like he believed her. Neither of them saw Will roll his eyes.

Sara plopped down into one of Will's visitor's chairs and started tapping away on her tablet. "I'll start working on some button designs and see if anyone still makes those. And I'll design some geofenced yard signs that people can see on their e-glasses when they walk past a supporter's house. Oh, and we have to write your platform and write position papers on each of the planks. One plank has to be against plasma gasification because it's a big government program. And we'll want to get the SCF to be your campaign team, and—"

"Sara. Sara. *SARA!*" Will half-shouted to derail her ramblings. "Settle down. I haven't actually accepted anything. I told Cody and Naomi that I would think about—"

Sara held up a finger. "Hold on, Professor Gant, my mom is calling." She walked out into the hallway. "Hi, Mom, how are—ow! Why are you shouting?"

"Students for a Conservative Future, Mom. Not the Nazis. God, you're always exaggerating."

"I will not! I started the thing! I can't quit now."

"Because Mom, we were tired of always—" Sara wandered away from the office, and Will and Kyle could no longer hear what she was saying.

"It sounds like you're not interested in running for mayor, Professor Gant," said Kyle.

"Well, I'm not *not* interested," said Will. "But I'm concerned about what this could do to my personal life. We may not have the partisan politics that we used to, but politics are still nasty and harsh, and they take a toll on everyone involved. My father-in-law used to say that the people who were qualified to run for office were smart enough not to and the people who wanted to run were too dumb to be qualified."

"Jesus, that sounds bleak."

"Yeah, well, politics before The Takening were bitter and mean, and they brought out the worst in people. Back in the early 2020s, when we had the COVID pandemic, people politicized health and safety. You were either for vaccines and protection, or you were against them. You were for the community, or you were for individual freedoms. That way of thinking just ballooned and got more hysterical on both sides until it happened again. At the time, we thought COVID was bad. But The Takening was much worse. We lost half the world over it. Literally."

"Yes, but the world is so much better than it was."

"Is it? Kyle, half the people in the world died. How can that be better? We lost four billion people in a few months because people couldn't agree on one simple issue, and it was all due to stubborn egos."

"Yeah, the Republicans."

"No, everybody's! Don't you see? Families were torn apart, children were orphaned, and parents lost their children. The Republicans wanted to 'stick it to the libs' and the Democrats ridiculed and mocked the Republicans for ignoring the science. The Democrats refused to offer empathy and support to their enemies, and the Republicans wouldn't ask their enemies for help."

"So we're to blame, too?"

"We're all to blame, son. All of us."

"They didn't teach us this in school," said Kyle. "They made it sound like the Republicans were just anti-science and didn't care about the people around them."

"Of course they did. That's the only way the survivors could deal with the fact that they shared the blame. Even now, many of them still have survivor's guilt and rely on some heavy-duty pharmaceuticals just to get through the day."

"Is it really that bad?"

Will's eyes welled up, and tears ran down his face. "I was thirty years old when it happened. My father caught it because he had attended a county Republican party and got whale spouted. He was a Democrat, but he believed in local politics, so he was attending a debate. He gave it to my mom, who used to go to protests when she was younger, but she had given a lot of that up when she got older. She was a librarian and loved books. And she loved my dad and let him play politics all he wanted.

"When the two of them realized they had it, they locked themselves in the house and were dead three days later. They called me the day before they died. I was across the country because I had just taken my first teaching position at Portland State University. I wasn't allowed to travel, so we said our goodbyes over video call. It was the last time we ever talked."

Will wiped at his face and sniffed as tears streamed down Kyle's face, too. Will continued:

"Tens of thousands of us volunteered to help clean up the bodies because so many people in the National Guard had it, too. We had to wear hazmat suits and oxygen tanks and be quarantined after each day. It was so hot that the sweat pooled in our boots so we squished when we walked. And the incinerators ran twenty-four hours a day because we couldn't let the virus survive. Besides, there was no room to bury all the bodies, and no one could have produced enough coffins anyway."

Will wiped his eyes again and blew his nose into a tissue from a desk drawer. "Politics and unreason killed four billion people when it didn't have to. The survivors bear as much of the blame as the ones who died. I sometimes think maybe the dead got the better end of the deal."

"How? We have peace, we don't have poverty, there are plenty of resources for everyone, the environment is on the mend, and people are more educated than they were before."

"Was it worth it, though? Who in your life did you lose?"

"Nobody, I guess. I was only a year old when it happened, so I never really knew what was going on. We were lucky because my family didn't have any conservative friends or family members. They had isolated themselves on the farm so they didn't have to associate with those people."

Will gave a sad chuckle. "'Those' people? When I was a kid, referring to anyone as 'those people' was enough to start a fight."

"It still is. The college banned the phrase. I shouldn't have even said it. It just slipped out. I apologize."

"We're not fucking Nazis, Mother! Stop calling us that!" Sara shouted from down the hallway.

"We're not fucking Nazis, Kyle. You don't have to apologize for every little slip."

"Sorry, it's a reflex action. Everyone gets offended at every slip of the tongue that it's become so ingrained."

Sara burst into Will's office again. "My fucking mothers. Good God, you'd think I wanted to eat children and murder old people! Why can't they—did I miss something?"

Will and Kyle both wiped their faces. "No, we were just talking. It's, uh, dusty in here," said Kyle. "Professor Gant's books collect a lot of dust, and we were, uh, sneezing."

"Uh-huh," said Sara, unconvinced.

"We were talking about The Takening," said Will. "I was telling Kyle what it was like when it happened."

"I was only two," said Sara, lowering herself back into her chair. She cleared her throat a few times before she continued. "Both my moms lost their parents. Mom Kelly was estranged from her parents for being gay, but Mom Samantha had a good relationship with hers. They fought for the chance to be married and faced a lot of hate and homophobia when they were younger. I think that's why they're so upset with me for starting the SCF."

"It reminds them of what happened," said Will.

"But we're not like that," said Sara. "We don't have to be like that. I don't see why we can't just be financial conservatives and leave it at that. Lower taxes, smaller government, pro-business. That kind of thing. We don't want to be arch-conservatives. We just want to be the loyal opposition to the powers that be. But maybe they're right. We should just quit."

"You can't quit," said Will, rising to his feet.

It was Sara's turn to wipe her eyes. "Why not?"

"Because I need you as my campaign manager."

"You're going to run?" asked Sara.

"Why not? Sheila Windsong is turning the mayor's office into a lifelong appointment, and I question some of her tactics. Now shake my hand." Sara and Kyle leaped to their feet, and each shook his hand.

"We have just formed The Committee to Elect Will Gant Mayor," said Will. "I need both of you supporting me if we're going to make a go of this."

"Professor Gant, this is so exciting!" said Sara.

"You know it, Professor. We'll bring change to City Hall," said Kyle.

"Call me Will. Professor Gant was my father." He winked at Kyle, who started feeling the dust from Will's books again.

CHAPTER 6

"We've got o-o-o-o-o-one! It looks like Appleseed's surviving adult Republican has thrown his hat into the ring for the race for mayor. Professor Will Gant, who many believed to be a moderate Democrat, revealed he was really a wolf in sheep's clothing after all. Gant is a professor of history at Appleseed College Of The Arts and is the faculty advisor to the Students for a Conservative Future, the far-right student group that threatens our way of life and our beliefs. Is the Nazi party returning to our fair city? Tune into WSED, Appleseed's TV News at 11 for more."

"The Republicans, who we thought were long gone, have slithered out from under their rock in America's Heartland, Appleseed, Ohio. We told you about the America-hating revolutionaries known as the Students for a Conservative Future, who invaded Appleseed College Of The Arts. Now it seems that the radical students' faculty advisor, Professor Will Gant, wants to goose-step his way into the mayor's office. He has announced his candidacy for mayor of the charming city of Appleseed. We here at WARB, Ann Arbor's Community Radio

Station, throw our wholehearted support behind Mayor Sheila Windsong and her vision for a brighter community. We'll speak to political historian Cheryl Clayton about it on our weekly politics show at 3:00 this afternoon."

"Don't forget, Appleseedians, it's the 48th annual Appleseed Apple Seed Festival this weekend. We'll celebrate all things Johnny Appleseed, apple trees, and of course, apple pie and coffee. Be sure to visit the artists' tents, the merchant tents, and the classic car show. Herb Purvis-Hatchett promises to show off his 1998 Pontiac Grand Am, which he has restored to factory condition. Stay tuned to WAPPL for more local news here on Appleseed's Golden Oldies with the hits of the 10s, 20s, and 30s. Next up, we're firing up the way-way-wayback machine with a little tune from the Spin Doctors."

"Looks like we've got problems at the college," said Enrique Medina. One of Enrique's jobs as the deputy mayor was to bring local news to Sheila since she couldn't be bothered to actually read any of the news stories or watch the TV news. Today, Enrique was wearing a mauve three-button suit with a white silk shirt and a gold chain hanging outside his shirt. He was also wearing a pair of canvas vintage basketball shoes that his grandfather had owned but never wore because they were a part of his prized sneaker collection. Enrique had inherited the entire collection and only wore them on special occasions.

"Again? Is this the fucking SCF again?" said Sheila Windsong. She was reclining in her office's lounge chair, which she used for meditating, mid-day naps, or strapping on her favorite VR glasses and taking skiing holidays between meetings. Today, she was skiing down Mont Blanc in France. She slightly swayed and leaned as an AI-generated skier navigated the twists and turns of the expert slope.

Enrique shivered a bit because Sheila had turned up the air conditioning to add to her enjoyment of the skiing experience.

"No, it's that history professor, Will Gant. You know, the, uh—" Enrique lowered his voice to a whisper, "*Black* guy. He's running for mayor against you."

"What the fuck? Ow, shit! Goddammit, you made me crash!" Sheila tore the VR goggles off her face. "Fuck, it's cold in here! Tiffani, set my office temp back to 72," she hollered to her administrative assistant.

"Sure thing," said Tiffani, a hint of disdain in her voice. "Computer, set the mayor's temperature to 72," she said loudly and slowly to remind Sheila how to do it herself.

"Thank you, Tiffi. You're a peach. I don't know what I'd do without you."

"Probably die," said Tiffani, only half-joking.

"Close the door, Enrique," ordered Sheila.

"Computer, close the door," said Enrique, matching Tiffani's tone. After the door was shut, Sheila ran her security sweep with her smartphone-looking device. The sweeper had a single app installed on it called BugSweep that her IT staff had designed so she could check her office for any listening devices and hidden cameras.

It didn't actually work; it just beeped and made pinging noises and always registered an all-clear. The IT department had figured no one actually cared enough about Appleseed's mayor that they wouldn't bother to bug her office. They issued occasional upgrades, such as changing the colors of the search waves or upgrading the database of devices it searched for, but it never delivered on the promise of the name.

If anything, the leaks from the mayor's office didn't come from listening devices; they came from Tiffani Stoudemire, who complained to anyone at The Hopping Frog who would listen.

That's where she spent most nights after work, wearing short plunge-neck blouses that showed off her enhanced breasts and her back tattoo in an attempt to pick up a wayward graduate student, her botox treatments and laser plastic surgery not quite fooling anybody. Or, if pickings were slim, she would settle for an enthusiastic college student with lots of energy and little experience. After a few vigorous rounds of sex, she would spend the rest of the night talking about how stupid her boss was. Her conquest of the night would end up leaving, citing an early class and strict professor, telling his or her friends about all the best gossip.

"I gotta quit fucking students," she would say to her cat Smudge, who licked his crotch in agreement.

"So what do you want to do about Will Gant?" Enrique asked after Sheila's successful sweep.

"Is he a serious threat?"

"No, not at all. We ran a quick poll this morning in the morning news feed, and most people supported you, seventy-five to twenty-five."

"Seventy-five percent? Did we drop?"

"Well, it's a five-point drop from the last poll, but I imagine it's just people who want to try something new. Plus, we had a lot of college students in the pool, and they always do stupid shit like that just to fuck with the polls. Remember that one where people said public nudity should be mandatory? Those dumbass students got all their friends to vote on it and skewed it to eighty-five percent of people supporting public nudity."

"Yeah, Tiffani wore a bikini to work that day. I mean, I know she looks great and everything with all the work she's had done, but that back tattoo is nearly hanging down to her ass crack now." Sheila shuddered at the memory. "Still, a five-point drop? It can't be a coincidence."

"So what if it isn't? You're still ahead in the polls."

"Not enough! Tomorrow, it's seventy points, and next week, I'm at sixty-five. And next election, I'm looking at a serious challenge by some hotshot gym teacher with a chiseled jaw and washboard abs."

"Yeah, but he's got one thing working against him."

"Oh yeah, what's that?"

"Will Gant. Is. A. *Moderate!*" Enrique hissed.

"So what?"

"So? So that's everything! Being a moderate is as far right as you can get in this country anymore, especially here in America's heartland."

"And...?"

"And we don't have to worry about fighting him on the issues." Enrique stared at Sheila, waiting for the penny to drop. Seconds ticked by.

"I don't get it."

"We just remind people that he's a moderate!"

"Still not following you."

Enrique threw up his hands. "That's the far right now! We label Will Gant as a far-right extremist who wants to destroy Appleseed's way of life, and we brand you as Appleseed's savior. You stand for inclusivity, diversity, and solid family values. And we say that, as a Republican, Gant wants to tell people how to live their personal lives, what to think, what they're allowed to say, and what they should believe."

Sheila's eyes widened as the penny finally dropped, and she got what Enrique was saying.

"There it is," he said.

"So, we just make the race about his politics, not my accomplishments?"

"Such as they are, yes."

"I've accomplished stuff!" Sheila protested.

"Mm-hmm. Of course, you have."

"I *have!*"

"And I believe you," Enrique said in a tone that said he believed no such thing.

"We raised salaries to $140,000 for beginning teachers."

"Uh-huh."

"It was $127,000 for the previous six years."

"Sure, that's a ten percent increase."

"And the funding for our artists' grants went up by four percent."

"Just like the national cost of living allowance."

"And... and.... goddammit, I've been the mayor for nearly twelve years. Surely I've done a lot more than that."

"Well, you did just sign the executive order to increase the two-day educational seminars to a four-day residential camp."

"See? I did that, too!" said Sheila, looking smug.

"Which people will hate."

Sheila's jaw dropped. "What? Why?"

"Because we're telling people how to live their personal lives, what to think, what they're allowed to say, and what they should believe. That's why we didn't tell anyone we did it."

"Ungrateful fuckers!" said Sheila. "We're helping them be better. We're helping people be better people—why can't they see that? Because we can't let people demean or denigrate others. They have to use people-first language and be tolerant and accepting of everyone so hate won't be allowed to flourish anymore! Do you remember what it was like before? Because I do."

"I know, but when we polled people about the re-education camps—"

"Educational seminars."

"—whatever—people responded very negatively. You only got twenty-eight percent approval."

"See? Some people like them," said Sheila, a glimmer of hope crossing her face.

"They had just come out of the camps."

"Seminars."

"Seminars. Basically, people don't like being told what to do, even with the best of intentions."

"Did you tell them they're voluntary?"

"We station armed guards outside the cabins and at the entrance to the gates."

"Armed? I thought we didn't have guns anymore."

"Well, with stun sticks and stun guns."

"Ah. So maybe I shouldn't mention the camps in my speeches."

"Seminars."

"Seminars. Shit, now you've got me doing it," grumbled Sheila.

"Now do you see why we need to make the campaign about Will Gant's politics? We accuse him of being soft on the arts, hating diversity, and wanting to increase military spending and roll back environmental regulations."

"We don't even have a military. And we have nothing to do with environmental regulations," said Sheila. She thought for a moment. "Ooh! I've got it!" She stood up so fast she had to put her hand out to steady herself. "Wait, wait, I don't got it. Hold on. I'm OK. Let me go. I'm fine."

Enrique let go of her arm and sat back down.

"I just got up too fast is all," said Sheila. "Why don't we make the PGP central to the campaign? By getting him to campaign against it and me campaigning for it, we can drum up a whole lot more support for it, right? We can also paint him as being against the environment."

"Well…"

"Yeah, more people will hear about it. Rather than just letting people decide for themselves what they should think about it, we'll be able to constantly campaign on it and run ads about its benefits and how Will Gant hates Appleseed and wants us to keep using unreliable solar and wind energy."

"I don't know if we should do that."

"Oh, yeah! It'll be great. I'll get my plant, and we'll be able to show that Will Gant is an out-of-touch dinosaur who wants to take us back to the Boring '20s."

"That's really not such a good—"

"Quiet, we're doing it. Get me a couple ad people, and let's start working on some campaign ads. I want to be ready to go when he officially announces his candidacy And get one of the political bloggers to ambush him about the PGP at his announcement press conference."

Enrique started tapping away at his tablet, trying to keep up with Sheila's rapid-fire instructions.

"Ooh, and we want to really make sure he gets his message out there. The more people think he's against the PGP, the more people will vote for me. With any luck, I could hit eighty, maybe even ninety percent of the total vote."

"Jesus, you only have to win the thing; you don't have to humiliate the guy."

"He's already going to be humiliated. This isn't for him. I want this to be a message to anyone who wants to run against me in the future. In four years, eight years, even in twenty years, I want people to remember that in 2053, Sheila Windsong got ninety fucking percent of the vote, and no one will dare run against me again. I'll be mayor for life!"

"How are you going to get people to do that? It doesn't sound like he's going to have much of a campaign. Those SCF kids are running the thing, so he doesn't even have a proper campaign staff, let alone money to do it."

"We'll give him some operating capital."

"What? Why would you give him your campaign money?"

"Not my campaign money, dolt!" said Sheila. "Roy Burkhart-Lanning's money. The guy from Braun McLaren."

"Why would he give money to the guy who's running against his company?"

"He won't. He'll give it to me to support my campaign, and then we'll funnel it over to Bert Welch at the university and ask him to give it to Will for his campaign."

"Your ex-husband? How will you even give it to Bert?" Enrique was aghast but intrigued.

"We'll ask him to design some campaign posters or some shit. Maybe give him a consulting gig or something. We'll pay him, and then he'll 'double-cross me'" Sheila used air quotes, but managed to do it wrong, "and give all the money to Will. That way, if anyone comes looking into it, it just looks like I got fucked over by my ex-husband."

"Even though it's totally illegal."

"It's not illegal. We'll really have him design some posters and write a report about what Foundlings these days really want out of politics."

"You know we're not supposed to call them that, right? You can't actually say that in public."

"Fuck those uptight little fucks! In my day, Generation Y was tough. We didn't have any of this trigger bullshit or whining about anxiety. We went through some shit."

"You were born in 1996," said Enrique.

"So?"

"So you were three months away from being in Gen Z. I mean, come on. You make it sound like you were a Gen Xer or something."

"Those decrepit old fucks? They're dying off. I mean, my mom is 84, and she looks pretty good for her age and everything, but Gen X is past it."

"I love her tattoo sleeves though. She's so badass. I got to hang out with her at your last holiday party, and she's a hoot. Who was Metallica though?"

"Forget that," said Sheila, waving her hand. "We need to think about the future. Computer, call Roy Burkhart-Lanning."

"Seriously, that's not such a good idea—"

"Shut the fuck—Roy! How's it going? Listen, I need your help with something. Can you swing by the office in the next few days? And bring your checkbook."

Sheila listened for a few seconds.

"It's a small book that has a ledger in it along with a pad of checks."

She listened again.

"It's a piece of paper that you write a note on to give a certain amount of money to another person."

Pause.

"Yes, like an electronic transfer."

Pause.

"Yes, on paper."

Pause.

"Right, like your Memaw did."

Pause.

"Because I wanted—look, it's just an expression, alright! Just show up here *with your electronic bank transfer codes* because I need your help with something. I can't go into it on the phone though."

Pause.

"Thursday is fine. Yep, 10 a.m. See you in a couple days. Bye-bye." Sheila tapped her glasses and then tapped them again. "Call Bert."

She waited for a few seconds. "Hey, it's me. No, that's not why I'm calling."

Pause.

"Because you're with Katie and I'm with Fallyn. Listen, I need you to do something for me."

Pause.

"Look, be at my office at 3 p.m. on Thursday because I want to hire you to design some campaign posters and write a report. I'll fill you in on Thursday. Right, right. I've gotta—I miss you, too—no, not like—no, don't bring Katie, I hate her—I've gotta—Bye-bye. Bye-bye. Bye-bye now."

"Alright, it looks like we've got ourselves a campaign to run."

CHAPTER 7

"**OK, what's so hot shit important that you** made me come here without my partner?" asked Bert Welch. It was the same afternoon, and he was sitting across from Sheila at her desk with Enrique seated nearby. Bert was wearing his favorite art professor outfit—vintage blue jeans and an old denim work shirt with the name "Earl" stitched onto a patch.

Bert liked to look like he wore vintage clothing, but he had given himself this outfit as a birthday present from Yesterdayville.com three weeks earlier. Even his leather work boots were vegan leather reproductions. He had his notepad on his lap and was ready to take notes.

"I need your help with my upcoming campaign," said Sheila. "I want you to give some money to Will Gant."

"Why can't you give money to Will Gant? And how does this help your campaign? Isn't he the opposition?"

"Yes, but he doesn't have any chance of winning."

"And you want to give him a chance? That seems awfully... uh, sporting of you?" said Bert, thoroughly confused.

"I just need him to be my King Pippin," said Sheila.

"Who?"

"Pippin Héristal?"

Bert shook his head. "I don't know who that is."

"From *The Short Reign of Pippin IV*? By John Steinbeck? It's almost a hundred years old?"

Enrique and Bert both stared blankly at Sheila.

"Jesus, doesn't anyone read anymore? Fuck, never mind. Just—" Sheila took a deep breath. "The French leaders needed someone to push and revolt against as a way to get the people interested in politics again, so they appointed Pippin to be the King. Then he was summarily dethroned as planned, and he returned to his life as an amateur astronomer."

"But Will Gant is a historian," said Bert.

Sheila buried her face in her hands and muttered, "Why did I ever marry you?" She raised her head to see if Bert had disappeared but was disappointed to see he was still there.

She continued, "I need someone to push against during my campaign, and I can't do that if he's running a shitty campaign on a shoestring budget. I need to get people interested in our local politics again, so it makes perfect sense that I get a far-right extremist as my opponent. He won't have any chance of winning, but I'll get the coverage I need to be in front of the voters."

"What are the issues?"

"You don't need to know the specifics—just understand that I want to run a good campaign and bring some of the most important issues to light. I can't do that if Will is nothing more than a flash-in-the-pan candidate who fizzles out three weeks after he starts."

"And how am I supposed to do that?"

"Roy Burkhart-Lanning is going to give some money to my campaign—$100,000, in fact—and you're going to give it to Will."

Roy was actually going to give $250,000 to Sheila's campaign, but she was not about to share that little tidbit with her ex-husband.

"Why would I do that?" asked Bert.

"Because I'm going to upset you."

"How so? You already had an affair with a woman and divorced me over it."

"Jesus Christ, will you ever let that go? It was thirteen years ago!"

"How can I forget? You were my first love! Sorry, Enrique. I didn't mean for you to get dragged into this," said Bert.

"Huh?" asked Enrique, who had been scribbling another poem on his own notepad.

History's past lives on
Bitter recriminations
Love's eternal sting

"Sorry, I, uh, I was writing notes about the campaign," Enrique mumbled.

"Look, do you want to help me or not?" asked Sheila. "I need you to design some flyers and write a report about what the Beta Generation wants out of local politics."

"And you'll give me $100,000 out of that?"

"Yes, and then I'll complain about the work, and you'll give it to Will in disgust."

"I want $125,000," said Bert.

"What?"

"I want $125,000," Bert repeated. "Then I'll give him $100,000 and keep the other $25K for myself."

This was going exactly as Sheila and Enrique expected, although they thought he was going to say $150,000, so this was a nice surprise for both of them.

"Fine," Sheila huffed. "We'll give you $125,000." She looked pointedly at Enrique who fought to hide a smile. "Then, we'll have a public disagreement, and you'll retaliate by giving $100,000 to Will. You can even become one of his most ardent supporters if you'd like."

"I just don't know how Katie will take it. She's very suspicious of Will and the SCF. Some of her best students are heading it up, and she's taking it all rather personally. But it may help her feel better if she thinks she's teaching them a lesson."

"Maybe we should funnel them some money as well?" mused Sheila. "Enrique, what do you think?"

Enrique started. "Huh? Oh, sure, Sheila. Whatever you say. That sounds good." He and Sheila looked at Bert.

"What? I'm not giving them anything. Do you know how far $25,000 goes these days?" He crossed his arms and tried to look serious; he looked like a petulant child.

"Can you give us a minute, please, Bert?" Sheila asked. "Just wait out there. Talk to Tiffani or something."

Bert glowered at Sheila and left the office.

"And close the door, please, Tiffani," she called.

"Computer, close the door," called Tiffani. The door shut as requested.

"Fuck, I thought we nearly had another $25K," said Enrique.

"Yeah, well, it's not like we were planning on it."

"That's three months' mortgage payment for me," said Enrique. He lived in the tiny home village west of downtown Appleseed.

"Oh, cry me a river. You already make ten times that much. Let's give it to him and have him give it to the SCF."

She crossed the room and opened the door. "Bert," she said, crooking her finger at him. He was staring at a painting on the outer office wall.

"Is that the one I gave you for your birthday?" he asked.

Sheila looked a bit embarrassed. "Yes, it is."

"And you liked it enough to hang it out in the main office?"

Sheila yanked Bert into her office and slammed the door. "Idiot!" she hissed. "I gave it to Tiffani for her sixty-fifth birthday because I forgot to get her anything."

"But I thought you liked it."

"Now is not the time, Bert!" She pushed Bert into his seat and resumed her chair. "Enrique and I talked it over. We managed to scrape together another $25,000 for you to give to the SCF. It was pretty tight, but we found it. You certainly drive a hard bargain."

Bert grinned and put his hands behind his head. "I wasn't captain of my high school debate club for nothing."

"Yep, you had us over the proverbial barrel," said Enrique.

Sheila silenced him with a glance. "Go back to your poetry," she said.

CHAPTER 8

"**P**ROFESSOR GANT?" ASKED BERT, STANDING over Will's table at the Johnny Bench Student Union a week later.

"Yes, uh…?" said Will, unsure of who Bert was.

"It's me, Professor Welch. Bert Welch. Professor Bert Welch. From the Arts Department."

"Oh, my goodness, yes! I apologize. I didn't recognize you outside the art studio." Will stood and shook hands with Bert.

Will was meeting with The Committee to Elect Will Gant Mayor campaign staff, which consisted of Sara, Kyle, Griffin, and Callie. They were meeting at the student union because Will didn't think it was ethical to do campaign work in a tax-payer-funded private office. Meanwhile, other members of the SCF were out knocking on doors and canvassing for Will, passing out real paper flyers at the mall and downtown as well as in several neighborhoods. The topic of paper flyers had caused a bit of a kerfuffle.

"People will love the novelty of paper. I'll bet they haven't seen it in years," Griffin had said at The Committee to Elect Will Gant Mayor planning meeting two days earlier. He had fully embraced Will's love of books and was even beginning to collect a few of his own, so the idea of using paper for a campaign appealed to him.

"Are we using organic and ethically harvested paper?" said Callie. "We need to make sure everything is organic and ethically harvested."

"Je-SUS, just give it a rest, would you? Everything is organic and ethically harvested these days. You can't find anything that's not organic and ethically harvested."

"That's a micro-aggression, Griffin McKenna. One more of those, and I'll report you on the personal justice app."

Years ago, Appleseed College developed a PDT app for students to report micro-aggressions in the classroom, either against other students or the faculty. In the first year, the system had overloaded when students were reporting every insult, eye roll, snide remark, and askance glance. Finally, the creators had set up an automated response that said administrators were being made aware of their report and would take it under consideration and respond if they felt it merited further discussion.

The developer had then written an algorithm that only searched for reports that indicated danger or violence and archived everything else. Anything else that included terms like "eye roll" or "pointed a finger" were immediately deleted.

The developer had long since left and failed to tell her successor about the algorithm, and no one at the College was ever the wiser.

"Is that a threat? Maybe I'll report *you*!" Griffin jabbed a finger at Callie.

"There's another one! I'm definitely reporting you, asshole."

"Oh, real mature, Callie. That's going in *my* report!"

"Please shut the hell up!" shouted Sara. "Seriously, you're supposed to be adults. Fucking act like it!"

Callie and Griffin looked at each other, then said in unison, "Computer, micro-aggression report on Sara Cooper-Wright."

"So, he's a Nazi?" asked Cal Goldtassel, a resident of Appleseed, Ohio.

Cal had been intrigued to hear a knock at his door. He was 78 years old and still remembered the days when real-life people would just pop in and say hello for absolutely no reason at all. So it was a real thrill that a young person would want to talk with him, something that hadn't happened since before The Takening. He longed for the days when he and his friends could sit around in a group and text each other, so this promised to be a real treat.

"No, sir, he's not a Nazi," said Trent Chang-Ramirez, who was volunteering as one of the student canvassers. They had been intrigued by the novelty of meeting new people; they were not any longer.

"Does anyone actually knock on doors anymore?" Trent had asked in The Committee to Elect Will Gant Mayor planning meeting. "Isn't that, like, illegal or something? That seems as archaic as actually calling people on their phones."

"Ewwwww!" shrieked The Committee to Elect Will Gant Mayor. Other than Will Gant himself, nobody on The Committee to Elect Will Gant Mayor was over the age of twenty-two. So everyone was skeptical when Will suggested they "go old-school," whatever the hell that was.

"You know, paper flyers and knocking on people's doors to talk to them," Will explained.

"Ewwwww!" shrieked The Committee to Elect Will Gant Mayor.

"I suppose you're going to have us watch television next," Griffin snorted. "Like on an *actual* television!" The Committee to Elect Will Gant Mayor howled with laughter. They looked at each other and rolled their eyes. *Oh, those crazy Zoomers*, they messaged to each other on their PDTs.

Trent and Grace Blasingame-Odoyo had been visiting people in their homes to drum up support for the last three hours, and the conversations had all been about the same.

"He's a moderate candidate, which in this day and age only appears to put him on the far right," corrected Trent.

"So, he's a far-right extremist?" asked Cal. "I thought they were extinct." Cal had known some far-right extremists when he was younger and enjoyed picking fights with them on social media.

"Noooo," groaned Trent, trying hard not to sigh or clutch their hair. "He's an old-school moderate. He's on the end of the current political spectrum, but he's still more closely aligned with liberal ideals than with historic conservatives." Trent had repeated this mantra over and over during the last three hours, and they wanted to quit politics forever. They wondered how Grace was doing.

Grace Blasingame-Odoyo also hated her job, and she hated people.

She had been talking with Dr. Kaitlyn Whitmer-Bradley-Brickman, a former life coach who was trying to get Grace to achieve her full potential and embrace her inner child.

"My inner child is fine," said Grace. "She just wants to tell you about Will Gant's campaign for mayor."

"Will Gant? Is he that Nazi?" said Dr. Whitmer-Bradley-Brickman.

"No, not at all, Ms. Whitmer-Bradley-Brickman."

"Dr. Whitmer-Bradley-Brickman," said Dr. Whitmer-Bradley-Brickman.

"Oh, no kidding? I was thinking about going to graduate school. What is your degree in?"

"Homeopathy and essential oils," she said in a haughty tone that implied she was looking down her nose at Grace.

"Huh. That's…interesting? Can I just call you Dr. Whitmer?" she asked Dr. Whitmer-Bradley-Brickman.

"No, you may not," said Dr. Whitmer-Bradley-Brickman.

"OK, thank you for your time," said Grace. "'Bye, Dr. Whitmer."

"It's Dr. Whitmer-Bradley-Brickman, goddammit!" shouted Dr. Whitmer-Bradley-Brickman as she slammed her door.

Trent and Grace met back on the sidewalk. "I've fucking had enough of this," said Trent.

"Me, too," said Grace. "Let's go back to the campaign office and see if we can hand out flyers instead."

"What can I do for you, Professor Welch?" said Will.

"Please, call me Bert." Bert Welch needed to get Will to trust him, and he couldn't do that by flexing his Ph.D. on another professor.

"Thank you. Call me Will."

"Will. Now, I wanted to help you in your campaign against Sheila Windsong."

"I thought she was your ex-wife."

"She is. That's why I want to help you win."

"Ahh," said Will, not understanding.

"She hired me to write a report about what the Foundl—er, Beta Generation wants from local politics and to create some artistic campaign posters. When I delivered the results, she called my work derivative and accidentalist."

"Er," said Will, not sure how to respond.

"We argued, and she said some pretty hurtful things."

"Like calling your work derivative?"

"And accidentalist, yes. So, I decided a great way to screw her over was to put the money she gave me into your campaign. I'm going to donate $100,000 to your efforts."

"Oh, Professor Welch, that's amazing," said Sara, springing to her feet. "That's going to make a big difference to our campaign."

"Sara, isn't it?" said Bert.

"Yes, Sara Cooper-Wright. We met at the Natalie Clifford Barney Hall protest last month."

"Oh, that's right. You were the ringleader."

"Well, co-leader, but yes."

"Professor Sartoris has talked about you and your work with the Students for a Conservative Future. I was impressed with your initiative and innovation, so I wanted to donate $25,000 to your group's efforts as well."

"Really? Oh my CHiP, that's so generous. Thank you so much!"

"You're welcome. It's good to see young people take an interest in politics, as I discussed in the report I did for Sheila. Which she now hates. So, I wanted to make sure I could help guide you. I'll zap the money over to you shortly, but I wanted to let you know why I sent it."

Kyle, Griffin, and Callie all stood and expressed their fervent thanks as well. Bert shook hands with each of them and wished them well.

"Mission accomplished," Bert voice-messaged to Enrique. "The package has been delivered. Repeat, tell Cactus the package has been delivered."

"Uhh, roger?" said Enrique, trying to think back to all the military movies he watched for his Understanding the Patriarchy class he took as an undergrad. "Cactus says well-done, Tango Mike."

"What?" said Bert.

"What?" shouted Katie when Bert informed her of his donations. "What do you mean you gave Will Gant $100,000? And $25,000 to those alt-right kids? How could you do that? They're the enemy!"

"The enemy? Whoa, that's not very accepting of you. They're just kids going through a rebellious phase and trying to figure out who they are."

"Pre-adults. And no they're not; they're close-minded conservatives! Not only do they go against everything this institution stands for, they're embracing everything that literally divided this world in half forty years ago."

"I think you're overreacting," said Bert.

"Oh, I'm not even close," said Katie. "Not only did you give comfort and aid to the enemy, but you just blew $125,000 on a no-win candidate. That's a decent entry-level salary for one of these kids—dammit, pre-adults!—when they leave college. Besides, you didn't even talk to me about it or ask my opinion."

"Why should I?" said Bert.

"Because we're a team! Because we're a couple. Because I thought we had a future together and that we talked about major financial decisions together. Hell, I asked you whether I should buy a new bicycle."

"And what did I tell you?"

"You mumbled 'whatever' and went back to reading."

"Right. Because it's your money. This is my money to do with as I please."

"So much for our partnership!"

"We can be independent partners. We don't have to be so enmeshed in each other's lives that we can't make a decision without the other person. I don't want that for us. I want you to be your own person, and I want to be my own person."

"But I wanted that! My parents had that when I was a kid, and they worked well together. I grew up admiring that, and I wanted that for myself."

Bert sensed this was not going the way he wanted it to, so he decided to try a different tactic.

"Look, we're veering off-track here. I was all set to take Sheila's money from her, but when she insulted my work, I wanted to get back at her. What better way to do that than to unseat her as mayor?"

"And so you thought giving away $125,000 of *your* money was going to hurt *her*? CHiP, are you really that dumb?"

"Whoa, whoa, micro-aggression!" said Bert.

"Oh, no," said Katie. "This is an out-and-out major aggression. I can't believe you would be so stupid."

"Don't call me stupid! I have a Ph.D."

"In art! You're a doctor of fucking art! You're a fucking art doctor. When someone says, 'Is there a doctor in the house?' it's not because they have a sick painting!"

"That's a very important field." Bert decided to try one more idea. "Alright, alright, never mind that. Now, listen, I'll tell you a secret." Bert put his hands on Katie's shoulders. "This is very important. Are you listening?"

Katie crossed her arms and rolled her eyes. "Whatever. Go ahead."

Bert looked around to make sure no one was listening even though they were in Katie's apartment. "It wasn't really my money."

"What?"

"Just what I said. It wasn't my money; it was Sheila's."

"Yes, and she gave it to you."

"To give to Will Gant and the conservative kids," said Will.

"Pre-adults."

"Whatever. The point is this was not really a question of me wanting to get back at Sheila. She wanted me to give it to them, and so we came up with the story of her pissing me off and calling my work derivative and accidentalist."

"I mean, that did sound like something you'd say. I can't imagine Sheila Windsong using words of more than three syllables."

"Exactly. But the plan was to funnel $125,000 to Gant and the SCF so they could oppose her plan to build the plasma gasification plant."

"But why would she want that? That's going to be good for the whole community."

"Yeah, but the community mostly doesn't care, and she's worried about her public support. But if she can get Will Gant some publicity, it will generate more interest in the mayor's race, and people will pay more attention to her. She's really looking to secure her future as the mayor, and so she wants everyone to see her win again."

Katie stomped over to the refrigerator and filled up a glass of water from the door. This was not going the way Bert expected. He thought she would applaud his genius and fawn over his political savvy. Plus, this would help the environment, which he figured would help him get laid tonight.

"But she's going to win. Of course, she's going to win," said Katie. She gulped down the entire glass and set it in the sink.

"Yes, but she's worried her support is slipping. It was at seventy-five percent last week, down from eighty. She wants to drub Will Gant so badly that no one ever runs against her again."

"Wait, so you're supporting Sheila Windsong by setting Will Gant up to fail?"

Bert grinned like a maniac. "Yes, exactly. Brilliant, isn't it?"

Katie shook her head. "No! That's terrible!"

"What? Why? I thought you'd like that idea." Any thoughts about getting laid quickly fled his head.

"It's sleazy! That's just more of the same political bullshit our parents used to tell us about."

"No, it's brilliant," argued Bert. "If anything, it's helping people. Gant gets to run a campaign and share his ideas. He can pay some people to do his campaign work which creates jobs. If anything, this is better for the community than if she did nothing at all."

"Oh, and so Sheila should be applauded for screwing Will and the SCF?"

"Exactly."

"No!"

"What do you mean 'no'? I thought you'd appreciate sticking it to those alt-right Nazis."

"First of all, you arrogant boob, they're not Nazis. They're conservatives, and they're not even that conservative."

"I thought you hated those guys."

"Second, of all the sleazy things you've done, this may be the sleaziest. I thought you were sleazy for suggesting an open relationship so you could sleep with my sister, but this tops that."

"I keep telling you, *she* came onto *me*."

"I don't care! The point is you're an amoral, unprincipled egotistical shithead!"

"Hold on. I did this for us."

"Oh, so *now* there's an us? Tell me, what twisted logic makes you think you did this for us?"

"Because I got another $25,000 for doing it."

"$25,000? You did all that for $25,000?"

"Hey, that's not nothing!"

"Whoop-de-doo! Do you want a fucking t-shirt? 'I sold my soul and all I got was this lousy t-shirt and $25,000!'"

"What do you mean 'I sold my soul'?"

"Because it's one thing to do a shitty thing because you actually believe in the cause. But you did a shitty thing because someone gave you money for it. You fucked over a decent human being and a bunch of kids who just want to figure out who they are for not very much money."

"You just said they were a bunch of close-minded conservatives."

"That's before I realized you were a major league shithead. They're not the enemy—you are. You and your shrew of an ex-wife."

"Whoa, calm down," said Bert, holding Katie's shoulders again.

"Calm down? Calm down? Get your fucking hands off me, and I'll calm down when you get the fuck out of my apartment!"

"You don't mean that."

"Wanna bet? Computer, revoke all access to Bert Welch from this apartment. No more key code access."

"Confirmed," said the apartment computer. "All access to Bert Welch is now denied. Bert Welch is now dead to us."

"Seriously? Because of a little political maneuvering? I did this for us," whined Bert.

"For us? You don't do anything for us. You haven't done anything for us in three years. So don't give me this selfless, caring bullshit now. You're a selfish, arrogant prick, and you haven't given me an orgasm in all the years we've been together, Mr. One-and-Done."

"That's a low blow."

"Yeah, and it's the last one you'll ever get from me. Get the fuck out, you... you... Trump-head!"

Bert clutched at his chest and stared open-mouthed in shock and horror, and Katie's hands flew up to her mouth. When it came to personal insults and disparagement, there was an unspoken line about what one was allowed to say or not say.

In 2053, you could insult a person's mothers, question their lineage, mock their intelligence, disparage their beliefs, demean their religion, and disrespect their fashion sense. You could call them a dildo-breathed, goat-fucking Nazi who wore open-toed combat boots. But in these enlightened and more harmonious days, there was still a line one did not cross, no matter how angry you might feel. Katie hadn't just crossed it; she dirty-bombed it.

Tears stung Bert's eyes, and he swiped at them with his tweed jacket sleeve.

"I don't care how much you ever apologize," he choked. "I will never, *ever* forgive you for that." He stormed out Katie's front door and slammed it shut.

Katie ran over and jerked the door open. "Good, you fucking Machiavellian prick," she shouted after him. "If I never see you again, it will be too soon!" She slammed the door shut. Then she yanked it open and slammed it shut again three more times.

Katie flopped down on her couch, tossed off her PDT, and sobbed herself to sleep. When she woke up two hours later, it was dark.

"What time is it?" she said to no one in particular.

"The time is 12:07 a.m.," said the apartment computer.

"Computer, message Will Gant. Schedule it for 6:30 a.m. Will, I need to meet with you this morning. I have important information about the donation you received from Bert Welch. Please message me when you're free."

CHAPTER 9

SUNDAY, AUGUST 31, 2053 — GORDON JUMP MEMORIAL PARK

"Mayoral candidate Will Gant spoke in front of a sizable crowd at Gordon Jump Park this morning, with nearly six hundred people in attendance. In his twenty-minute speech, Gant talked about his rather frightening vision for local government, business taxes, and his view on arts funding. We have snippets of some of the most damning phrases from Gant's speech, plus our drone footage captured the crowd's reckless, if not dangerous, enthusiasm. We also interviewed several protestors who peacefully demonstrated in the city-approved free-speech zone two hours after Gant's speech. We'll have more news for you tonight at 11:00 on WSED, Appleseed's best TV news station."

"Al-right dog whistler Will Gant gave a speech today in a park in Appleseed, Ohio this morning to a teeny-tiny crowd of fringe supporters and curious onlookers. Many attendees were Appleseed College students, which raises the question, 'Is Will Gant indoctrinating our young people?' Before The Takening, conservatives often

accused colleges of indoctrinating their students, but now it looks like the far-right has adopted its own rhetoric and is doing everything it can to turn our impressionable young people against their parents and their community. We believe Appleseed College should investigate Gant, revoke his tenure, and throw him out. We'll have an analysis by political historian Cheryl Clayton tonight about sounding the alarm about the growth of the alt-right in the Midwest. That's tonight at 7 p.m. on the Declan Russell-Lambert Political Hour, here on Ann Arbor's Community Radio Station, WARB."

"Good evening, Appleseed. Big news out of Gordon Jump Park today! We had a great turnout at the Appleseed Chili Fair and Arts Cook-Off—excuse me, the Arts Fair and Chili Cook-Off—today as organizers tell us there were a few thousand people in attendance, many from all over the Midwest. Visitors, uh, visited the artists' tents, merchant tents, and the classic car show. Today, JoAnn Yeoh-MacGregor showed off her fully restored 1995 Chevrolet Monte Carlo, complete with real leather seats. Stay tuned to WAPPL for more local community news here on Appleseed's Golden Oldies with the hits of the 10s, 20s, and 30s. Next up is an old favorite for our friends at the Appleseed Pet Rescue Center, the Baha Men's 'Who Let the Dogs Out.'"

"Good morning, Appleseed. My name is Will Gant, and I'm running for mayor of Appleseed because I believe in this city and its people, and I want to bring important changes to the way we do business in this city."

A crowd of three hundred supporters had gathered in front of the music stage where a local classic rock was set to perform in about an hour. The organizers of the Appleseed Arts Fair and Chili Cook-Off had invited both Will and Sheila to speak at the event, but Sheila begged off, saying she had prior engagements. The engagement in question was that she and her wife Fallyn had driven up to Mackinac Island on the previous Thursday for an extended vacation and wouldn't drive back until tomorrow morning. She already believed she had the election in the bag, so she planned on coasting into office come November 4.

"I believe that this city can grow, improve its finances, and create even more jobs and opportunities for its citizens and people who come here looking for a better life."

Several people from the crowd cheered while most of them remained silent. There were a few uncomfortable coughs. Sara and Kyle stood shoulder-to-shoulder in the front with several other members of the SCF and The Committee to Elect Will Gant Mayor.

"That's my line!" whispered Sara. Kyle held his hand up, and Sara high-fived him. Sara and Kyle had spent several hours with Will writing his speech and preparing him for any number of questions he might get.

"And I also support reducing the overreach of our local government and its drive to grow in size and scope even as it seeks to put more of our fellow Appleseedlings under its thumb."

"That was mine!" Kyle whispered. The two high-fived again, and the crowd started to pay closer attention. They liked the idea of not being under anyone's thumb.

"But what about the plasma gasification plant?" shouted a crowd member.

"I'm glad you asked," said Will. "I support the plasma gasification plant, but I don't think we need one as large as the system my opponent has suggested. She wants to spend $50 million of taxpayer money on a bond issue for a $150 million plant. But the proposed system is too large. If we followed her plan, we would need to import fuel—literal garbage—from other communities within a year. Based on my analysis, the surrounding communities would run out of garbage in eight to ten years.

"That means we would have to pay to have fuel trucked in from farther and farther distances. By then, the PGP would be our sole source of power, and we would be so dependent on outside fuel that we would have to pay more and more just to keep up with the demand. We might even have to start importing garbage from Canada just to power our city.

"I propose a PGP half its size that can easily handle the amount of waste produced in this city and within a hundred-mile radius. The costs are more manageable, and we won't become dependent on foreign garbage."

The crowd applauded, and people were murmuring that this made a lot of sense.

Will paused and looked out at the crowd. He knew he was about to make or break this speech, but it was important to address the elephant in the room.

"Now, you may have heard that I'm an alt-right candidate or Nazi sympathizer."

Many people in the crowd booed. Whether it was in response to the rumors or because they hated Nazis, no one knew.

"Go home, Nazi scum!" one person from the crowd shouted, and many people cheered. Now they knew.

"This is a complete lie," said Will, ignoring the Nazi haters. "I'm not a Nazi. I'm not on the alt-right. I'm not a far-right nutjob. The people who say these things are lying. It's a common political practice for the opposition to exaggerate, tell half-truths, and outright lie about their opponents. I'm happy to let my views speak for themselves, but my opponents are afraid of those views."

More cheers from the crowd with fewer boos.

"They call me names, they lie, and they stir up fears that we thought were buried in our past. But none of them are true. As a Black man who grew up in the 21st century, I have been called all kinds of names and experienced all kinds of hatred. Those of you who are old enough to remember the 20-teens and 2020s know what I'm talking about."

The crowd grew quiet as many of them remembered what it was like in the first three decades of the 21st century. It was a dark, shameful time that many of them had lived through. And while attitudes changed after The Takening, there were still tendrils of systemic and overt racism that could be felt in today's liberal society.

"But despite all that, I'm a moderate. That means that, before The Takening, I was between the left and the right. I was neither liberal nor conservative. After The Takening, the moderates became the furthest right on the political spectrum. But rather than try to run on her own merits and her own record, my opponent chooses to lie and exaggerate my beliefs and my experiences. She doesn't want you to look at her own record; she only wants to make you question my beliefs."

The crowd cheered again, and there were almost no boos.

Is this actually working? Sara thought. *Are people actually listening and being persuaded?*

"So let me tell you what I believe. As a moderate, I believe in a commonsense approach to politics, the economy, the arts, and social issues. I believe in equal rights for everyone, I support the arts, and I believe in a common-sense approach to government spending."

"What's wrong with the government?" shouted another person.

."It has gotten too big and created an unnecessary tax burden on the people of Appleseed. The current local tax rate is eight percent, not to mention a national flat tax rate of twenty-five percent. I believe businesses should pay more in corporate taxes and carry some of the load."

The crowd cheered at this idea. Everyone loved paying lower taxes, no matter which side they belonged to.

"I propose cutting three percent from the local tax rate, but I also propose increasing the tax on local businesses by two percent. That will balance out any lost revenue."

The crowd cheered again.

"And I believe we are putting too much money and emphasis into the arts."

A distinct chill fell over the crowd. Will looked down at Sara and Kyle, his brow furrowed. The three of them had discussed this for nearly an hour last night, debating whether or not Will should share his idea about funding for the arts.

"People love the arts," Kyle had said. "That's the sacred cow in this community. You can't just take away the arts from Appleseed. You'll be lucky to get ten votes if they think that's what you're going to do."

"Oh, shit, he's going to lose them," hissed Sara.

"Fuck, I knew it!" Kyle hissed back. He made a slashing motion across his throat as Sara shook her head vigorously.

Sara shouted up to Will, "Tell them about STEM!"

Will held up his hands. "Don't get me wrong—I love the arts. I think the arts were neglected for far too long, and now we have elevated its place in society to the point where everyone is free to pursue their dream of being any kind of artist."

The crowd was not convinced, and people were murmuring their disapproval. This was going to turn ugly in a minute.

"But what about the scientists and technologists?" Will asked. "We're ignoring the people who want to pursue careers in science and technology, what used to be called STEM. We're ignoring their dreams and their goals."

The crowd calmed a bit.

"Let me ask you a question: Who has had an idea for an app for your PDT, but you didn't know how to make it? Who has wanted to fix their car engine or create a gadget that makes their life easier but didn't have the skills? Raise your hand and let me see you."

A few people raised their hands.

"Who got a special thrill from doing math in school or learning about chemistry?"

More people raised their hands.

"Who enjoys getting their hands dirty building things or fixing things? Who has unclogged their own pipes or restored an old machine from a hundred years ago?"

More hands went up.

"Right now, there are only a lucky few who get to make a living working with their hands, writing computer code, or repairing mechanical systems. Most work, including manufacturing, is done through AI engines, which leaves us free to pursue our interests. There are plenty of people who get to work in their dream job in the arts, and I support them. We need art in the world, and we need people who can make great art. We are at a time in our world's history where we are seeing unprecedented arts creation. It's the Renaissance of the 21st century, and I am here for it."

People cheered again. Sara breathed a sigh of relief as Will was getting them back on track.

"But we're neglecting the people who want to build, to create, to engineer. We're neglecting the STEM kids—science, technology, engineering, and math—the kids who think with their left brains, not with their right.

"They're having a tough time finding their way into their dream jobs. So, I propose that we bring STEM back into the schools. Give the kids who want to learn about science, tech, engineering, and math a chance. Stop telling them it's a dream or something they can do on the weekends. STEM is vital to life!"

The crowd cheered again. Many of them had pursued math or science on the weekends and as a hobby. No one told them this was something they could do as a career, and they were eating it up.

"STEM helps us understand the world!" Will shouted into the microphones. "It lets us see how the world works and our part in it. STEM has been critical to human growth and advancement. It's a tool for the exchange of knowledge, education, and expression."

The crowd went wild. "STEM is the collective knowledge of our society. Scientists, engineers, and mathematicians preserve our way of life. The things that we know and that we have created all have a basis in STEM, and I plan to support STEM in our schools as your next mayor!"

TUESDAY, SEPTEMBER 2, 2053 — GORDON JUMP PARK

"Will Gant hates the arts!" Sheila said to a crowd of supporters. "And he clearly hates Appleseed. He's a traitor to our city and wants to keep us down."

It was two days after Will's big speech at Jump Park, and she was in panic mode. Enrique had called her on Sunday and shared the videos of Will's speech with her.

"Shit! That fucking fucker is going to fucking fuck us!" she had yelled the second Enrique answered his phone. Enrique jerked the phone away from his ear.

"We have to jump on this. This could really hurt. The *Mail-Journal* poll now has you at sixty-eight percent approval," he told her.

"What are you worried about then? That's more than enough to win."

"You dropped seven points in less than three weeks!" Enrique hissed. "At this rate, you're going to be in the thirties by Election Day."

"Oh, fuck!" she said.

"'Oh fuck' is right."

So now she was giving a campaign speech back at Jump Park in the same place Will had spoken less than forty-eight hours before. The crowd was a lot smaller—about fifty people or so, most of them city employees getting paid their regular wage to attend—so they disguised this fact by having everyone cram close together and cheer wildly at the appropriate lines. Enrique ran around with his mobile phone to cover the livestream and make it look more crowded.

"He's opposed to free energy from our proposed plasma gasification plant."

The crowd booed.

"He hates the arts and thinks we should abolish them completely."

"Booo!" the crowd responded less-than-enthusiastically. They had all seen Will's video, too.

"He advocates replacing it with boring old science and math."

"Booo!"

"And he wants to cut your taxes!"

"Booo?" the crowd asked.

"By raising taxes on our businesses. That will hurt job creation and put people out of work."

"Booo!"

"That means your kids will be forced to leave school and go to work in factories just to pay your rent. Or you'll end up homeless and living on the streets! Now, as you all know, I've worked tirelessly to end homelessness, but if Will Gant has his way, we'll soon return to the way things were forty years ago."

Appleseed had not had a homeless person in the last twenty years. After The Takening, there were so many vacant houses that homeless people were able to easily find a home, and homelessness was all but eliminated. Plus, the increased social spending helped people get better treatment for mental health issues and drug addictions. Those things still existed, but there was enough social spending that the community was able to get it under control. Sheila had nothing to do with any of it, of course, but she always made sure to make it sound like those issues were resolved the day she took office and completely discounted all the efforts of the people who came before her.

"Now, Will Gant says he wants to slash the city's arts budget, raise everyone's taxes, and gut our education spending."

"Booo!" the crowd dutifully booed. They knew this was complete bullshit, but they weren't getting paid to point out Sheila's lies. They were getting paid to boo whenever she paused.

"Will Gant is guilty of treason against this fine city of Appleseed and all its citizens. He hates the arts, he hates the environment, he hates education, and he hates all of you!"

Enrique pointed at one of the people in the crowd, and he began chanting. A few people picked it up and joined in. More people heard what was being shouted, and they followed along. Soon, all fifty people were chanting the same thing: "Lock him up! Lock him up! Lock him up!"

CHAPTER 10

"**S**HHHHH," SHUSHED BENNA WESTON-GEIGER, a junior majoring in political science and conflict resolution. Benna waved their hands downward in a large shushing motion. "Shhhhh," they shushed again.

A large group of Appleseed College students were crammed into the student government meeting room, taking up all of the seats, standing in the aisles, and spilling out into the hallway. More of them also filled up an overflow classroom, watching the proceedings on a large-screen television that took up an entire wall. The meeting had garnered such attention that several faculty members, including ACOTA's president, Dr. Grogan, were in attendance. Will Gant, as the faculty advisor, was watching the live video stream from his home, which was in the same apartment building as Katie Sartoris, although neither of them knew it.

Sara, Kyle, Griffin, and Callie, as well as several other members of the Students for a Conservative Future, were all clustered together in the front rows.

"Shhhhh!" Benna tried one more time, waving their hands. "Excuse me! Excuse me, people!"

"HEY!" shouted Inge Fitzhugh-Jensen, a junior majoring in sustainable business. She stood up and clapped her hands several times. "That's enough, people!"

The crowd still didn't respond, so she grabbed the gavel in front of Ben and held it over her head. "I will use this if I have to!" she shouted once more.

The crowd fell silent. "Threats of violence give me anxiety," said one voice in the crowd. Several others agreed loudly.

"Not *on* you!" said Inge. "On the table."

"That's still violent," said the voice.

"Whatever," said Inge and dropped the gavel back in front of Benna with a clatter. Several people gasped audibly; Inge rolled her eyes. Thirty-seven people reported Inge's eye roll on the school's micro-aggression reporting app, where they were promptly ignored.

Benna and Inge were seated at a long conference table with three other students trying their best to look somber and stern.

Benna set the gavel back in its proper position. "This meeting of the Appleseed Student Government Judicial Committee will now come to order," they said. "The first item on the agenda is the new Student Nazi Party."

The crowd booed and jeered as Benna waved their hands again. A chant began at the back and slowly filled the room: "Hey-ho, Nazi Party's got to go!"

Sara leaped to her feet from the front row. "We're not the Nazi Party!" she shouted to be heard above the boos. She turned to Benna and Inge. "We're not Nazis, and I resent being labeled as such."

"Hey-ho, Nazi Party's got to go! Hey-ho, Nazi Party's got to go!"

"Can't you do something about this?" shouted Sara toward the people at the front table.

Benna pointed at their ear and shrugged. Inge looked like she was debating grabbing the gavel again so Benna moved it out of her reach.

"Hey-ho, Nazi Party's got to go! Hey-ho, Nazi Party's got to go!"

"We're not fucking Nazis!" Sara tried to raise a counter-chant, but since there were only four SCF members, it wasn't having an effect. "We're not fucking Nazis! We're not fucking Nazis!"

The crowd was really getting into it and rising to their feet.

"Can't you fucking do something?" Sara shouted at the Sub-Committee leaders with no effect. Kyle tugged at her arm and showed her what was in his backpack. She grinned and reached in and retrieved the item.

"Hey-ho, Nazi party's—OWW!"

Sara smiled and released the siren button on her bullhorn again. She raised the microphone to her mouth. "Now, I'll say it again: We're not the Nazi Party."

"Ms. Cooper-Wright, that's entirely out of order," said Benna. "We will call this meeting to order, and we do not require your help."

"Really? Your hand-waving didn't seem to be working."

"This is not helping your cause."

"Yes, but we're not Nazis. That's entirely inaccurate."

"But you're conservatives."

"That's not the same thing. We're not alt-right Nazis like the ones our parents and grandparents fought against. And our great-great-grandparents who fought against actual Nazis over 100 years ago."

"What's the difference?"

"Seriously? Aren't you a political science major?"

"Fine, noted. Now, as I was saying, the first item on the agenda is the Students for a Conservative Future."

The crowd began to boo again, so Sara hoisted her bullhorn, and the boos quickly died down.

"We've got this under control, Ms. Cooper-Wright," said Benna, who didn't have this under control. "Now, as I was saying, it has come to this committee's attention that we have a group of Naz—" Sara glared at him, "alt-right—" Sara's glare blazed, "I mean, conservative students who have formed a group on campus. This meeting is to decide whether the group should be allowed to continue, or if they're a threat to the peace and tolerance that Appleseed College is noted for."

"We're a threat?" said Sara, who had not yet sat down.

"Yes, because you want to... what is it you want to do exactly?"

"We just want to have something to protest against."

"But we have entire classes dedicated to protests," said Benna.

"And we were in danger of failing ours. There weren't any additional school-approved protests to match our class requirements, so we started our own group."

"But that's no reason to embrace something so hateful," said Benna. The crowd applauded and cheered.

"But we're not hateful," said Sara. "We aren't modeling ourselves after the conservatives of the 21st century. We're more interested in the Republicans from the 1970s and 1980s, the ones our great-grandparents grew up with."

"How are they different?"

"Well, they believed in smaller government, lower taxes, increased military spending—"

"So you're pro-war?" shouted another voice from the crowd.

"Not at all," said Sara. "But we do believe in limiting government spending and lowering taxes. We also support reducing restrictions on businesses so they can hire more people and create more jobs."

There were a few murmurs and mumbles passing through the crowd. This was not something they had considered. Benna could sense a slight shift in the crowd.

"But the point remains you have chosen to side with a radical political philosophy that has been deemed reprehensible and antithetical to our way of life."

"Use smaller words!" shouted a third voice from the crowd.

"They bad; we good!" Benna said in a sing-songy tone they would use with a two-year-old.

"Fuck! You!" the voice shouted back in the same tone.

Benna grabbed the gavel and made as if they were going to bang it on the table. The crowd quieted down again, waiting to see what happened next. A student passed around a bag of organic, cruelty-free popcorn.

Sara continued, "Look, I know the conservatives from this century were all pretty horrible, but that's not our model. We've learned from speaking with Professor Gant that a society is most successful if there's more than one person making a decision, more than one group having a viewpoint, and each group has the freedom to express those views. When one group has someone to push against and to hold them in check, then we avoid the problems of excess and corruption."

"Are you saying we're corrupt?" said Benna.

"What? How do you even get that? That's not what I said at all."

"Oh, and now you're accusing us of not listening?" Benna tapped their PDT. "File a micro-aggression report against Sara Cooper-Wright and the Student Nazi Party."

"Now who's not listening?" Sara shouted. "All I'm trying to say is that we wanted to be able to express ourselves and try to find a positive way to protest without having the faculty spoon-feed our protesting opportunities to us. We wanted to engage in a healthy exchange of ideas and to learn from each other. We can't do that if you stamp out any ideas that are different from yours."

"I don't need to hear any more of this," declared Benna, banging their gavel. Dozens of the general student body booed. The SCF members looked around, surprised that they were getting more support from the people who had just been booing them.

"I will have order in this forum. I will have order," shouted Benna. "President Grogan, can you please make them come to order?"

President Grogan decided this would be a good time to approach the table. He stood in front of Benna and held up his hands. The room immediately fell silent.

"Finally, someone with real authority," said Irene, sneering at Benna.

"Good evening, learners. I'm very pleased to see such interest in student government and student politics. I've long believed that student involvement in the political process now helps you understand what's going on in society as you get older.

"Unfortunately, this is such a divisive issue, the same one that divided this country twenty years ago. We couldn't come to an agreement on anything then, and we know what happened.

"It would be so easy for me to just step in and make a decision, but that would make me no better than the dictators and despots who were overthrown right after The Takening. If history has taught us nothing else, let us at least remember that no one should wield absolute power and that people need to come together to make decisions that benefit everyone. So rather than exert my authority, I'm going to leave it to the duly elected student government to decide on the fate of the Students for a Conservative Future group. Thank you."

With that, President Grogan smiled, pressed his hands together, said, "Namaste," and left.

The crowd erupted into chaos, but the cheers against the SCF were now heated discussions about what the SCF stood for versus what had happened in the last four decades. Benna, Inge, and the other three students huddled together, Benna arguing one side, the three nodding, and Inge jabbing her finger at them. The phrase "phallocentric intimidation" was bandied about for a time.

After several minutes, Benna asked a question, and they and the three students raised their hands; Inge did not. Benna asked another question, and the four raised their hands again with Inge abstaining. A third question yielded the same result.

As this was going on, people in the crowd argued amongst themselves while Sara and Kyle engaged with a couple of students who had approached them with questions.

Finally, Benna stood and raised their hands again to no avail. Not only were they actively ignored, the crowd seemed to get louder.

"People, please!" Benna raised their hands higher.

"Jesus Christ, you're so lame," said Inge, seizing the gavel and holding it over her head again.

"Ableist! Computer, report Inge Fitzhugh-Jensen for an ableist slur." The computer wasn't able to actually discern Benna's voice over the noise, and Benna instead upgraded their cable package to its premium Big Sur level.

Sara blasted the siren on her bullhorn once more, and the room quieted down amid howls.

"That wasn't necessary, Ms. Cooper-Wright," said Benna.

"It clearly was."

"Nevertheless, the Appleseed Student Government Judicial Committee has voted, and we are prepared to render our decision."

Everyone sat down, and the room grew deathly still, like a doctor showing up in a hospital waiting room to deliver news to a patient's family.

"First, this committee strongly condemns the existence and philosophy of the Students for a Conservative Future. We believe they have aligned themselves with the deplorables of this century, and we need to stamp out dissent and disloyalty in any form."

"Disloyalty?" shouted Sara. "We are anything but disloyal. Haven't you heard of the loyal opposition?"

Benna ignored her. "To that end, we offer our full-throated recommendation to the Student Government Association and the Student Activities office that this group be terminated."

"Terminated?" yelled Sara and Kyle, who leaped to their feet. Sara tried to charge the table, but Kyle and Callie held her back.

A small chorus of boos filled the room as even more students cheered and applauded. The rest of the SCF began to shout, "Now who's the Nazi? Now who's the Nazi?" Benna waved their hands again, and surprisingly, everyone quieted down.

Benna shot Inge a look and said, "See?" only to realize Inge was holding the gavel above her head again.

"Second, we will recommend to President Grogan that he expel all members of the Student Nazi Party—"

"We're not fucking Nazis, you ass!"

"Computer, report Sara—you know what? Never mind, you're going to be expelled anyway. As I was saying, we recommend that President Grogan expel all Nazis from Appleseed College."

There were even more boos and jeers from the crowd.

"Finally," Benna shouted over the crowd, "we will write a strongly worded letter that recommends termination for Professor Will Gant for indoctrinating students with such harmful ideas and philosophies that have led these misguided students down a dark path."

"You are such an arrogant fucking asshole!" shouted Sara. She tried to rush the table again, but Kyle and Callie had not released her. They grabbed her and carried her out. The rest of the SCF followed them out, humming "The Battle Hymn of the Republic."

"This isn't over, you power-hungry fuck!" she screamed, struggling against the two. "You can't stamp out ideas, and you'll never take our *freeeeedoooommmm!*"

The crowd booed and jeered even louder, and Benna smiled until they realized the boos were directed at them. Several students began to follow the SCF founders out of the room, holding their middle fingers high in the air. Inge slammed the gavel onto the table, snapping off the head. She dropped the handle in front of Benna, flipped both fingers in front of their face, and followed the growing crowd out of the room.

Sara was pacing furiously around the classroom where they had met in the past. Several of the current SCF members had joined them and were sitting around, moping, and drafting emails to their parents saying they might need a moving truck and a ride home soon.

Outside, Grace Blasingame-Odoyo and Trent Chang-Ramirez were talking with several of the students who had followed them out of the meeting.

"Can you fucking believe this?" Sara shouted to no one in particular. "That jumped-up little dictator thinks they can tell us whether we can be a group or not!"

"Sara," said Kyle.

"Who the fuck do they think they are? They call *us* Nazis but won't listen to anyone themselves. Themself? Themselves? What's the right word here?"

"It's Themselves," said Trent, who was also nonbinary. "English grammar rules still apply."

"Sara," said Kyle again.

"And they want to expel us? *Expel* us? Who gave them the fucking authority to do that?"

"Oh God, can they really expel us?" said Callie, who could see her dreams of being selected by a public school in the teaching draft circling the drain.

"No, they can't fucking expel us," said Sara. "And they can't fire Will either. Because we'll sue the shit out of those bastards, especially that Benna Fucking Weston-Geiger."

"Sara!" shouted Kyle.

"*What?*" shouted Sara.

Kyle stood up and put his hands on her shoulders. "Take a deep breath. Just relax."

"If you tell me to calm down, I'm going to kick you in the nuts."

"I won't. CHiP, give me some credit."

Sara closed her eyes and took a few deep yoga breaths. "OK, what?"

"First of all," said Kyle, "they can't kick us out. Remember, they only said they would recommend expelling us. But

President Grogan is pretty cool. If we just tell him what the SCF is about and that we're just students trying—"

"Learners."

"What?"

"He says 'learners.' He doesn't call us 'students' anymore."

"Whatever. Anyway, we're just *learners* trying to develop our own philosophy or that we were conducting our own independent study, he wouldn't kick us out."

"What about Will? Can they fire him?"

"No. For one thing, he's tenured. Also, the faculty senate doesn't really have any powers at all. Also, they can't fire him just for his political beliefs unless he were to say or do something really terrible. Also, he hasn't done anything wrong."

"That's a lot of also's," said Sara.

"So, what about us? Can they kick us out? Oh God, they can't kick us out, can they?" cried Callie Wong.

"No," said Sara. "Will you calm down? Your career is safe."

"Says you! I knew I shouldn't have gotten involved in this stupid committee. My dreams of becoming a teacher are dead before I've even started. Now I'm going to have to become a poet or some stupid shit."

"Hey!" shouted a poetry major from Birmingham, Alabama.

"Oh, come on, Dylan, like we need yet one more poet. Didn't Shakespeare say 'First, kill all the poets?'"

"It was lawyers," said Dylan.

"Hey!" shouted a pre-law major from Mt. Pleasant, Michigan.

"Whatever," said Callie. "We're still going to get kicked out."

"We're not going to get kicked out!" said Sara.

"How do you figure?"

"For one thing, it's the judicial committee. What power do they actually have? None. The worst they can do is recommend to the actual student government and the Student Activities office that our group be disbanded. But the judicial committee can't actually do it. Benna's got delusions of grandeur if they think they can."

The murmured conversations around the room stopped so they could all listen to what Sara was saying.

"But even if they did, who cares? All having a student organization means is that we can use campus resources and take advantage of student funding. So what if we don't have access to that? We can always meet at the Appleseed City Library or have people over to our off-campus housing."

People in the room were sitting up and listening to Sara, and she could sense the mood lifting, so she carried on.

"Besides, isn't this what the group was formed for? To have something to protest about? To do something that actually had meaning? What's more meaningful than speaking out against bullies and despots like Benna Weston-Geiger?"

Cries of "nothing! and "Get 'em, Sara!" filled the classroom.

"We wanted to protest against something, so this is our chance, right?"

"Right!" everyone shouted.

"We wanted to fight the good fight, right?"

"Right!"

"We wanted to do something with the same drive and energy as our parents and grandparents, right?"

"Right!"

"So I say we protest against the Student Government Judicial Committee! Who's with me?"

The small crowd of students leaped to their feet and cheered wildly but quickly fell silent as the door opened and Grace Blasingame-Odoyo stepped inside.

"What'd I miss?" asked Grace.

"We're getting ready to go protest against the SGJC," said Sara. Several people cheered their agreement.

"Do you think this is enough people?" said Grace.

Sara looked around the room and did a quick count. "Well, we've got seventeen people here, and I'll bet we can call up a few more. Do you think that's enough?"

"I don't know. But I've got forty-one newly minted members of the SCF downstairs, and they're wanting to do something today."

"Sounds like we've got our protest group!" shouted Kyle. "Now, where's the SGJC?"

"They're in their office," shouted a voice from out in the hallway.

"Who's out there?" called Kyle.

"It's Inge Fitzhuhgh-Jensen," said Inge Fitzhuhgh-Jensen, stepping through the door. Several people booed and hissed.

Sara and Kyle quickly shushed everyone. "What the hell do you want?" said Sara.

"I want to join you," said Inge.

"How? Why?" said Kyle. "You're with the SGJC."

"Not anymore. I quit," said Inge. "I'm so sick of Benna being such a power-hungry dickhead. They just became the chair of the committee three weeks ago, and the power went to their head. You're the fourth group they've recommended be disbanded. The last one was the Vinyl Record Appreciation Society for playing Beastie Boys twelve-inch vinyls at a party. I didn't want to be a part of their bullshit anymore, so I quit and followed you guys over here. Can I join you?"

"Make that forty-two members," said Grace.

"You're in," said Sara. "Now, come on. Let's get the people downstairs and go launch a protest." She looked at Inge. "And I know just the place."

"Count me in," said Inge.

"Where?" said Kyle. "Where are we going? Sara, where are we going? What are you doing?"

CHAPTER 11

"*Mayoral candidate Will Gant's campaign team is showing their true colors by inciting riots and rabble-rousing on the Appleseed College campus. Following the Students for a Conservative Future's crushing defeat in a fight with the Student Government Association, they have gathered outside the SGA offices and are demanding that SGA member, Benna Weston-Geiger, be handed over to them for CHiP knows what. Mayor Windsong has urged citizens to stay away from the area and accused her opponent of indoctrinating these students with the ideas of political dissent and hatred of the government. We'll have more news for you tonight, including dramatic footage from our news drones, at 11:00 on WSED, Appleseed's best TV news station.*"

"*Protests are rocking the tiny Appleseed College Of The Arts in Appleseed, Ohio, just two hundred miles due south. The alt-right con-servatives have infiltrated this institute of higher learning. The group, the so-called Students for a Conservative Future, was being reviewed by the duly-elected Student Judicial Committee, when the founder of the group, Sara Cooper-Wright, lashed out at the SJC chairperson and stormed out of the hearing, screaming threats and vile invectives. The group has now amassed several hundred protestors in front of the Student Government Association building and is undoubtedly seeking to overthrow the rightfully elected student government. We'll have an analysis by political historian Cheryl Clayton tomorrow morning about whether our listeners need to worry about the alt-right influence in their own community. That's tomorrow morning on Ann Arbor's Community Radio Station, WARB."*

"We've got big sports this weekend! The Appleseed College Fighting Summer Tanagers Ultimate Frisbee team will face off against the Ball State Cardinals in the Midwest regional bracket in this year's NCAA tournament. The winner of this regional will go onto the Final Four, which will be held in the coastal city of Valdosta, Georgia at the Rosalynn Carter Memorial Stadium.

And closer to home, it's the 19th annual Found Items Trunk Show and Swap Meet. Bring your gently used and worn items and clothing, whether yours or a family member who has passed on, to Gordon Jump Park between 8 a.m. and 5 p.m. Be sure to visit the artists' tents, the merchant tents, and the classic car show. Andrea Calvert-Martin promises to show off her 1990 Chrysler LeBaron, which she has restored to brand-new conditions. Stay tuned to WAPPL for more local sports news, here on Appleseed's Golden Oldies with the hits of the 10s, 20s, and 30s. Next up is a little love song from 2003 with Fountains of Wayne's 'Stacy's Mom.'"

"Call Professor Will Gant," said President Grogan, tapping his PDT. A few seconds later, there was a response.

"Hello, President Grogan." President Grogan could hear Will through the PDT's bone-conducting earpiece. "I'm sorry for calling, but I'll get straight to the point. Do you know what your learners are doing?"

"My students? You'll have to be more specific. Do you mean in my classes?"

"Learners. I prefer to call them learners."

"Yes, of course," said Will, rolling his eyes.

Privately, he hated the term "learners," and he refused to use it when the university had passed its "Learning Over Studying: A Proposal for Recontextualizing the Higher Education Experience" proposal eight years ago.

The idea was President Grogan's brainchild, coming to him after he had met with two groups of students who were protesting the Appleseed faculty's use of old-school teaching methods: video learning, independent study, gamification, audiobooks, textbooks on tablets, and collaborative learning groups.

The protestors were actually made up of two different philosophies, but there had only been one available time slot in President Grogan's busy schedule, so representatives from both sides agreed to approach him together to air their grievances.

One group was upset that the faculty was failing to challenge them and wanted them to adopt new, more modern teaching methods. The other group was upset that the faculty were too challenging and wanted them to reduce the reliance on old-school teaching methods.

Both sides were adamant that they did not like classroom lectures, which is what the professors ultimately wanted to use. After all, they had spent years and hundreds of thousands of dollars pursuing their Ph.D.s, and by God, they weren't going to let them go to waste on some dumbass collaborative learning system.

Both sides also demanded that the professors stop referring to them as students because "it implies a superior-subordinate relationship."

"Well, duh," said the professors, who despite living in an egalitarian society believed that having a Ph.D. meant they were, in fact, smarter than everyone else.

President Grogan promised the newly minted learners that he would create a blue-ribbon commission to look into the ways the faculty could somehow be both more challenging and less challenging at the same time.

The school briefly toyed with unlearning, the philosophy that all learning can be self-directed without following a specified curriculum, but they stopped after dozens of angry calls from parents who were paying $30,000 per semester for their precious children's learning experience.

The net result of the whole process was that students were now called learners, and absolutely nothing else had changed.

Will Gant thought the whole thing was stupid and refused to call them learners, although he sometimes forgot to hide that fact when speaking to President Grogan.

"So what, uh, learners are you referring to?" Will said.

"The Students for a Conservative Future. They really should be called Learners for a Conservative Future. Anyway, do you know what they're doing?"

"No, I don't," said Will. "I was watching the video feed of the Judicial Committee meeting, and when it ended, I turned it off."

"Well, first of all, I don't want you to worry about being fired," said President Grogan.

"Oh, I'm not."

"Oh," said President Grogan, a little disappointed. He had been hoping he could provide some reassurance to Will and put his mind at ease.

"No, I'm tenured, and I haven't done anything wrong. Plus, Janice Montgomery-Lee is the president of the faculty senate, and she told me she wasn't even going to entertain their motion, should it actually reach her desk."

"Oh," said President Grogan again.

"I get at least one call for my resignation each month for any number of reasons. Most of the time it has to do with my politics. Sometimes it has to do with teaching about some piece of history that a student is triggered by."

"Well, I apologize for that. You're one of our most valuable educators, and I appreciate all of your work with our learners. But that's not the reason for my call. I wanted to talk to you about the, er, Students, er, Learners for a Conservative Future. Do you know where they are right now?"

"No, I'm afraid I don't."

"They're protesting."

"Well, that is what they wanted to do, so I'm glad they're—wait, are they at your office?"

"No, they're—"

"They're not at your house, are they? That's a bit out-of-bounds."

"No, they're not at my house. The last time students protested at my house, Mrs. Grogan yelled at them and chased them away. I was going to offer them cookies, but she frightened them off."

"Then where are they?"

"They're at the Student, er, Learners Government Association office, protesting against the chair of the Judicial Committee."

"Hey-ho, Weston-Geiger's gotta go! Hey-ho, Weston-Geiger's gotta go!" chanted the sixty-seven members of the Students-er-Learners for a Conservative Future. The forty-two people who had left the Judicial Committee meeting just thirty minutes ago were now outside the SGA office, which was in a small house that had been purchased by the College many years ago in case the school ever decided to expand, chanting for the removal of Benna Weston-Geiger.

"Computer, report major aggressions against the Nazis outside!" screamed Benna, trying to make sure they could be heard over the chants coming through the locked door. Benna and the three other students who had voted against the removal of the SCF and expulsion of all its members were cowering under desks, visions of guillotines and bonfires dancing in their heads.

"Oh, my, that is... well, not unexpected," said Will.

"Can't you do something?" said President Grogan.

"How? What am I supposed to do?"

"You're their faculty advisor, are you not?"

"Yes, but I'm not in charge of them. I mean, I can advise them to stand down, but this is what they wanted. Besides, they're just kids."

"Pre-adults."

"Pre-adults. They're doing exactly the thing we taught them."

"Yes, but it's not school-approved!" protested President Grogan.

"Protest has never been approved, President Grogan. You and I both know that through bitter experience. The squeaky wheel gets the grease. Public conflicts and protests have been more effective because they get media attention."

"Excuse me, I'm Carla Walters-Fenstermacher. I'm from Protest Accreditation Registration Empowerment. Have you registered this protest with our office?" said a short Black woman with twisted locks in her hair. She was wearing khaki pants, a navy-blue polo shirt with the PARE logo, and a button that said, "Ask me about approving your student protests!" She was carrying a tablet inside a high-impact case.

Sara jumped at the figure appearing at her shoulder. "Jesus!" she gasped and jumped.

"No, just me," said Carla Walters-Fenstermacher, repeating her favorite joke since she often startled people by appearing behind them.

Carla Walters-Fenstermacher was the daughter of two people who had originally met at the Occupy Wall Street protest in 2011. The 22-year-olds had met over a shared cup of patchouli chai, held hands while holding signs, and then asked to be handcuffed together when police finally cleared out the park. The two were married in the overnight lockup by a police chaplain and left the country on a trust fund-funded world honeymoon with stops at the anti-austerity movement in Spain, copper mining protests in Ecuador, the Faure Gnassingbé protests in Togo, and the 2012 Catalan independence demonstration before living in Ireland for nearly a year as part of the anti-austerity protests, where Carla was conceived.

She was born in the U.S. but traveled with her parents for several years, receiving a thorough home education before settling down in Chicago, getting her degree at Illinois State University in Peace and Conflict Resolution. She had been with the PARE department for the last eight years as the Student Advisor and Strategist.

"I'm sorry. What did you say?" asked Sara, still clutching her chest.

"Have you registered this protest with our office?" repeated Carla Walters-Fenstermacher.

"Have we…? Registered? Why would we register a protest?" said Sara, not quite understanding.

"All student protests must be registered and approved."

"Approved protests? People actually approve our protests on campus?" She was getting a little annoyed.

"Sure," said Carla Walters-Fenstermacher. "How else do you think you get class credit for them? Your protests are submitted through our online forms, usually by a faculty member who's offering the protest for class credit. It gets reviewed by our committee at a bi-weekly meeting, and then the protest gets scheduled."

"A committee approves them?" said Sara, shouting to be heard over the other chanters. "That's the dumbest fucking thing I've ever heard!"

"I agree, actually," said Carla. "I've been pushing my colleagues to begin using artificial intelligence so we can get immediate approvals with our new app, but they're a bunch of old stick-in-the-muds—or is that sticks-in-the-mud?—and prefer doing things the old school way."

"No, we didn't submit this for approval! You don't get approval for protests!"

"Actually, you do. But that's OK. We can give you conditional approval right away, and we just have to formalize it later for the credit to actually count. I just need you to give me your name, facial scan, and signature, and then I can get the ball rolling for you."

"No! We're not doing that. This is a protest against the bureaucracy and stupid-ass student fascist government that just voted to disband our group. We don't need anyone's approval. It's our constitutional right to gather and protest."

"Then I'm afraid you won't get any credit for this protest," said Carla Walters-Fenstermacher.

"Get the fuck out of here!"

"But I'm here to help," protested Carla Walters-Fenstermacher.

"You're part of the system we're protesting against. You've got to go!"

"Hey-ho, Weston-Geiger's gotta go! Hey-ho, Weston-Geiger's gotta go!" chanted the now eighty-nine protestors outside. As more people heard about the protest or watched the video feed of the meeting, they all came to the office to join the protest or at least watch it all unfold. But even the watchers got caught up in the emotion of it all and joined the chanting themselves. Within fifteen minutes, the crowd had grown to more than four hundred people, which was more than most of the school-approved protests had ever attracted, even when it was required for class credit.

Occasionally, Benna or one of their cronies would pop their heads up to look out a window and identify some of the protestors by name, and then report them on the school's micro-aggression reporting app, and the chants would begin anew.

Each report was analyzed by the micro-aggression app's algorithms, which would see one of the terms that indicated violence or danger and refer it to the campus police department. Sam Violet-Paisley, ACOTA's campus police captain, was standing next to her patrol car, watching the protest, and decided this didn't look that dangerous, even after report after report pinged her PDT. She set the PDT to mute as the pinging started to wear on her nerves.

The protestors had attempted a chant of "No Benna, know peace," but many of the students thought they were chanting "No Benna, no peace" and didn't want to be seen as supporting violence while others didn't want to be perceived as chanting "Know Benna, know peace," which sounded too supportive, so the whole thing was quickly abandoned.

Now, they had settled on "What do we want? Benna's resignation! When do we want it? Now!"

Inside, Benna was tapping their PDT like a telegraph and screaming "Report Ellie Meghnot-Wilkins for major aggressions! Report Jesse Lampert-Peppers for Nazi behavior! Report Jean Washington-Shields for illegal protesting!" and so on.

"I think we should just let them go and see what happens," Will was telling President Grogan. "We've spoon-fed these kids—er, learners—their successes, and it created some problems for them, which is why they created the SCF in the first place. I suggest we let this play out and see what happens."

"It's just... unseemly," said President Grogan.

"What is?"

"Learners protesting against learners. The whole point of protests is to speak truth to power, to buck the status quo, and to advocate for change. To punch up. This seems like they're punching down. Or sideways."

"Yes, but the SCF felt like they weren't listened to. They were being pre-judged, falsely labeled, and were lied about. The Judicial Committee made its intentions clear when they called the SCF a bunch of Nazis and wouldn't quit."

"But what about Weston-Geiger? Who will protect them?"

"Maybe Weston-Geiger will learn a hard lesson about why it's important to listen to everyone without prejudging them. If they can remain in office, they can use this experience to become a better leader."

"And if they are forced out?"

"Then they can use it to become a better person."

Around the city of Appleseed, people received an alert over their PDT and their mobile phones (Zoomers over the age of 50 had refused to give up their mobile phones amid concerns that "kids these days" spent too much time on their PDTs) about a breaking story out of the local college. Clicking the link or accepting the alert showed a video of Carmen Cowen and Sara standing together, twenty yards away from the chanting crowd, close enough to have to shout, far enough to still be heard.

"This is Carmen Cowen of the *Appleseed Mail-Journal,* 'Bringing you the good news of the day.' I'm outside the Student Government Association office building at Appleseed College Of The Arts where approximately four hundred students are protesting against the Student Government Association and its chairperson in particular. I'm here with Sara Cooper-Wright, one of the leaders of this student protest movement."

"Hi, Carmen, thanks for having me," said Sara.

"Sara, what exactly are you all protesting against?"

"We're protesting specifically against the Judicial Committee of the Student Government Association here on campus. They tried to disband our group, showed a complete unwillingness to hear our defense, and called us hateful and hurtful names in the process."

"Really? And what did they call you?"

"Mostly Nazis and alt-right deplorables."

"And what's the name of your group?"

"We're called the Students for a Conservative Future."

"But you're not Nazis?"

"Not at all. We know the damage that the Nazis caused thirty years ago and one hundred years ago. We simply stand for reduced government spending, more responsible social spending, and reduced regulations and fewer taxes on businesses so they can hire more people."

"And that's it? Nothing about prejudice against LGBTQQIP2SA or people of other races?" asked Carmen.

"No, that was all true of the old conservatives, even in the 1970s and 1980s. We're still socially liberal, but we're economically conservative. We believe in smaller government without interfering with people's right to live their own lives."

Even as the news broadcast was going on, dozens of little hearts and thumbs-up emojis were floating up past the two women as viewers and listeners signaled their approval—what the *Mail-Journal* and other media outlets called "viewer-votes"—for what was being said. The more votes, the higher and longer the story appeared on their website.

"What made you start the Students for a Conservative Future?" asked Carmen.

"We believe that for there to be true change in society, there needs to be a loyal opposition. This is how new ideas and new ways of thinking happen. In the business world, this is what makes innovation happen. But we don't have it anymore. So, we started the group and then threw our support behind our faculty advisor, Dr. Will Gant, in his campaign for mayor."

"And what is Dr. Gant's platform for his mayoral campaign?"

"Pretty much the same. He's opposed to the rampant spending of the local government and has raised some questions about the proposed plasma gasification plant. We think it could create a dependence on other people's garbage to power our city and may encourage people to increase consumption just to keep the thing running. We're worried that our taxes will increase to pay for it, which is a problem since we believe in lower taxes for everyone."

The hearts and thumbs-up emojis swarmed up the screens as people shared their viewer-votes by the hundreds.

The total approval rating for the story ended up around the seventy-nine percent range, which was unheard of for most stories about politics. Not since the last conservative president had stepped down from office after ninety-nine percent of his voters had died during The Takening had there been a political story that garnered more than a forty-six percent approval rate. A rating that high earned Carmen Cowen a Trendsetter badge on her KNCLD score and a $2,000 bonus in her paycheck that week.

"Fuck, we've got a problem," said Enrique Medina. He tapped his PDT. "Call Sheila."

CHAPTER 12

"Hello, and welcome to Appleseed's mayoral debate for 2038. My name is President Caden Grogan, president of Appleseed College, and I will be your moderator tonight."

President Grogan looked out over the audience at Nikki Giovanni Memorial Auditorium. It was a packed house with more than 2,400 people eagerly waiting for the debate between incumbent Sheila Windsong and challenger Will Gant. There were several small video cameras stationed around the stage as the College's student video production team was streaming the debate online and making the live feed available to the multimedia news stations throughout Chapman County.

As far as anyone could remember, this was the most interest the mayoral campaign had ever generated, including before The Takening. Even then, the best they could ever hope for was a twelve percent voter turnout. This year, the pundits were predicting that number could easily reach a history-making forty-seven percent.

Last month's protest against the Student Government Association led to a few notable changes in the campus. Benna Weston-Geiger had stepped down as chair of the Judicial Committee, which no one had cared about, left Appleseed to return home, which no one had noticed, and was writing their memoirs, which no one would read.

More importantly, the SCF was allowed to retain its membership as nearly four hundred students joined the organization and had promised to conduct Appleseed College's first-ever student government recall in its history if the group were forced to disband.

Additionally, the resulting media coverage of the protest and Sara's interview had fired up people's interest in the mayoral election. Even her own mothers were pleased and said they better understood what their daughter was going through. They offered both their emotional and political support and said they were proud of their daughter for standing up for her ideals.

People in the city who normally couldn't be bothered to attend City Council meetings were showing up in droves and were asking some hard questions about the plasma gasification plant as well as the city's spending and high taxes.

Sheila had been able to answer most of the questions, but when they got too difficult, she resorted to belittling the questioner for asking such a dumb question and refused to engage any further. It was a tactic employed by the last conservative president the country had ever had, which he had learned from his own father during his political career.

The media attention on Will Gant's candidacy had eroded Sheila's approval rating to 58%. His campaign team smelled blood in the water and determined that if Sheila's popularity continued to drop at its current rate, she would be at 38% by Election Day, and Will's victory would be a cakewalk.

This concerned Will because he still didn't want to be the mayor. He enjoyed being a history professor at a small college in a small Midwestern town and never figured he would actually win. He had seen enough and done enough advocacy in his younger days that he was happy just to teach and shape young minds. The thought of being the mayor worried him.

What if he actually won? What would he do? Could he keep his job at Appleseed College? Will had only gone along with Cody and Naomi's plan because he didn't think this would actually go anywhere and now it looked like he may actually have to become the mayor and leave behind the warm embrace of academia.

So he was baffled as to why he had ever agreed to Kyle's suggestion of a mayoral debate.

Sheila's campaign manager Enrique had leaped at the chance. He was panicked at the sudden drop in Sheila's popularity, and his fashion had suffered. He stopped wearing his vintage outfits and his highly-valued shoes and had taken to wearing organic cotton sweatpants and cruelty-free t-shirts complete with vegan chili stains.

He also had trouble sleeping most nights and had resorted to taking Nar-co-lapse pills and turning up the green noise generator next to his bed just to catch a few hours of sleep. His dreams were filled with images of Sheila driving staples into his body, one for each vote she lost by, before being shoved into a wastebasket next to her desk which turned into a plasma gasification vat, and he woke up screaming just as she slammed her hand on the large green START button.

Sheila, on the other hand, wasn't worried at all. She surprised everyone by actually being thrilled at the competition.

"It's about time I had a real challenge," she would tell people. "This will only strengthen my image and brand for the future. If I can overcome this, then people will see that they can't mess around with Sheila Fucking Windsong."

Enrique and Sheila's wife Fallyn exchanged PDT messages that Sheila wasn't aware of the danger she was in. Sheila told them both to quit worrying because everything was under control. And when Kyle's invitation to the debate came, she declared, "Finally! Now we'll show these mouth breathers what real leadership looks like!"

Sheila had two conditions for accepting the debate challenge. First was that President Grogan served as the moderator. The two had known each other since Sheila had been his student in his Dismantling the Patriarchy Through Free Verse class in her junior year at Appleseed. She hoped their history would make him a little more predisposed to putting his thumb on the scales during the debate if need be, not that she needed it. But she definitely wanted his support during the campaign because he held a lot of sway over the ACOTA community.

Second, she insisted that she be placed on the audience's left and Will on their right so they could be reminded of his political leanings. Which is where the two candidates could be found, President Grogan placed squarely in the middle, his few remaining hairs at the top of his head dancing hypnotically under the breeze from the auditorium's ventilation.

"To my right, your left," he said, "is the incumbent and my former student, Mayor Sheila Windsong."

The crowd cheered and applauded politely.

"And to my left, your right, is the challenger and one of Appleseed's fine educators, Professor Will Gant."

The crowd exploded with cheers and thunderous applause. Sheila's brow furrowed, and she wrote herself a note on her digital pad—"Fucking Enrique!"—to chew out Enrique for selecting the college as the debate venue. She wrote another one to remind herself to clean the voter rolls before election day: "Fucking voters!"

"Welcome to you both," said President Grogan. "We had a coin flip backstage before we started, and Professor Gant won the toss, so he gets the first question, and Mayor Windsong will respond. Then the next question goes to Mayor Windsong and Professor Gant gets to respond, and so on. Is that clear?"

Will and Sheila said they understood, so President Grogan asked the first question.

"We've heard a lot about the plasma gasification plant proposal that's before the city council right now. Professor Gant, please summarize your stance on the proposed plant and why it's beneficial or harmful to the city."

"Thank you, President Grogan, and thank you to Appleseed College for sponsoring this debate. I think it's important to point out that I'm not opposed to the plasma gasification plant as a whole," said Will, which elicited a small gasp and murmur from the crowd.

"My big concern is that our city becomes wholly dependent on it for our primary energy source, which will require us to begin importing fuel from other cities in order to operate it. Eventually, those other cities will run out, and we'll have to bring in fuel from farther and farther away. Either that, or we will need to increase consumption in order—"

Sheila interrupted him. "That's not true. Your figures are clearly misleading and skewed in your favor."

"Madame Mayor, you will have your turn in a few moments. Let me remind you to follow the rules that you agreed to," corrected President Grogan.

Fuck, thought Sheila. *So much for his thumb on the scale.*

"Thank you, President Grogan," said Will. "Now, what happens if a few more nearby cities decide to install their own plants? We'll eventually have to either bring in fuel from farther and farther away, start paying the other cities for their fuel, or abandon the plant entirely and switch back to our current wind and solar generation efforts. If anything, I'm in favor of a smaller plant that subsidizes our energy but doesn't make us dependent on so-called 'foreign fuel.'"

The audience thundered its approval, and Sheila wondered for the first time if maybe she was going to have a real challenger in Will Gant. Regardless of what happened at the debate, she was going to have to come up with a different strategy to get him out of the race. She made another note on her tablet: "Fucking *with* Gant."

"Mayor Windsong, your response?" said President Grogan.

"Thank you, President Grogan, and I would also like to thank Appleseed College for hosting this debate as well as your support for my mayorship these last twelve years. I believe in the continuity of leadership and feel we would be taking a step backward as a city if we were to change horses midstream."

There were a few murmurs at Sheila's obvious gaffe as very few people rode horses anymore because it was seen as a cruel humans-first practice. But she ignored it and pressed on.

"And while I appreciate Professor Gant's support for my proposal, I'm surprised at his small-minded thinking. I've held many discussions with Braun McLaren Energy as well as several of the mayors in a 100-mile radius of our fair city. We've had great conversations, wonderful conversations. And they have reported to me that they would support the largest possible plasma gasification plant we can have built, and they would pledge to send us their fuel for the next fifty years. Braun McLaren would also guarantee that they would not build another plant within a five-hundred-mile radius of Appleseed, thus protecting our investment.

"Also, the PGP won't just generate free energy, which will lead to lower energy bills for all Appleseedlings—including all of you—it will also create several new high-paying jobs for the area. These will be important jobs that can help boost Appleseed's already-strong economy. Thank you very much."

"What kinds of jobs?" asked Will.

"I'm sorry?" said Sheila.

"You said they will create high-paying jobs. What kinds of jobs will they create?"

"I, uh, I don't, uh, that is, isn't it my turn to be asked a question?" said Sheila, feeling a bead of sweat run from her arm down her side.

"Yes, yes, that's right," said President Grogan who was actually a little taken aback himself at Will's unexpected breach of protocol. On the other hand, he was curious himself.

"The next question is for you, Mayor Windsong." He paused and looked at the audience then back at Sheila. "What kinds of jobs?"

"Shit," hissed Enrique from the wings, stage right. He was standing on Sheila's side of the backstage, and his face smoldered darkly, and his glare was so fierce, Sara and Kyle could see it from the wings on the other side of the stage, stage left. Sara felt like she could even hear it.

Fucking shit, Sheila thought. "Well," she said, "we're still working out the exact details with Braun McLaren's guidance. We'll need fuel technicians, of course. And, uhh, sanitation engineers, maintenance people, and so on."

"So, people to dump the garbage in the vats? How much will those people be paid?" Will said. He was clearly not following the debate protocol, but nobody seemed to notice. Except Enrique, who was jumping up and down and waving his arms.

"Well, a lot of that will be automated," said Sheila, and then immediately wished she hadn't.

"That means there will only be a few jobs because the robots will be doing the rest?"

"Uhh..."

"How many jobs will there actually be at this plant?"

"We won't entirely know for sure until we know how big the plant will be."

"If we could return to the answer and response model, please," said President Grogan, finally realizing where he was and attempting to wrest control of the debate back from its participants.

"Actually, we do," said Will.

"I'm telling you, we don't!"

"Maybe you don't, or you just don't want other people to know. Because I know."

Sheila opened her mouth to protest and closed it again. She wiped the sweat off her forehead.

Will continued, "I spoke with a representative of Braun McLaren this week, and she told me that a plant of this proposed size will need only five people to run it. Two 'fuel technicians,' which is the term for the people who make sure the garbage gets into the vat, two energy techs to maintain the machines, and a senior director."

"But I don't, that is, we can't just—"

"They also estimate that, based on the current size of plant you've proposed, we will run out of fuel in eight to ten years, depending on how efficiently we operate and whether we increase electricity consumption. But with a smaller plant, we can reach an annual breakeven point if we use it to supplement our power needs, not replace our current methods. Of course, the PGP will need to be placed about two miles closer to town and not on their proposed location."

"I haven't heard anything about that," said Sheila. Both she and Enrique knew what was coming next and knew that she was powerless to stop it, like watching a car accident happen in slow motion. Enrique covered his eyes with his hands, but Sheila could only stand and watch. Beads of sweat began dripping down her back and her armpits, and the auditorium suddenly felt like someone had pulled on the thermostat like they were trying to stop a runaway train.

What the fuck is wrong with me? thought Will. *I don't even want this job. Why the hell am I fighting for it?*

He continued, "Of course, what most people don't realize is that the original location for the proposed PGP is a family farm—"

The auditorium was plunged into darkness, and a collective gasp erupted from the audience as some of the older Zoomers turned on the flashlights on their mobile devices. People chattered and tried to figure out what was happening when they were interrupted by an ear-splitting buzzing and were bathed in a red flashing light.

After several seconds, the lights came back on, and Enrique ran out onto the stage and over to Sheila, saying something in her ear. She looked out at the audience, looked at President Grogan, and darted off the stage. He then crossed over to President Grogan and said something to him as well.

President Grogan looked at Enrique and said, "Seriously?" Enrique nodded and ran after Sheila. President Grogan tapped his microphone and said, "If I could have everyone's attention. Please evacuate the building immediately and proceed across the street. If I could ask everyone to please evacuate in a calm and orderly fashion and proceed across the street."

People stood up and did as they were asked, filing out as quickly as they could without actually trampling each other.

Will, Sara, and Kyle had joined President Grogan in the middle of the stage.

"What's going on, President Grogan?" asked Kyle.

"We have to evacuate the building immediately," said President Grogan, his face taking on an eerie look from the red flashing lights. "There has been a bomb threat. I suggest you evacuate immediately."

"You all go now," said Will. "Exit the building through the back way and make sure you take anyone else backstage with you. I'll meet you out front."

"Where's the nearest exit?" asked Sara.

"That way," said Will, pointing across the stage where Sheila and Enrique had fled just moments before.

"President Grogan, Professor Gant, what's going on?" a voice called from the front of the stage. It was Carmen Cowen, the reporter from the *Appleseed Mail-Journal* and she was wearing a small video camera rig on her shoulder. She had been streaming the entire debate on the *Mail-Journal* media page.

"Ms. Cowen, I must ask you to evacuate the building. It seems someone has called in a bomb threat, and we must evacuate immediately."

"A bomb threat?" shouted Carmen, forgetting her journalistic training.

"A bomb?" someone at the back of the evacuating crowd repeated. "They said there's a bomb."

"It's only a bomb threat," shouted President Grogan into the microphone in order to calm everyone down. It didn't help. "Please remain calm and evacuate the building in an orderly fashion."

Cries of "There's a bomb! They said there's a bomb!" made their way up through the evacuating crowd, and people started pushing and shoving their way out of the building. A few older people fell and were in danger of being trampled. Will jumped off the stage and waded into the crowd, Sara and Kyle following him. They helped the people who had fallen and shielded some of the less mobile people from being knocked over again.

"Please remain calm," shouted Will. "We'll all make it out safely. Just remain calm."

Carmen jumped up onto the stage and zoomed her shoulder camera in on Will, Sara, and Kyle. The people who were watching at home saw Will and the leadership of the SCF helping several people even as they listened to Carmen's commentary on what they were all seeing.

"I don't know where Mayor Windsong or her advisor, Enrique Medina, have retreated to, but they are nowhere to be found, having exited the moment the lights came back on. Meanwhile, President Grogan, Will Gant, and two members of the Students for a Conservative Future are remaining behind and ensuring that the slowest and least mobile of the audience members are safe."

A firefighter in full gear entered through the backstage entrance and shouted to President Grogan, "What are you people still doing in here? You need to evacuate immediately!"

"We know, but we need to make sure that everyone else is out safely," said President Grogan.

"That's our job, Dr. Grogan," said the firefighter.

"Good evening, Chief Price-Ward."

"Good evening, sir," said Brittany Price-Ward, Appleseed's longest-serving fire chief. "We appreciate your concern for your people, but we'll make sure we get them out. And that means you have to get out, too. You as well, Ms. Cowen."

Carmen continued to video everything, turning her body to catch different parts of the action.

"Not until the last of them are out," said President Grogan. He looked up and saw that nearly everyone was through the doors with Will, Sara, and Kyle helping the final people to the exit. Will turned and gave President Grogan a thumbs-up and was the last one to leave through the front.

"Now that Professor Gant and his campaign team have ensured that everyone else is out of the building, it's now time for President Grogan and I to evacuate so the fire service and bomb squad can do their jobs," Carmen said.

They followed Chief Price-Ward out the backstage exit through the stage right wings. Sheila and Enrique were nowhere to be found. They weren't out front with the rest of the crowd either.

Out on the street, traffic had stopped and was being diverted by Captain Sam Violet-Paisley of the Appleseed College Police Department and three of her officers. Several fire trucks, police cars, and a bomb disposal unit truck were all stationed in front of the Nikki Giovanni Memorial Auditorium. Chief Price-Ward and a police lieutenant were standing on the other side of the bomb disposal truck, communicating via two-way radios with their staff.

Two officers and their bomb-sniffing beagles entered the auditorium, the dogs on high alert for any kind of explosive. While society had moved on from most humans-first practices, bomb and drug-sniffing dogs were still deemed acceptable.

Will, Sara, and Kyle stood with the rest of the crowd, answering questions and talking with President Grogan. Carmen Cowen stood nearby, interviewing people on the scene, even while she kept an eye on the front entrance for any news from the first responders.

After forty-five minutes, Chief Price-Ward crossed the street, followed by the two bomb disposal officers, their dogs, and Lt. Fitzhugh House-Dupree. The entire crowd had stayed for what they told their friends was a concern that everyone was OK. In actuality, they were hoping to be able to see an explosion. By the time Chief Price-Ward gave the all-clear, more than 30,000 total minutes of PDT and mobile footage had been uploaded to the various social media channels in the hopes of capturing the explosion live.

Carmen slowly crept over to President Grogan as the three responders approached.

"False alarm," said Chief Price-Ward. "Looks like someone called it in as a hoax."

"Do you have any idea who might have done it?" asked President Grogan.

"No clue," said one of the bomb techs. "We never received any call ourselves. We checked with Appleseed dispatch, and no one reported any kind of bomb threat. In fact, we haven't had one in twelve years, so this was a bit of a surprise."

"Really? So why does Appleseed have a bomb disposal unit?" asked Kyle.

"I don't know," said the bomb tech. "We've always had one, and it doesn't hurt to be prepared. And aren't you glad now that we had one?"

Kyle couldn't argue with that logic; no one could. "Good point," he said.

"If you didn't get a call, then who reported it?" asked Sara.

"Enrique Medina told me after he told the mayor," said President Grogan.

"Whenever a fire alarm is pulled, we immediately receive an alert, and the trucks roll out," said Chief Price-Ward. "We saw on Ms. Cowen's livestream that there was a bomb. Then Deputy Mayor Medina called and said he had received a call about a bomb threat and pulled the alarm himself."

"Where is the mayor now?" asked Sara.

"I haven't seen her out here," said President Grogan.

"I think she left right when President Grogan gave the evacuation order," said Will.

"No, she left right before," said Carmen who had been standing nearby, still recording everything with her shoulder camera. "I watched her, and then I double-checked the student feed. Enrique Medina whispered something in her ear, and then she left through the backstage door while Enrique told President Grogan, and then he followed her out."

"I'll ask our arson investigator to liaise with the police department on this if that's alright with you, Lieutenant House-Dupree," said Chief Price-Ward.

"That'll be fine," said Lieutenant House-Dupree.

"Chief Price-Ward, could I get a quick interview for my story?" said Carmen.

CHAPTER 13

"A bomb threat hoax interrupted Appleseed's mayoral debate between incumbent mayor, Sheila Windsong, and the challenger and pre-Takening conservative holdover, Will Gant, last night. Gant, you will remember, is the faculty advisor to the Students for a Conservative Future, the alt-right student group that led an unsanctioned protest against noble watchdogs Benna Weston-Geiger and their student judicial committee, forcing Benna to withdraw from Appleseed College Of The Arts for their own mental health. We'll have coverage of Mayor Windsong's press conference at 11:00 this morning. Tune into WSED, Appleseed's TV News, at 6 p.m. for more."

"More news from America's Heartland and our siblings to the south in Appleseed, Ohio. The Nazis are starting to emerge from their dank cave as they disrupted a mayoral debate between the Right Honorable Sheila Windsong and alt-right candidate, Professor Will Gant. According to our inside sources, Mayor Windsong had the America-hating upstart on the ropes when one

of his cronies—allegedly—called in a bomb threat to the mayor's deputy mayor, Enrique Medina. Mayor Windsong and Mr. Medina informed the moderator before wisely evacuating the building. We'll speak to political historian Cheryl Clayton at 3:00 this afternoon about what this means for political watchers here on Ann Arbor's Community Radio Station, WARB."

"Good morning, Appleseed. This weekend is a big one: It's the 19th annual Found Items Trunk Show and Swap Meet. Bring your gently used and worn items and clothing, whether yours or a family member who has passed on, to Gordon Jump Park between 8 a.m. and 5 p.m. Be sure to visit the artists' tents, the merchant tents, and the classic car show. Francesca Coy-Pessoa promises to show off her 1985 Chevy Citation, which she has restored to factory condition. Stay tuned to WAPPL for more local news here on Appleseed's Golden Oldies with the hits of the 10s, 20s, and 30s. Next up, we're firing up the way-wayback machine with a little tune from La Grand Dame herself, Lady Gaga."

"Are you sure about this?" Sheila asked Enrique.

"Absolutely," said Enrique. "We need to counteract the news about our early departure last night. And, uh, other things." He jerked his head toward the third person in the room.

The two were in her office as a makeup artist applied the finishing touches to Sheila's appearance. The woman's eyebrows were bold and strong, her blonde hair was a rich platinum, and her pink lipstick and blue eyeshade were especially vibrant. It was a must for anyone appearing on today's 96K video terminals, explained the makeup artist, Mistress Blueberry.

Mistress Blueberry came highly recommended by those West Central Ohioans who were in the know about such matters. TV anchors and regional politicians swore up and down by Mistress Blueberry's methods and evangelized her talents to anyone who could afford her hourly rate.

"You vant people to vocus on your eyes and mouth, *dahling*," said Mistress Blueberry, affecting Zsa Zsa Gabor's accent even though she was from Coldwater, Ohio, just up Interstate 75. "And I vant your cheeks to absolutely *shine*." She applied another layer of Blazing Shitrus, a shade of TV makeup made popular thirty-seven years ago.

"And ze boobies! Ve must ample up ze boobies!" She made up-sweeping motions with her hands before putting them on the Right Honorable Cleavage and trying to fluff them up.

Sheila looked at Enrique and twirled her hand to make him turn around. She adjusted herself and looked at Mistress Blueberry. "Well?"

"Very good, *dahling!*" declared Mistress Blueberry.

"Thank you, Mistress Blueberry," said Sheila. "Now could you give us a few minutes, please?"

"Ja, ja, zat is good. You look vonderful, dahling. Not to be gauche, but I will wait outside for my payment."

"I'll take care of it," said Enrique. He tapped the temple on his PDT. "Pay Mistress Blueberry from the campaign fund."

"Thank you," called Mistress Blueberry from the outer office after her PDT pinged and notified her she had just made $2,500.

"Tiffani, can you close the door, please?" Sheila called.

"Computer, close the door," Tiffani hollered in response.

"Now, let's go over it one more time," said Enrique once the door closed. "What happened last night?"

"You received a call from a potential terrorist threatening to blow up the auditorium. You notified me and then President Grogan, and he ordered the evacuation."

"Right, and when did we leave?" said Enrique.

"As soon as President Grogan ordered the evacuation," said Sheila.

"Not before?"

"No, I waited to see what he was going to do."

"And what were you going to do?"

Sheila looked up as she tried to remember. "If he didn't order the evacuation, I was going to."

"How do you know it was a bomb threat?" Enrique asked.

"You told me."

Enrique sighed. "Yes. But how did I know?"

"Because they said 'tell the Windsong bitch this is her last debate.' By the way, did you call your phone to show that call?"

"No problem. I did it last night from an old phone my mom used to own."

"You carry your mom's old phone?" Sheila snickered. "How cute. Do you keep her toaster, too?"

"It's a really good toaster. Also, you never know when you're going to need an old phone."

"Like calling in fake bomb threats?"

"I have no idea what you're talking about," said Enrique.

"What's wrong with you? Are you having a stroke?"

"No, that was a wink!"

"Jesus, you're really bad at that. Don't do that. How do you even scrunch up the whole half of your face like that? I really thought you were having a stroke."

"Fuck off. I wink great. Now, who do you think called in the threat? Why would they do it on the night of the debate?"

"It was one of Gant's Nazis—"

"Ah-ah. We can't say it *was*. We have to speculate and imply. We can't say it was at all. And we certainly can't say it was a Nazi."

"Why not?"

"Because that would be slanderous, and he could sue the shit out of us. So you can only speculate and imply."

Sheila sighed and checked herself in her office mirror one more time. "I don't know who it was, but it was likely someone who didn't want us to do well in this debate, and so they sought to disrupt the very foundation of American democracy."

"Good enough. Now, do you have your speech?"

"Yep," said Sheila, tapping her PDT and giving a thumbs-up. "Let's do this."

"Great. *Please* don't say Nazis though."

"Yeah, yeah, whatever. You worry too much."

Sheila and Enrique strode into the city council room where a lectern had already been set up and several wireless microphones installed by the various members of the media in attendance. Fire Chief Brittany Price-Ward, Chief Colin Sipe-Lockwood, and Lt. Fitzhugh House-Dupree of the Appleseed PD and Captain Sam Violet-Paisley of the ACOTA PD stood behind the lectern, looking somber and serious.

There were at least forty-five media people in the room, not only from the local media outlets but several other local and regional media outlets. They all looked rumpled and bedraggled as if they had all traveled overnight to be there, which they had. There hadn't been a bomb threat or a conservative political candidate in twenty years, so people from all over the Midwest were clamoring for more information.

Also, journalists had not changed their appearance in over 120 years.

When news of the bomb threat first hit the local news, it immediately went viral. Viewers were treated to images of

Will and his campaign staff heroically trying to usher people out of the auditorium and protect them from being trampled, even as a bomb was ticking toward its ultimate purpose.

Will Gant's popularity and campaign donations went through the roof. He had raised nearly $3 million in campaign contributions, and he was now leading the polls with fifty-three percent. Different news outlets sent reporters to Appleseed and told them to cover the news conference and to get as many interviews as they could with both candidates and local Appleseedlings.

When Sheila and Enrique saw how widespread the video had become and realized Will's KNCLD score could only decrease, they began to worry. That turned into a panic attack when social media comments slammed Sheila and Enrique's early departure, and the #runawaysheila and #flylikethewindsong were trending. And they went into full-blown panic when Sheila's approval rating dipped below fifty percent for the first time in twelve years. It took a two-hour massage and some of Enrique's edibles to finally calm her down.

"Good morning, everyone," said Enrique, standing at the lectern. "Mayor Sheila Windsong will read a short statement, and then she'll answer your questions." He moved aside, and Sheila stepped up to the bank of microphones.

"Good morning. Thank you all for coming. Last night, at 8:27, the Appleseed mayoral debate was interrupted by what we believed to be a real bomb threat which later turned out to be a hoax.

"My deputy mayor, Enrique Medina, received the call. Out of an abundance of caution, Mr. Medina cut the house lights in order to get everyone's attention, pulled the fire alarm, and then turned the lights back on.

"He then informed me and Dr. Caden Grogan, president of Appleseed College, about the threat. Dr. Grogan ordered the evacuation of the building, and we immediately complied.

"Thanks to Mr. Medina's fast thinking and heroism, we were able to evacuate the building quickly and efficiently and get everyone to safety. After a thorough check by the fine men, women, and nonbinary members of the Appleseed police and fire departments, the all-clear was given, and it was discovered there had never been a bomb in the first place. It was confirmed to be a hoax."

"Who do you think called in the threat?" asked a young man from the *Fortville-McCordsville Reporter* in central Indiana.

"If you could hold your questions until the end, that'd be great, mmm-kay?" said Sheila. "Now, our investigators are working diligently to trace the call and the caller, but they aren't having any luck. If anyone has any information about this horrible incident, we would appreciate it. The city is offering a $250,000 reward for any information leading to the capture of this Nazi terrorist."

"Goddammit," muttered Enrique. The microphones, which were some of the industry's most sensitive thanks to the much-vaunted Clymer upgrade, were not able to pick it up as the room erupted into heated discussions and questions being lobbed at the mayor and the first responders at the front of the room.

"Are there Nazis in Appleseed?" someone shouted.

"Are we under attack? Should we be afraid?" shouted someone else.

"Have we tried diplomatic measures?" hollered someone from the back.

But the question being asked the most was, "How do you know it was a Nazi?"

Enrique stepped back up to the microphone. "People, please." He bounced his hands up and down in an attempt to get people to quiet down.

"That shit just doesn't work, does it, Dolly Purrton?" Benna Weston-Geiger said to their cat as they both watched the livestream on their home computer. "Bet Sara Cooper-Fucking-Wright would be all over that shit."

"We will answer your questions once we can calm down and use our inside voices," said Enrique. The crowd soon settled back down, and Sheila stepped up to the microphones again.

"No Nazis, goddammit," Enrique hissed in Sheila's ear as they passed.

"I guess we'll go with the first question," said Sheila.

"Motherfucker!" hissed Enrique.

"How do you know it was a Nazi?" said the reporter from the *Fortville-McCordsville Reporter*.

"I misspoke when I said that. We don't actually know who made the call, so we have no way of knowing who the actual terrorist is."

"But what makes you think it was a Nazi?" said a young blonde woman from one of the remaining TV-only news stations in Cincinnati.

Sheila looked over at Enrique, gave a half-smile, and shrugged. "Well, like I said, we don't actually know who made the call. But I find it curious that the call came in the middle of the debate when Professor Gant was struggling."

"Actually, Professor Gant seemed to be doing quite well," said Brooklyn Hazel-Stinebaugh, a reporter from the *Celina Daily Standard*.

Other reporters echoed Brooklyn Hazel-Stinebaugh's assessment.

"Maybe to someone who doesn't understand how political debates work," said Sheila, beginning to sweat a little bit.

Brooklyn said she understood perfectly well how political debates worked, having worked on Capitol Hill for twelve years. Sheila turned back to Enrique and raised her eyebrows as if to say, *Well, what now, genius?*

Enrique pursed his lips in a way that said, *I told you not to mention Nazis in the first place. Why did you even bring them up? All you had to do was cast aspersions on Gant's knowledge of the bomb, and we would have been in the clear. But noooooo, you had to bring Nazis into this.*

Sheila flared her nostrils. *You know, sometimes you can be a real asshole.*

Enrique cocked one eyebrow. *Frosty bitch.*

"Did you coordinate with the Appleseed first responders at all? No one has reported seeing you at the scene," said Carmen Cowen of the *Appleseed Mail-Journal*.

"Absolutely. As the mayor, I support the fine men and women and nonbinary members of the Appleseed first response agencies."

Carmen continued, "But were you actually still at the site?"

"Next question."

"Who do you think is actually behind all this?" asked Emily Brown-Yelich, the news anchor from WAST in Midland, Michigan.

Sheila looked out over the audience from left to right. She cleared her throat and took a drink from the glass of water on the lectern. She swept her gaze over the audience again. This was it. This is what she and Enrique had discussed as the way they were going to get the voters back on her side and cast doubt on Will Gant's heroics. She cleared her throat one last time.

"What I find curious," she said, "is how calm Will Gant and his students seemed during the so-called threat. Mr. Medina and I left the building immediately, as we were instructed to do so, especially once we were aware of the threat. But Professor Gant took all the time he needed to play the hero, almost as if he knew he was going to be safe."

The room exploded once more into rapid-fire questions and shouts.

"Are you saying Professor Gant was aware of the hoax?" shouted the reporter from a media station in Dayton.

Sheila stared out over the audience and said nothing as questions continued to be shouted at her. She spoke softly into the microphones, so softly that no one could hear what she was saying, and everyone quieted down to hear her.

"What I'm saying," said Sheila, "is that I'm asking Police Chief Sipe-Lockwood to investigate this bomb hoax closely. I will also be speaking to our city's prosecutor about possible treason charges against whoever is found to be involved."

"How do you think Will Gant was actually involved?" shouted Carmen.

"If you were actually good reporters, you would ask those questions yourselves instead of waiting to be spoon-fed your stories," Sheila said. And with that, she walked out of the room, Enrique trailing behind her, leaving a stunned audience in their wake.

"What time did the call actually come in, Enrique?" Carmen called after Enrique. He froze briefly, for just an instant, but it was enough for Carmen to notice.

"Gotcha," she whispered.

CHAPTER 14

"We need to respond!" shouted Sara, slam-ming her hands on her table. "We can't let this stand. What she said was libelous!"

"Slanderous," said Griffin. He and Sara were seated at her kitchen table with Kyle and Callie. They had just finished watching the live stream of Sheila's press conference and were understandably angry. They had tried calling Will several times, but he wasn't answering. They had also checked his home and office, and he wasn't there either. They weren't sure what they should do, so they decided to focus on a strategy they could present to Will for his approval.

"What?" said Sara.

"Slanderous. Slander is spoken. Libel is l—well, written."

"What do you suggest we do, Sara?" asked Kyle. "It's not like we can prove anything. She didn't actually say anything concrete or that we could sue over. So how can we counteract it?" Kyle walked over to the coffee machine on the counter and poured himself a cup of mushroom coffee with almond milk creamer.

"Lettered?" offered Callie.

"Literary?" said Griffin.

"Literal?" said Callie.

"I don't know," said Sara. "But we need to respond, otherwise people will think that Will ordered that bomb threat. We were doing so well in the polls until Sheila Breakwind lied about us. Her and her fucking lapdog. Bunch of fucking Zoomers. They got the world into this mess and then leave it for us to clean up."

"Ooh, libel is lies!" said Callie.

"So is slander," said Griffin.

"Shit," said Callie.

"WHOOOO!" hollered Trent from the nearby living room. He and Grace were playing a skiing video game on their PDTs, bodies contorting as they navigated the Olympic downhill slalom course from the Albertville Olympics in 1992.

"Man, can you believe all this snow?" said Grace.

"I know, I've never seen this much snow," said Trent. "I'm getting cold just seeing it all."

"Look at these ski fashions! Everyone looks so puffy and cozy."

"If we could all just focus, please," said Kyle. "Also, you're thinking of legible."

"Hey, that's it," said Griffin. "Slander is spoken; libel is legible."

"Or lettered," said Kyle.

"Even better!" said Callie. "Slander is spoken; libel is lettered."

"WIPEOUT!" shouted Grace.

"Dude, you ate it hard!" jeered Trent.

"Come on, you guys!" said Kyle. "We need to focus up here."

Grace and Trent tapped their PDTs, went to the coffee machine for their own mushroom coffee, and sat down at the table.

"Now, what kind of response can we come up with?" asked Sara. "We need something to counter Sheila's pack of lies during that last press conference."

"What about a response video?" asked Grace. "I was watching these old, old videos by this guy named Jon Stewart. My parents used to love this guy and showed me some of his videos when I was a kid. He'd do these little rants about the politicians of his day and then show video clips of stupid things they had said or done. Those people were some real assholes! Anyway, we could create a video like that and show some examples from the debate about how Sheila was floundering when Will called her out on some of the bullshit about the PGP?"

"That could work," said Sara. "You start on that."

"What about a press release?" offered Trent.

"About what?"

"Just Will's statement about what happened and how Sheila's comments are clearly made out of desperation because she doesn't have anything of substance that she can say. I'm majoring in Advocacy Journalism, so I can write that up."

"Excellent. That's all yours," said Sara. Trent pulled his tablet and keyboard out of his backpack and began typing.

"Did he say that? How do you know what he said?" asked Kyle.

"I don't," said Callie. "I haven't talked to him today. But that's OK. I'll write up the statement, then we'll show it to him and get his approval. That's what he does with our other press releases."

"What about placing a story with Carmen Cowen? It was her story from the debate that went viral," said Kyle.

Sara said, "I could call her. Maybe she could interview Will and—Weird, she's calling me right now." She tapped the side of her PDT. "Hi, Carmen, what's up?"

"Hey, Sara, do you have a minute?" Carmen's voice came through the bone-conducting earpiece.

"Sure, what's up? Hold on. I'm going to put you on broadcast. We're all in a meeting about last night." Sara double-tapped her earpiece and said, "Computer, conference in the Gant For Mayor group." Within two seconds, everyone else in the room received an alert on their own PDTs. They tapped their earpiece and were looped into the call.

"I was wondering if you all had a response to Mayor Windsong's press conference this morning."

"Well, uh, we were just formulating a response to—"

"Great. I just need something fast for a new story. First, what is Professor Gant's response to the Mayor's allegations?"

Sara looked around at everyone, but no one seemed to have any ideas, so she shrugged her shoulders and plowed on. "Well, Professor Gant categorically denies Mayor Windsong's outrageous accusations. Anyone who was watching the debate could tell she was floundering once the truth was revealed about the financial benefits she was receiving. Not to mention, she and Enrique Medina fully left the building the second she found out about the bomb threat. They didn't wait for President Grogan to order the evacuation. And they certainly didn't stick around afterward to see what had happened."

"Did you actually see her leave?" Carmen asked.

"Absolutely. Kyle and I were standing in the opposite wings, stage left, and we could see Enrique in the wings, stage right. Plus, we could see the backstage exit from where we were standing. Once Enrique whispered in Sheila's ear, she exited right out that door. And after he spoke with President Grogan, he followed her out the door. I didn't see where they went after that because Professor Gant and a few of his students were too busy helping people to evacuate."

"Did you see them at all outside after you left?"

"Not at all. We left through the same door, and I didn't see them in the alley and not out front where everyone else had gathered. I even walked around a bit to see if I could spot either of them, but I couldn't find them."

"Mayor Windsong said she was coordinating with the first responders on their efforts," said Carmen. "How far were you from where the responders had set up?"

"We could absolutely see them from where we were standing," said Sara. The others all voiced their agreement.

"I was watching them even while Sara was walking around," said Kyle. "Chief Price-Ward and Lt. House-Dupree were coordinating efforts from behind the big truck the bomb disposal people came in."

"And did Mayor Windsong ever communicate with them?" asked Carmen. "Did she maybe show up and leave, or was she on her PDT with them from the crowd?"

"No, not even once. She never showed up where the responders were stationed," said Kyle.

"And I walked through the entire crowd, and she was nowhere to be seen. There were only a few hundred people there by then," said Sara. Everyone in the room said they had been in different parts of the crowd but had not seen Sheila or Enrique anywhere in the crowd. "Why? What's going on?" continued Sara.

"I can't say too much, but I'm working on a story about the timeline of last night's events. Although I can tell you that I don't quite think things happened the way Medina says they did. They just don't add up."

"What do you mean?" said Sara.

"I can't say anymore because I don't have all the details, but the times between the call, the lights out, and the evacuation aren't in the order you would think."

"Are you saying the call was faked?" said Sara.

"Well, we already know it was a hoax," said Callie. "That's what a hoax means."

Sara made a face at her. "I don't mean that. I mean, was there actually not a call at all?"

"I can't tell you anything right now, but when I publish the story, you can read all about it. In the meantime, let Professor Gant know that he needs to watch his back."

"Why?"

"Because I think Windsong and Medina have more in store for him." The members of the SCF collectively gasped. "Have you talked to him at all since last night?" asked Carmen.

"No, we've all tried calling him, and we've been to his house and his office, and he's not around at all. Have you?"

"I've tried calling him, and I've emailed him, but I haven't gotten any response. I also went to his house and checked out his regular jogging trails. You need to find him because I think he's in trouble."

Sara grew pale. "What are they going to do?"

"I don't know. But keep looking for him and tell him to lay low and to get rid of his PDT. They can track him through it. I have to go. Talk to you soon." Carmen disconnected from the call, and Sheila looked at her friends.

"What's going on?" Kyle said.

"I don't know." She tapped her PDT. "Call Will Gant."

"We're sorry, but the party you are trying to reach is not available at this time," said the recorded voice.

"Leave a message," said Sara.

"I'm sorry. I'm afraid I can't do that," said the recorded voice.

"Shit." She tapped her PDT again. "Call Will Gant." The recorded voice apologized once more.

"What's happening?" asked Griffin.

"Locate Will Gant," Sara said, panic creeping into her voice. "Is he at the library?"

"Will Gant cannot be located," said the recorded voice. "Will Gant has left the library."

"Call Will Gant's office," Sara said, panic rising in her voice.

"Sara, what's wrong?" Kyle stood up; the others followed suit.

"There is no answer at Will Gant's office," said the recorded voice.

"Oh, God," said Sara. "I can't find Will. He's missing."

CHAPTER 15

WILL GANT STOPPED AT AN INTERSECTION, SWEAT pouring down his face and soaking his shirt. He put his hands on his knees and gasped for breath.

"Come on, Gant! Give it up," said a voice behind him. "You can't keep this up forever."

"Shows what you know," said Gant. "I've still got a few tricks up my sleeve." He turned around to look at his pursuer.

"Really? You're gasping so hard, I'm about ready to call the EMTs on your saggy ass."

Gant laughed. "Double or nothing?"

"You're on." The light changed, and the two broke into a sprint down the block. Gant's stride was smooth, his arms moved effortlessly, and he was as relaxed and poised as an Olympic sprinter as he easily outpaced the other person by ten yards.

"Good God, you're still too fast for me," said Katie Sartoris.

"Benefits of being a track star at Tulane."

"Were you setting me up?"

"Wisdom and experience, youngling. When you don't have youth and speed, you rely on wisdom and experience," said Will.

"Fine, first beer's on me."

The two trotted into Clap Hands Bottles and Cans Brewery, a local craft brewery, and looked for a spot on the patio. They found an empty table under a big cooling fan and sat with their legs spread, huffing and puffing, enjoying the cool evening breeze and the air from the fan.

"Who won today?" asked their server Bonnie.

"Who do you think?" Katie said with a wry smile.

"Congratulations, Will," said Bonnie. "What can I get you?"

"Two waters and two wheat beers, please," said Will. "Is that alright? I don't mean to presume."

"No, no, that's fine," said Katie. She pulled a microfiber cloth out of her pocket and mopped her face. Will did the same, and the two perused the menu.

Nearly a month after Katie and Bert had broken up, she was still furious at him, which caused her feelings to spill over into other parts of her work, which meant getting furious about her students launching the SCF group. She decided to shout at Will Gant about brainwashing them into a conservative lifestyle in the hopes that this would make her feel better. He was in his office with the door open, seated at his desk, when Katie burst in.

"Who the hell do you think you are, indoctrinating these impressionable young learners into your alt-right bullshit?"

"I what? Indoctrinating who?" asked Will, rising to his feet. "I'm sorry. Who are you?"

Was this a crazy woman he was going to have to deal with? Or an angry parent? A local political crank? He occasionally dealt with upset parents who didn't like that Will examined both sides of an argument in his political history classes. Was this another irate parent? It wouldn't be the first time one of them traveled to Appleseed to yell at him. Or was this someone who objected to his mayoral campaign? It wasn't the first time someone got upset that a Black man was running for political office against a White woman.

"Sorry. I'm Dr. Katie Sartoris. I'm in the Educational Psychology department."

"Oh, right, Dr. Sartoris. Sara Cooper-Wright has mentioned you. She speaks very highly of you." Will extended his hand, and Katie shook it. "You were her advisor for the Barney Hall protest in August, right?"

Shit, this was not going the way she wanted. She wanted to yell and vent at Will, get into a shouting match, so she could unleash some of this anger she was feeling. But he was being rather nice and disarming. "That's right. Me and Bert— uh, Dr., um, Welch."

"I know Dr. Welch. He's an, uh, interesting guy."

"Yeah, that's one word for him." Katie wiped at her eyes.

"Oh, I'm sorry. Did I say something wrong?" Will reached into a desk drawer, took out a box of tissues, and held it out to Katie.

"No, no, you didn't. It's fine," said Katie, snatching one out of the box and dabbing at her eyes. "I just... I don't know."

"Why don't you sit down for a minute?"

Katie sat down in the chair in front of Will's desk, and he returned to his own. He waited as Katie dried her eyes.

"Is there anything I can do for you?" asked Will. "Can I get you some water?"

"No, thank you. I just need a second," said Katie. She started to cry again, tears streaming down her cheeks. After a few moments, she said, "Can I have another tissue?" She took another one from Will's box and blew her nose, a loud, ungraceful honk. "This is not going at all the way I wanted," she continued.

"How did you think this was going to go?" asked Will.

"I was going to come in here and yell at you for being an alt-right indoctrinator."

"Ah. And now you've realized I'm just a simple history professor?"

"No, I just lost the urge." Katie looked like she might cry again.

"So I'm still a serious threat to democracy and liberalism?" Will smiled and held the tissue box out to her again.

Katie snickered. "You don't seem like one, but I haven't decided yet."

"Fair enough. So what's going on with you?"

Katie couldn't explain it, but she felt safe with this history professor. He was soft-spoken, tall, slender, wore glasses and sweater vests, and didn't strike her as an alt-right anything, let alone a money-grubbing, power-hungry politician. He was the complete opposite of what she had conjured up in her imagination leading up to this moment.

She told him about her time with Bert Welch, his selfishness and self-centeredness. And she relayed the story of their breakup, including how he had worked with Sheila Windsong to funnel her funding into Bert's campaign.

"Yeah, I figured something was up with that," said Will. "I thought it was weird that Sheila Windsong's ex-husband would be giving us $100,000 out of spite. The guy's about as subtle as a rhino playing hide-and-seek. We haven't touched that money, and I notified the state election board about it. They haven't responded, but I'm getting ready to return it."

"What about the $25,000 he gave to the SCF?"

"They're holding onto it as well. Technically, they don't have to return it. And since the group has been disbanded by the SGA, and Dr. Welch—unwisely, I think—gave it directly to Sara, it's technically private money. She's thinking about donating it to a mental health support group."

The two talked about politics, Will's work in the history department, what first drew Katie to educational psychology, and the cognitive development of pre-adults and young learners. ("You're right, they can be pretty dumb! But then they surprise me with their insights.")

As it grew dark outside, Will's office lights automatically turned on, and he looked at a clock on the wall, a gift from his ex-wife many years ago.

"Oh, my CHiP," said Katie. "Is that the time? It's been over two hours."

"I completely lost track of time," said Will.

"Do you want to get dinner?" Katie asked. "I, uh, don't feel like going home right now."

The two walked to the Clap Hands Brewery, where they continued to talk well into the night, about their lives, their careers, and their marriages and subsequent divorces.

Will's divorce happened fifteen years earlier when he was teaching at the University of Illinois. He learned his wife Yasmine, a professor of literature, had been sleeping with her department chair for nearly two years, so Will reported both of them to the university. The department chair was dismissed because of the power imbalance of their relationship, and the university promoted Will's wife to department chair in an effort to keep her from suing them. The department chair got another job at Penn State University as the dean of the humanities department. Will left the university and took a teaching position at Appleseed College.

Katie's husband Devon left her because she got tenure and he did not. She was a rising star in the Appleseed College academic scene, winning awards and accolades, and was granted tenure a full two years early. Her husband was a professor in the Communications department. He conducted mediocre research and failed to get published in enough academic journals, and four years into his tenure journey, he realized he wouldn't be able to make it up, so he blamed Katie and her successes for overshadowing him and making him lose his confidence.

Devon was now running a maple syrup co-op in Vermont, working as an adjunct professor at a local college, and sleeping with as many of the undergraduates as he could before he got too old and they started saying he reminded them of their dads.

"I guess I keep going for the insecure academic types. Bert always tried to flex his Ph.D. on other people and insisted people call him Dr. Welch, including other professors. I just never cared and let my students call me Katie. That used to bother him because he said I earned my doctorate, so I should be proud of it."

As the servers were stacking chairs on tables and sweeping the floor, Will said, "So have I answered all your questions about my alt-right indoctrination attempts?"

Katie snorted. "I'm really sorry about that. I guess my learners were just pushing to be rebellious like I did when I was a kid."

"I get it. My parents were dyed-in-the-wool liberals, and they thought they had failed when I said I just wasn't as interested in politics as they were."

"And that's when you became a moderate?"

"Yep, I became a radical moderate. I refused to attend protests. I never signed petitions, never marched for a cause, and never really got involved in anything. My parents were heartbroken that I didn't grow up to follow them into the family business."

"Don't you care about those things?"

"Ultimately, yes. But I don't want to spend my energy on them. I have a good job, I have hobbies, I like to read, and I love to explore history. I want to read about it, not make it. I leave that to people braver than me. I'd rather just stay in my office or my study and watch it from afar."

"That sounds ... cozy," said Katie. "My parents were both teachers and constantly encouraged their students to do bigger and greater things. I got my love of education from them and developed an interest in psychology on my own. So I thought my degree was a way to do both those things."

"I'm sorry, but we have to close now," said their server Bonnie, who had been waiting patiently, hoping the stacking of chairs and vacuuming of carpets would give them the hint, but it clearly wasn't working.

"Oh, shit, I'm sorry. We completely lost track of time," said Will. "Dinner's on me."

"No, I'm happy to—"

"Next time," said Will. He tapped his smartwatch on the server's reader and paid the bill, leaving a generous tip.

"Do you need a ride home?" asked Will. "I can give you a lift. My car is in the parking garage across the street."

"Um, sure, I would like that," said Katie, whose car was parked in the same garage.

The following morning, Katie woke up smiling for the first time in weeks. "I could go for an omelet," she said out loud.

"Sounds good," said Will, next to her. "Do you want me to cook?"

Katie turned to face him and propped herself on her elbow, not bothering to cover up. "No, I'd be happy to do it."

Will propped himself up, too. "I know, but I don't want to look like I'm expecting it just because you're a woman." He leaned over and kissed her.

"That was the furthest thing from my mind," she said. "I just make a pretty mean three-egg omelet. Tomatoes, onions, peppers, and a little cheese. Plus, I like to cook."

"Real eggs or F'eggs?" Will asked.

"Ew, no. F'eggs taste like shit." F'eggs, or fake eggs, had become a staple in most vegetarian and vegan homes, but some people like Katie and Will bought real eggs from local farmers who raised free-range chickens. "I picked up a dozen eggs at the farmers' market this weekend for only twenty-four bucks."

"That's pretty good," said Will. "I paid thirty at the Tri-N-Save a couple weeks ago. Are you sure you want to use that many eggs though?"

"You bet! One per orgasm."

"Mine or yours?" Will said, smiling. He kissed Katie again and brushed her hair back behind her ear. The two kissed more deeply and settled down into the bed again, wrapping their arms around each other.

An hour later, the two finally got out of bed and showered together. Another hour later, they were sharing omelet duties, Will chopping the vegetables and Katie beating the eggs.

The two were soon spending each night together, trying to keep their distance during the day. The goal was to keep their relationship a secret for as long as possible, knowing it wasn't likely on a small campus like Appleseed College. Their relationship wasn't frowned upon, as long as they weren't in a superior-superordinate—like Will's ex-wife had done—or educator-learner role—like Katie's ex-husband was doing less and less as he got older.

The two registered their relationship with Appleseed's HR department, filling out the necessary forms and signing the appropriate liability waivers the university made any couple sign after three consecutive days of a romantic relationship.

They would meet for lunch and have sex in each other's offices among the sandwich wrappers and reusable soda bottles. Or they would take turns spending the night at each other's apartments, happily discovering they lived in the same building. Katie even began volunteering with Will's campaign staff, but the two called each other "Professor Gant" and "Professor Sartoris" to keep things hidden for as long as they could.

They were outed one Saturday afternoon while the executive sub-committee of The Committee to Elect Will Gant Mayor—Sara, Kyle, Griffin, and Callie—was meeting in the Bench Student Union and arguing about whether they needed more paper flyers or if they should spend money on more PDT ads in the *Appleseed Mail-Journal*.

Katie was running a few minutes late and rushed in, out of breath and sweating slightly.

"Sorry I'm late. Hello, everyone. Hello, Professor Gant."

"Good morning, Professor Sartoris." The two briefly shook hands.

"Oh, geez, get a room, you two," said Kyle, clapping his hand over his mouth as soon as he said it.

"Wha-a-a-a-at?" said Will, pretending to be surprised. He took a few steps away from Katie and put his hands behind his back.

"What are you talking about?" said Katie. Her face and neck flushed a deep scarlet, and she fumbled with the fringe on her purse, not sure where she should look.

"Oh, come on. Everyone knows," said Sara.

"I have no idea what you're talking about," said Will. "Do you know what they're talking about, Professor Sartoris? I don't have any clue what they're talking about."

"Neither do I, Professor Gant," said Katie. "They clearly seem to be projecting their own youthful desire to ship two people they respect and admire into a relationship that clearly does not exist. We talked about this in my ed psych classes a couple weeks ago."

"Oh, come on! It's so obvious!" said Kyle. "Nobody on campus is this formal with anyone else."

"You never call each other by your first names," said Callie.

"You always make it a point not to sit next to each other," said Griffin.

"You never make eye contact," said Sara.

"You always show up to a meeting exactly thirty seconds apart," said Kyle.

"I told you counting to thirty was too predictable," hissed Katie.

"And Will usually has a faint smell of Katie's perfume on him," said Callie.

Will pulled his sweater vest to his nose and sniffed it.

"But mostly, we saw you kissing outside your apartment building last Friday night," said Sara.

"Passionately," added Griffin.

Katie and Will looked at each other, feeling both happy and guilty at the same time.

"Yeah, OK, fine," said Katie. "We've been seeing each other for a few weeks. I went to his office to yell at him for indoctrinating you guys, and we ended up talking for hours."

"Indoctrinating us?" said Sara. "Nobody indoctrinated us to do anything. My mothers keep saying that. Mom Kelly called and yelled at Will after the bomb threat."

"Tell her I said hi," said Will. "How's she doing?"

"Pretty good. Her pumpkins came in really well this year," Sara said. "Anyway, we chose this stance by ourselves before we even met Professor Gant."

"Right," said Kyle. "I mean, if you were going to indoctrinate us for anything, it would be to quit smoking pot before class, am I right?"

"You smoke pot before class?" said Will.

"Did I say before class? I meant before an Ultimate tournament."

"That's not better, dumbass," said Griffin.

"Yes, I realize it's not indoctrination now," said Katie. "But you have to admit, when students go away to a college, their eyes are opened to all kinds of new ideas, and it's easy for them to be influenced to experiment and try new things and new ideas. It's a big chance for them to rebel and do the things they never would have done at home."

"That's just part of being a college student," said Callie. "You did it when you were a college student, didn't you?"

"Well..." said Will and Katie together.

"That's personal," Will added.

"And private," said Katie.

"Look, if we could truly be indoctrinated, wouldn't you just indoctrinate us into turning in our assignments on time or not skipping class?" said Sara. "If we could truly be indoctrinated, college students wouldn't get into so much trouble in the first place. We'd all be good little automatons who only go to class and study."

"Fair point," said Katie.

"Wait," said Will, "you saw us when you all stopped by with the new campaign flyers?"

"Yeah," said Sara. "We were driving up and saw you, so we went to the coffee shop and hung out for twenty minutes before we came back."

"I thought you were all acting weird that night," said Will.

"We're sorry we didn't say anything earlier," said Kyle. "We thought you deserved your privacy."

"Well, we'd appreciate it if you could keep it to yourselves," said Will. "It's not that we need to keep it a secret from the administration. It's just that we don't want to throw a wrench into the campaign just yet. It could give Sheila an edge. Since Bert is secretly supporting Sheila's campaign, we don't want to give him any ammunition to give to her."

"No problem," said Sara. "Right, guys?"

"I object to the patriarchal label of guys, especially by another woman," said Callie.

"CHiP, Callie! It's been a gender-neutral term for the last thirteen years. And that's not the issue right now. Can you keep this a secret?"

"Oh, yeah, no problem. That's a given."

"Then quit being such a pedant."

"Have you decided what you want to order?" Bonnie asked, snapping Will and Katie back to the present moment.

"Sure, I'll have the black bean burger," said Katie, "with an organic side salad."

"I'll have the same, but I'll have the cruelty-free tater tots," said Will.

"By the way, Will, one of your students called looking for you two," said Bonnie. "They said it was an emergency."

"We left our PDTs at home while we went for a run. Did they say what it was about?" asked Will.

"Someone named Sara. She said you needed to make yourself scarce."

"That's weird. I wonder what she meant by that," said Katie.

"Mr. Gant," said a deep voice. The two looked and saw three looming figures of indeterminate gender standing at the entrance to the patio. They were members of the Appleseed Counseling and Enforcement Division, dressed in riot gear, comforting sweaters, and armed with both a taser and a Master's degree in Counseling Psychology and Unarmed Combat.

The largest of the three figures, Sergeant Patrick Graham-Steuben, stepped forward. He was wearing a blue-and-green tartan sweater vest and had a pair of high-impact glasses on a breakaway chain around his neck. "Mayor Sheila Windsong has invited you to attend a completely voluntary period of re-education at our local Inclusivity Counseling Center at the YMWNBCA."

"Oh, that," said Katie.

CHAPTER 16

"**S**O WHY DID YOU WANT TO MEET WITH ME?" asked Dexter Jonson-Johnson, his voice tinged with suspicion. "You weren't just 'in town,' not with everything happening up in your city. Besides, you haven't called me in eight months."

"I need your help," said Carmen, playing with her beer mug, making designs with the moisture rings from the condensation. She had driven an hour south to Cincinnati to meet an old friend-with-benefits for lunch at the Big Red Cuisine restaurant along the Ohio River. The walls were paneled with reclaimed lumber harvested from old barns in the Ohio Valley, and they were covered with photos from the local major league baseball team, the Cincinnati Reds.

"Oh, no! No more. I already told you last time was the last time," said Dexter.

"But it's important."

"You said that last time." Dexter Jonson-Johnson was a computer engineer with QuantumSonic Communications and was their Director of Customer Support and Monitoring Department. He was short and gangly with dirty blond hair. He wore glasses, although they were mostly for effect since people could now take medication to fix their vision problems.

Dexter and Carmen had gone to college together at Bowling Green State University just a few years before, dating on and off during those four years. For the last few years, Dexter had helped Carmen with her stories in the past whenever she needed to track calls or get recordings of conversations between politicians and their illicit lovers. He had the ability to copy—some might say illegally if they actually knew—these recordings without QuantumSonic's system detecting they had ever been accessed, let alone saved to an old-style USB drive hidden inside the replica of a human thumb on his keychain. It was his own little joke with himself.

The two would meet up, he would hand her the keychain, she would hand him $500, and the two would have hot monkey sex at his condo for hours. Once, when Dexter asked Carmen about her journalistic ethics in sleeping with him for information, she said, "I'm paying for the information. I'm fucking you because I want to."

"So you'd have sex with me even if I didn't give you any information?"

"Mmmmmmm, sure. Why not?"

Carmen grabbed a french fry from Dexter's plate, dipped it in some organic curry ketchup, and popped it into her mouth. She licked a bit of ketchup from her lip in what she knew was a sexy and alluring manner.

"Stop doing that," said Dexter.

"What? Stealing your fries or licking my lips?"

"Both. I'm not helping you."

"Come on, Dexter! Dexy! Sexy Dexy. Pleeeeeease!"

"I can't. I could lose my job."

"We both know that's not true. You've never been caught; you're too good. Besides, don't you run the whole department?"

"Yeah. So?" Dexter looked a little worried. He took a drink from his beer mug, licked the foam from his pencil-thin mustache, and pushed up his glasses.

"So, who monitors the activity within your department? Is there someone looking over your shoulder who can see what you can do?"

"No, not as such. I mean, there's a VP that I report to, but she's as dumb as a post when it comes to computers. Fucking Zoomers can be so technophobic. I don't even know how she got her job, let alone stays in it."

"Hmm, if only there were some way you could find out without anyone knowing..." Carmen ate another french fry and did the ketchup-on-the-lip trick again.

"That's not working," Dexter said. "I'm immune to your charms. Besides, you missed a spot."

"Spoilsport." Carmen wiped her lip and drank the rest of her beer. "Can't blame a girl for trying." She wrapped her hands around her mug. "So what would it take?"

"Nothing."

"Look, this time, it's serious. I think I'm really onto something big. You know the mayor in my city?"

"No, not at all."

"You haven't been reading my stories? I watch your fucking video blog every week."

"Alright, alright! Yes, I do. What about her?" Dexter ate a few more fries.

"She's crooked as a pig's pecker."

"Is a pig's, um, dick crooked?"

"I don't know. It's something my grandfather used to say. He used to be a pig farmer in Coldwater and thought the city government and the police were 'crookeder 'n a pig's pecker.'"

"Were they?"

"No, probably not. But my grandfather hated them just the same."

"So, what does your grandfather have to do with your story?"

"Nothing. He just had a pithy saying about pig's peckers. But the mayor, Sheila Windsong, she's the crooked one. I think she's responsible for the bomb hoax that got called in during the debate. I think her toady Enrique called it in. Based on some of the backstage security footage I saw, Enrique killed the lights right when Sheila was on the ropes. I matched up the video footage to the footage I was shooting of the debate. Right when she starts floundering, the lights go out, and then they come back on, and then Enrique pulls the fire alarm."

"So? Maybe he flipped the wrong switch."

"Not a chance. The lights were inside a breaker box, and the fire alarm was 20 feet away. I looked at the breaker box, which is about three feet tall, and the house lights were clearly labeled, and they were down near the bottom, so it's not like he accidentally flipped them. No, he flipped the lights off and on and then ran over to the fire alarm. It's almost like he did his first idea and then had a different one a couple seconds later."

"So let's say he did do this," said Dexter.

"Because he did."

"As you say. Anyway, let's say he did do what you say. What can I possibly get for you? It's not like he would have called anyone and said, 'Hey, I'm killing the lights to end the debate.'"

"Right because he would have been with the only person he would have told. No, what I want to do is see when that supposed bomb call came in. I think it came in after he pulled the alarm, not before. The backstage video shows that he was not on his phone or PDT at all, even when he ran out on stage to tell the mayor and President Grogan. But after he left, he used one of those old-fashioned flippy phones. He dialed a number and then answered his regular phone."

"His phone and not his PDT?"

"No, his actual mobile phone. Just for three or so seconds. I saw him on the backstage video footage, and then I got some footage from a drug store's security camera at the corner of the alley. I zoomed in and hit the cleanup button, and I could see him on both phones. Then he and Sheila got in her car and drove off."

"So how does he explain that the call came in after the alarm?" asked Dexter.

"It hasn't come up. I don't know if the police are incompetent or as crooked as—"

"A pig's, uh, penis?"

"As you say," said Carmen, smiling. Dexter was not really comfortable with dirty talk, even when they were having hot monkey sex. She often had to coach him on the things she wanted him to say.

She continued, "I really just think it's a question of incompetence combined with fear for their jobs. The police aren't too eager to investigate the mayor for calling in a bomb threat, so they're going along with her official story and looking to blame Will Gant for the bomb threat."

"What? Really?"

"Oh, yeah," said Carmen. "They're accusing him of orchestrating the entire thing and saying he or his staff did it because he was the one struggling during the debate. I mean, our video footage is on our website, and most people believe it. But roughly thirty percent of the reader comments have all been accusations of 'fake news' and that we fabricated the evidence. They refuse to believe we haven't doctored the footage, even though the Deep Fake Foundation has certified the video to be original, and the AI Detection software results show it to be one hundred percent original."

"God, people can be such fucking morons!" Dexter rubbed his face with his hands, exhausted with people. "This is why I work in IT, so I don't have to deal with people. I like having conversations with my AI friends and not dealing with the actual customers who use our products."

"So, if I can show that Enrique not only got the bomb call after he pulled the fire alarm but that he's also the one who made it, it'd blow this whole fucking story wide open! So, please, Dexter. I need your help. This one is important."

"You said that about Congresswoman Charlton-Tyrell and her funneling campaign funds to her lover."

"That was important," Carmen protested. "But this is bigger. Much bigger!"

"Bigger than a corrupt Congresswoman?"

"All politics is local. That makes this the biggest story of all."

Carmen stared at Dexter and didn't say anything further. She let the silence hang between them. It was an old negotiating tactic: don't be the first to speak when trying to close a deal. Whoever spoke first lost. Dexter was not an expert at negotiation; Carmen learned the trick from conducting numerous interviews. She found that if she asked a question and then just waited, her subjects would avoid the uncomfortable silence and tell her whatever she wanted to know.

"Goddammit," growled Dexter. "Fine! Fucking fine! But this is the last fucking time."

"Absolutely," promised Carmen, not meaning it.

"How soon do you need it?"

"Today would be great."

"I can't send it to you though. That will definitely show up on the system monitors."

"The USB trick will work again. I can just copy it over to my laptop." She handed his "thumb" drive to him; she had kept it from the last time he gave her information.

"I don't get off work until 5:00, and I won't be home until 5:30. I can give it to you then. What are you going to do in the meantime?"

"I'll just work at a coffee shop for a few hours and pre-write the story. I don't want to run any of it just yet. I have a few more details to confirm besides this one before I can publish it. Is that place near your house still open? What was it called? Deja Brew?"

"No, that's the one by my old place. You're thinking of Afternoon Delight."

"Speaking of which, I don't have to be home until tomorrow..."

"I thought you didn't exchange sex for stories."

"I'm not. I just wanted to have a little fun before I go home."

"Ohhhh, CHiP! That was amazing!" Carmen said, rolling off of Dexter's sweaty, naked body, equally sweaty and naked herself. "So what did you find out?"

"Jesus, let me recover first!" said Dexter.

"Sorry. You were so great. Yes, yes, my mighty steed. I have never been rogered so vigorously."

"You're being sarcastic, but I'm having that engraved on a plaque to hang over my bed. What does 'rogered so vigorously' even mean?" said Dexter

"It's from the diary of some dude who lived in Virginia in the early 1700s. I saw it on the internet once," said Carmen. "Now, what did you find out?"

Dexter stared at Carmen and waited.

"Oh, come on! We had sex first! I at least waited that long."

Dexter sighed. "Just give me five minutes, please. I'd like to catch my breath and maybe cool off a bit. Can we just lay here and enjoy the post-coital cooldown?"

Carmen huffed and slammed her arms rigidly down at her side. Patience was not one of her virtues, and she was going to lay here and use all her psychic mental energies to make Dexter get his lazy ass out of—a-a-a-and three minutes later, she was snoring.

Dexter crept out of bed and padded naked to the shower. When he returned fifteen minutes later, Carmen was still asleep.

Dexter went out to the kitchen. On the way home, he had picked up a frozen vegetarian lasagna, and he popped that into the oven. He was making the garlic bread when Carmen came out of the room wearing Dexter's bathrobe.

"Oh, man, I must have been more tired than I thought. How long was I asleep?" she asked.

"About an hour," he answered.

"Wow, you must have rogered me more vigorously than I thought."

"You know, it sounds creepy when you say that."

"Yeah, well, you don't like doing dirty talk, so I'm trying to protect your delicate sensibilities. Now, what did you find?"

Dexter sighed. "The thumb drive is on my keychain in the bowl by the door."

Carmen retrieved the thumb drive and her laptop. She plugged in a USB reader and powered up her laptop. As she listened to the phone call on her earbuds, her eyes widened.

"Holy shit! Is this for real?" she said.

"Absolutely."

"And the time stamp is accurate?"

"I'm offended you would even ask that."

"I need to make absolutely sure because if I'm wrong about any of this, they could sue the shit out of me and the *Mail-Journal* and put us out of business."

Dexter sighed again. "Yes, it's accurate."

But Carmen was already pounding away on her keyboard, filling in the last details of her story. "This is huge!" she said, more than once. "This is fucking huge."

"I wish you would have said that an hour ago," Dexter said, but Carmen was too engrossed in her story to hear him.

Dexter sat down at the dining table with his tablet and played some word games while she worked. He looked at the kitchen timer to see when the lasagna would be done, but otherwise, the two worked in silence. Carmen stopped typing just as the kitchen timer dinged.

"Food's done," said Dexter. "Let's eat."

As they were seated at the dining table, Carmen's computer set to the side, uploading the story to the *Mail-Journal* servers for editorial review, the two talked about the results.

"Did you get a chance to listen to the call?" asked Carmen. She took a bite of lasagna. "Oooh, Chef Dexter, you have worked your magic yet again."

"No, I didn't get to listen to it. What was on it? And thank you. It's an old family recipe from Great-Grandma Stouffer." The two clinked forks as if they were toasting and took another bite.

"OK, so basically, Enrique called his own phone from the flip phone two minutes after he pulled the fire alarm."

"Well, we knew that, right?" asked Dexter.

"Not quite. All we know is he placed a call from something that wasn't his regular phone. The info you got for me also showed he deleted the call from his phone so it wouldn't show up in an examination. But Enrique is a moron for three reasons."

"Just three?"

"For our purposes, yes. First, that phone he called from? It's registered to his mother, Juliana Ramirez-Medina, deceased."

"Seriously? Why would he have his dead mother's phone?"

"I don't know. But I checked the morgue—"

"Eww!" cringed Dexter.

"Oh, grow up. That's what we call the place where all our old issues are stored. In the 20th century, they kept old copies of the newspaper bound into huge books. Nowadays, they're all in the cloud, going all the way back to the 1890s. Anyway, Juliana Ramirez-Medina died five years ago. She must have had one of those old flippy phones. How were you able to get her phone records anyway?"

"We've got our own morgue, I guess. Our digital records go all the way back to the 1990s when we were just a long-distance carrier that was part of the old Cincinnati Bell system. Enrique may have deleted the call from his phone, but that doesn't delete the call from the system."

"OK, he's a moron for four reasons."

"And when I did a search for the number his phone received, I just pulled all records related to that number, including all of the calls and texts it ever made, and there was nothing after 2033."

"That's why there weren't any calls for five years until the night of the debate. My guess is Enrique never actually cut off the service and has just been carrying it around all these years for something just like this."

"So what's the third reason he's a moron?"

"Because when he called from his mom's phone, he must have known he needed to keep the call a certain length of time. He couldn't just call and then hang up immediately. So he said, 'Blah blah blah, this is a bomb threat blah.' It's a good thing he didn't know you guys record all the calls."

"Yeah, the government makes us do it, but we don't publicize that little fact."

"And finally, number four: He made the bomb threat call *after* he killed the lights, pulled the alarm, then turned them back on. The time stamp of the video coincides with the time of the phone call he made." Carmen sat back, looking triumphant, resisting the urge to rub her hands together. Then she gave in and rubbed them like a mad scientist taking over the world.

"Holy fuck! So what are you going to do now?" Dexter asked.

"Well, after we're done eating, I say we go back to bed for some more rogering," said Carmen.

"Gross."

"Fine. I'm going to fuck your brains out."

"Better. And after that?"

"I uploaded my story, and my editor and the legal team are going to review it, along with all of the evidence. For something this big, it will be a few days before the story actually runs because we have to confirm everything, plus we'll want to interview the Appleseed PD, and then—hold on one second."

Carmen tapped the temple on her PDT. "Hey, Sara, what's up?"

"They took him!" shouted Sara. Carmen could hear that she was crying and out of breath. "He's gone. They took him!"

"What? Who? What are you talking about?" Carmen looked at Dexter, eyes wide.

"What?" he mouthed, holding his palms up.

Carmen held up a finger. "One minute," she mouthed back.

"The police came and took him, and we don't know where," said Sara, not any calmer.

"Sara, relax! Take a deep breath. What's going on?"

"It's Will. They arrested him. But we don't know where they took him. We called the police department, and nobody knows anything about it."

"Breathe some more. Slow down. I'm serious. Breathe through your nose and out your mouth." She listened to Sara's breathing. "Good. Again. OK, one more time. Alright, are you calm?"

"No."

"Good. Now, start at the beginning. Tell me what's going on."

"We just got a call from Katie Sartoris, Will's, uh, friend."

"You said that weird. Do you mean they're romantically involved?" asked Carmen.

"Well, they've been spending time together, and we've seen them kissing outside Will's house."

"His partner?" asked Carmen.

"They've only been together for a couple of weeks," Sara clarified.

"Lover?"

"Gross!"

"Paramour?"

"Meh."

"Girlfriend?"

"It seems weird for college professors with Ph.D.s to call each other 'boyfriend' and 'girlfriend,' don't you think?" asked Sara.

"Fine, whatever. They were two people who enjoyed boning. Get on with the story."

"Right. Anyway, they were eating at Bottles and Cans when the police showed up in their riot gear and took Will away in their wagon."

"Did they say anything?"

"Only that he was being invited to their voluntary seminar camp."

"Do you know what that is?"

"Not really," said Sara. "The college is pretty insulated from what's going on in the city."

"The re-education camps are where the mayor has been sending people who disagree with her decisions. It's nothing very serious. They go through some indoctrination for a few days, and they're none the worse for wear when they get out. I've interviewed a few of the participants before; they all say the same thing. There's no psychological torture or anything, and they're not mistreated. But the idea that they can be taken against their will and held for a few days is enough to get people to back off from their stance. It's just political bullying and intimidation."

"But why would she do that to him?" Sara said, her breath coming in shudders.

"She's trying to get Will to drop out of the race. If nothing else, she can use his political stance and time spent in the camp to show that he's more conservative than he actually is. She wants people to think he's unhinged and mentally unstable. Her popularity has been slipping, so rather than try to improve herself, she'd rather tear him down."

"What can we do about it?"

"Nothing."

"What do you mean 'nothing'? We've got to get him out of there."

"I know. But the people who could get him out of there are at home, and they won't take too kindly to you interrupting their personal time. Not after President Clinton passed the Mandatory Work-Life Balance Act a few years back. Government employees can actually get in trouble for working past 5:00, and that includes at the local level, so they won't answer their PDTs, let alone do anything on your behalf."

"But we have to do something!"

Like a dog with a bone, this one, thought Carmen. "OK, listen. You can't tell anyone, but I'm working on a story that will show the truth about the bomb hoax at the debate on Wednesday. Once this publishes, it will clear up a lot of things and will make Will's placement at the seminar look like retaliation."

"What did your—"

"No, I can't tell you anything. Don't even mention that the story exists. Not even to your friends. I probably shouldn't have said anything, so you just have to trust me." Carmen tapped the left temple of her PDT. "It's, uhh, 8:53 right now. I'm down in Cincinnati and will head up tomorrow morning. The story won't drop until Monday morning because it has to be vetted by the legal department, plus that's the bigger news cycle. By then, Will will probably be out of the seminar."

"So we just have to let him sit in there over the weekend?"

"Yes, I'm afraid so. And Sheila will definitely make sure there are plenty of media people there getting photos and videos of him leaving on Monday morning."

"What do we do when the news breaks about his 'participation'? It'll probably happen tomorrow. I just got a call from one of your coworkers at the *Mail-Journal*, but I didn't answer. She left a voice mail that she'll call back later."

"It probably *will* break in the afternoon, so most people will get the breaking news alerts. Be prepared with some talking points because you're going to be hammered by the media, and not just the *Mail-Journal*. They're already against him, so be prepared for tough questions. Rehearse your answers and make sure they're consistent every time you give them. Don't say anything negative about the mayor because that gives her ammunition. Or wait! Better yet, just say it's retaliation by the mayor because of her falling in the polls. Make everything about her polling numbers and retaliation."

"OK, I can do that," said Sara.

"I'll leave here early tomorrow morning, and I'll see what else I can find out. We'll get this figured out. I'm just too tired to drive back safely tonight," said Carmen.

"That's great. Thank you. But why are you helping us?"

"Because I'm a fucking Foundling."

"Huh?" asked Sara.

Carmen disconnected the call.

CHAPTER 17

"**A**LRIGHT, PARTICIPANT, PLEASE EXIT THE vehicle in a departing motion as you are able," said the figure. Will looked up from where he was sitting in the back seat and saw one of the people who had arrested him. They had opened the door and held it open like they were a doorman at a fancy hotel welcoming him to their little corner of luxury.

"Do I have a choice?" asked Will.

"Uhh, no, not really," said the figure. "I can always drag you out."

"I need you to help me out. I can't get out with handcuffs." Will absolutely could get out of the car, but he decided he was going to passively resist as much as he could just to be the biggest pain in the ass possible.

Will had been arrested at Bottles and Cans and placed in handcuffs while Katie raged at them about civil rights and his Fourth Amendment right against illegal search and seizure.

"Hey, where are you taking him? What gives you the right?" Katie shouted as they put the cuffs on Will. Two of them were escorting Will to their all-electric, matte-black SUV while the third turned to face Katie, stopping her in her tracks. The figure was dressed in what looked like police riot gear and a bright red cardigan with a zipper down the front as well as a matte-black helmet and a dark-tinted plastic visor covering the person's face. The figure flipped up their visor, and Katie saw a young face with brown eyes and a light brown complexion.

"Sir, ma'am, or preferred nonbinary honorific," said the figure. "I am Officer Kirby McHenry-Anisetta, they/them, of the Appleseed Counseling and Enforcement Division. We are transporting Professor Gant to a completely voluntary time period of re-education at the Inclusivity Counseling Center. Professor Gant will remain there for a window of time of not more than four days."

"What? Why? That's the craziest fucking thing I've ever heard of!"

"We don't say things like 'crazy,' sir, ma'am, or preferred nonbinary honorific."

"Just 'ma'am' is fine," sighed Katie.

"We prefer to say 'living with mental health issues.' I'm sure you can be in an understanding mindset about how that's better," said the figure, more politely known as Officer McHenry-Anisetta.

"That's not the point. The point is you're taking Will away in handcuffs but calling it voluntary."

"So?"

"So that's not what voluntary means!" shouted Katie.

"Professor Gant is free to choose to leave at any time, ma'am," said Officer McHenry-Anisetta.

"Will!" called Katie. "Will, they said you can leave at any time."

"Great. I don't want to go," Will said to one of the two other counselors, stopping in his tracks.

"That's an excellent choice, sir, ma'am, or preferred non-binary honorific," said Officer Helen Booth-Eskamani, on his right.

"Just 'sir' is fine," said Will.

"Yes, sir, a very good choice," echoed Sergeant Patrick Graham-Steuben on Will's left.

"So you'll let me go?"

"No," they both said.

"But you just said he could leave at any time," Katie called.

"No, we said he was free to choose to leave at any time," said Officer McHenry-Anisetta. "According to the new Appleseed statutes, which were created by executive order by Mayor Windsong in August, citizens can be voluntarily remanded to the Camp Breakthrough Inclusivity Counseling Center for voluntary re-education for up to ninety-six hours."

"Then why did you say he was free to choose?" demanded Katie.

"We are all free to make our choices in life. Professor Gant is free to try to leave, although we will do everything in our power to prevent that, and the detainee will face conse-quences if he does so," said Officer Booth-Eskamani.

"Exactly," said Sergeant Graham-Steuben. "We understand that this is quite the dilemma, but we have been informed by our departmental psychologists that it's important to offer participants a choice, even if there are dire consequences to be faced by that choice being made. They designated it as a, uhh, umm... What's that...?"

"Hobson's choice," offered Will.

"Stop helping them!" said Katie.

Will just shrugged. "That's what it is," he said.

"It's some fucking bullshit is what it is!" shouted Katie. By now, a large crowd had gathered to watch the arrest that wasn't really an arrest, and people were uploading video footage from their phones and PDTs to various social media sites. Within an hour, #FreeWillGant had begun trending on the big social networks, as well as #WillGantisaNazi, which Sheila and her dirty tricks staff had paid to boost in an attempt to bury #FreeWillGant.

The members of the Inclusivity Counseling Department force bundled Will into their SUV and drove him to the local camp owned by the YMWNBCA—the Young Men's Women's and Non-Binary Citizens' of America, also called "The Y"—for his weekend retreat.

"Participant, please exit from the vehicle in a departing motion," repeated the figure, snapping Will back to the present moment. He looked up to see Officer Kirby McHenry-Anisetta holding the door open. He stepped out of the SUV and looked around.

It looked like any other summer camp with twelve cabins placed around a large open field, a dining hall, and a non-denominational chapel down by a pristine lake. Pine trees and oak trees shaded many of the cabins, and several people dressed in khaki pants and teal or turquoise golf shirts walked around, accompanied by others in olive green pants and navy blue golf shirts.

"Participant, please move with me in a following motion to the intake office so the facility's intake processing procedure may begin."

Will thought about running, just sprinting back the way they came. He was still in good shape and had just finished a run with Katie less than an hour ago—*My CHiP, was that just an hour ago? It seems like last week*, thought Will—but the barbed wire fence and electric gate made him rethink that idea. He might have gotten away from Officer McHenry-Anisetta, but he wouldn't have been able to clear the fence or outrun the vehicles on foot.

As he walked, Will mentally reviewed the history of non-violent resistance and passive resistance of some of the notable figures he had studied—Martin Luther King Jr., Gandhi, Nelson Mandela, and John Lewis. He knew he wouldn't be able to fight his way out, but he could at least be a pain in the ass while he was there. He assumed Katie would fight to get him released, so he was determined to be the biggest non-violent pain in the ass he could be while he was here.

"This way, Participant," barked Officer McHenry-Anisetta. "We will proceed in a forward-acting motion toward that structure that lies approximately thirty yards ahead." The structure in question was a small white clapboard hut about the size of a garden shed. Officer McHenry-Anisetta extended his arm as if motioning Will to pass him and then fell in step next to him. They kept a hand on the taser on their belt.

Officer McHenry-Anisetta had also removed their helmet. Will saw a young person in their mid-20s with light brown hair, shaved closely at the sides, slightly longer on top. They were White with a tattoo of a flamingo on their neck.

They quickly reached the shed and stopped at the door. Officer McHenry-Anisetta knocked, waited two seconds, and then stepped inside.

"Good afternoon, Officer McHenry-Anisetta," said an older grandmotherly woman with white hair seated behind a long wooden desk and a large laptop. A nameplate on the desk identified her as Kayla. There were three guest chairs in front of the desk, and she motioned Will to have a seat. Officer McHenry-Anisetta remained standing behind Will, trying to look menacing, which was not hard to do, despite wearing a bright red cardigan with a zipper down the front.

"Well, hello, Professor Gant," said Kayla. "Welcome to the Appleseed Inclusivity Counseling Center."

"Why am I here?" asked Will.

"Well, I'm not exactly sure. They don't tell me anything. I just welcome our guests and help with their intake. But I would imagine the Mayor or her assistant, Mr. Medina, felt you needed some additional training and support to remain a positive and contributing member of the Appleseed community."

"But I already am a positive and contributing member of the Appleseed community."

"Well, surely not, or else you wouldn't be here. The Mayor and Mr. Medina would never make a mistake about that." Will realized she was going to say "well" every time she opened her mouth, and it was all he could do not to shout at her to stop it.

"Are you sure it's not because I'm Mayor Windsong's opponent in the upcoming election?"

"Well, I wouldn't know anything about that," said Kayla; Will grimaced. "As I said, I'm only here to welcome our guests and help with their intake."

"So what determines whether someone becomes a so-called 'guest' of your little happy camp?"

"Well, it could be anything. They may have made an insensitive remark, such as saying something racist or sexist. They may have said something that was unsupportive or hostile to a member of the LGBTQQIP2SA community. They may have made unwanted sexual or romantic advances toward another person."

"And if I've done none of those things?"

"Well, it could be that your KNCLD score dropped so quickly that it was important to bring you here to help you amend your ways and return your score to a more societally acceptable level."

"What's my KNCLD score?" Will asked.

Kayla's fingers clattered over her keyboard. "Well, that's, uh—that's unusual."

"What's that?"

"Well, your KNCLD score is a, uh, oh my! A 57?"

"That's pretty good, isn't it?" Will said.

"Well, sure. That's very good. The average person is somewhere in the high 40s. Many of the people we get in here are in their 20s, so I don't know why you would be here for that."

"Then that means I'm free to go?" Will started to rise until he felt Officer McHenry-Anisetta's hand on his shoulder.

"Please, sir, remain seated."

"Well, no, not really. I don't know what's going on, but it's really not my place to question it. So let's just get you processed and into the system. Name?"

"You know my name."

"Oh, uhh... well, I guess I do!" She beamed. "What's your favorite color: teal or turquoise?"

"Green," said Will. "British Racing Green."

"Well, I'm afraid that's not a choice. You only get to choose between teal and turquoise," said Kayla.

"That's a false dilemma," said Will.

"What's that?" Kayla looked so confused she forgot to say, "Well."

"That's when you're only given two choices even though there are other options available. You asked my favorite color, and that's what it is."

"Well, we don't have British Racing Green," said Kayla.

"So I'm not actually choosing my favorite color then."

"Well, I guess not." Kayla was finding it harder to keep her down-home folksy charm in place.

"Then what am I choosing exactly?" asked Will.

"You're choosing your uniform shirt color," said Officer McHenry-Anisetta. "We want you to feel empowered during your time here, so you are free to choose."

"Great, I choose to leave."

"That's not a choice."

"You just said I was free to choose. So I choose to leave the whole place entirely."

"That *is* your choice," said Officer McHenry-Anisetta, "but your refusal to participate in our learning system could result in negative effects on your employment and, more importantly, your KNCLD score."

"That's not very empowering."

"Plus, we may have to resort to more ... corporal methods."

"Corporal or corporeal?" said Will. Officer McHenry-Anisetta stared blankly at him. "Physical punishment or ghostly, Officer McHenry-Anisetta?" clarified Will.

"Ah," said Officer McHenry-Anisetta. "Physical punishment."

"But you can't keep me here longer than ninety-six hours, right?"

"That is correct. On Monday morning, Mayor Windsong has ordered you to be released and allowed to leave."

"Wait, she did this on Monday already? So I can leave now?" Will asked.

Officer McHenry-Anisetta rubbed the bridge of his nose with his gloved fingers. "Goddammit," he whispered. "Look, would you just quit being such a pain in the ass and pick a fucking shirt? I'd hate to have to tase you for being such an asshole."

"We're in agreement then. I'd hate for you to tase me."

"Pick! A! Color!"

Will sighed and rolled his eyes. "Fine. Turquoise, I guess."

"Well, what a coincidence. That's my favorite color, too," said Kayla.

"I'll bet you say that to all the inmates," said Will.

"Participants," corrected Officer McHenry-Anisetta.

"Participants," corrected Kayla.

"Jesus Christ," said Will.

The next morning, Saturday, Carmen was racing north toward Appleseed on I-75, her all-electric Ford Flagstaff humming along quietly. "You have an incoming call," said Carmen's PDT. A little notification popped up on her windshield's heads-up display, which was also showing traffic conditions as well as alerting her to police speed traps, an unauthorized app Dexter had helped her install a few years ago during a previous journalistic booty call. The PDT and her car were interconnected, so she could receive data information from her car as well as display short messages on her windshield display.

Carmen double-tapped her right temple. "Who's calling?" she asked the PDT.

"Unknown number," the PDT replied. "The caller ID is blocked."

"Record this call," Carmen ordered her PDT.

She double-tapped the left temple. "This is Carmen Cowen."

"Carmen? This is Tiffani Stoudemire, Mayor Windsong's assistant." The voice was a whisper, so the PDT amplified the call and removed the background noise.

"Hi, Tiffani. Why are you whispering?"

"I need to talk to you about Mayor Windsong," said Tiffani. "She's been doing some bad things, and I can't work for her anymore."

"What has she been doing?"

"I can't tell you now. Someone might hear me. We have to meet. Now."

"Where are you?"

"At the Cool Beans Coffee Shop on Braeburn."

"I need more information than just 'doing bad things.' Besides, I'm driving up from Cincinnati, and I won't be back for another forty minutes."

"Why can't we just meet in two hours at a different location?" whined Tiffani.

"Because something could happen to you before we get there. You and I have both watched enough mystery movies to know something always happens to the person who says, 'We have to meet. I have important information.' They die before they reveal anything. I'm not taking that chance."

"Oh, my CHiP! Do you think someone's going to kill me?"

"No, but then again, your boss did just have Will Gant confined to a re-education camp."

"Inclusivity center."

"To-may-to, to-mah-to," said Carmen.

"But someone may overhear me."

"Then go outside. Make sure no one is standing near you."

"I don't know..." Tiffani moaned.

"Look, I at least need to know what you're going to tell me about so I can be prepared when we meet. I'll drive straight to the coffee shop and pick you up, and you can give me all the details, but I at least need to know what we're going to talk about."

"You have to understand I've worked for Mayor Windsong for twelve years. Before that, I worked for the previous mayor until he retired. And the mayor before him until he retired."

"I understand," said Carmen.

"I take my work very seriously, and I believe in the sanctity and integrity of the mayor's office of Appleseed, Ohio. But she doesn't share the same beliefs."

"I get it," said Carmen, not getting it. "What has Mayor Windsong done to, uh, sully the reputation of the mayor's office?"

Tiffani hesitated, trying to figure out whether Carmen was mocking her. She finally blurted it out in a whisper. "She's been taking bribes from Braun McLaren!"

"The plasma gasification people?"

"Exactly. The land where they want to place it is owned by Mayor Windsong's family, only no one knows she owns it. And they're paying more than the land is worth. A lot more."

"How much more?"

"They're leasing it for $775,000 per year, plus they're paying her a $10 million 'consulting fee.'"

"Holy shit, that's huge!" said Carmen. "I'm in the wrong line of work!"

"Tell me about it. I've worked for the Mayor, but do I get anything out of it other than my paltry public servant's salary? No! I barely clear $90,000, and I've had the same title since I got here!" Tiffani was getting worked up.

"How do—"

"Instead, it's 'Tiffani, close the door,' 'Tiffani, hold my calls,' 'Tiffani, get me a coffee.' How about you get your own fucking coffee? And the fucking door closes on a fucking voice command, you breathless moron!"

"Are you OK, Tiffani?"

Tiffani took several deep breaths. "Yes, I'm sorry. I just get worked up sometimes. I'm OK now."

"How do you even know all of this?" Carmen asked.

"Oh, I've been bugging her office for years. I need to gather material for my book."

"Your book?"

"Yes, I'm going to write a tell-all book one day. I'll share the audio files with you when we hang up. You know, in case something happens to me."

"I thought the mayor checked her office for bugs every day."

Tiffani roared with laughter. "That thing? That's a toy that the IT guys rigged up to make beeping noises. It goes off any time someone turns on the microwave in the break room. Her clock radio even set it off once. But that thing couldn't find a bug if it was sitting on top of one."

"So, where did you put the bug?"

"Where do you think? Inside the bug detector."

Thirty-eight minutes later, Carmen pulled up in front of Cool Beans Coffee and Treats, an Appleseed mainstay for the last twenty-seven years. Tiffani was standing against the wall, clutching her purse to her ample chest, a gift from her third husband on her fiftieth birthday. Carmen pulled to a smooth stop, rolled down the window, and said, "Get in."

Tiffani looked left and right before darting into the car. "Go! Go! Go!" she shouted.

Carmen pulled slowly away, checking her mirror before she pulled back out onto the street. She looked in her rearview camera and saw that no one was following them.

"Did anyone follow you?" demanded Tiffani.

"No," said Carmen, a little defensive. "Did anyone follow you?"

"Of course not! I stayed at Cool Beans like you said, keeping a sharp eye out for anyone looking suspicious."

"Well, I think you're fine then. Let's drive back down to Cincinnati. I've got a place we can hide out while you tell me your story."

"No, absolutely not!" Dexter had said when Carmen called him thirty minutes ago to tell him of her plan.

"Please, Dexter. This is important," Carmen said.

"I swear to CHiP, you told me that less than twenty-four hours ago. You said it would be the last time."

"No, you said that. Besides, this is something different. I don't need any information from you, just a place to stay for a day."

"I don't even know this woman," Dexter protested.

"Oh, you'll love her. She's great. Her name is Tiffani with a heart over the 'i'. She had it legally changed forty-three years ago. She's like everyone's grandma. She's even got a belly-button ring and a back tattoo."

"My grandma had a back tattoo," said Dexter. "And tattoo sleeves on both arms. She was kind of a badass."

"Mine had a pair of dragon wings on her back," said Carmen. "Plus, a Chinese symbol on her forearm that she said meant 'fierce warrior,' but I later found out it said 'breakfast.'"

"Fu-u-u-u-uck!" growled Dexter, which Carmen took to mean his begrudging acceptance of her plan.

"Thanks, Dex, you're the best. I'll make it up to you one night real soon."

"Goddammit, Carmen. You owe me so much more than one night."

"Love you!" Carmen had said, disconnecting the call and then feeling horrified that she had just used the L-word with her friend-with-benefits. She hoped he didn't read too much into that.

Carmen looked at Tiffani and said, "OK, I'm going to record all this, and I want you to tell me everything you know while we drive down. Also, I need you to share all the recordings with me, and I'll work on my story."

She then addressed her PDT AI personality. "Iris, record everything said in this car."

"Can do, Carmen," came a voice in Carmen's ear as well as over the car speaker.

Tiffani started her tale. "Sheila wasn't always so bad," she said. "In the beginning, she was a pretty good mayor. She was no Mayor Bart, the mayor before the last one. I tell you, he was something else.

"Appleseed used to be a tiny little town, but Mayor Bart made affordable housing and economic development his two top priorities, and the city grew. We were nearly seventy-five thousand people until The Takening. Then, we lost forty percent of our population, which was better than a lot of cities.

"Some cities in the South were nearly wiped out with only a few people surviving. Mayor Bart invited all the people from the different small cities and brought a lot of them to Appleseed, which saw us grow rather quickly."

Tiffani sighed and stared out the window at the fields whizzing by. "I tell you, he really was something else." She sighed again and sat for a few seconds before Carmen prompted her to continue.

"Oh, sorry!"

"Mayor Bart must have been pretty hot, huh?" said Carmen.

"He was!" Tiffani confirmed. "And that man could go all night!"

"Uhhh..." said Carmen.

"Oh, yeah, just what you think. The guy was sixty-two years old, but he didn't need any pharmaceutical assistance, if you know what I mean."

"Anyway, he retired, and Mayor Lori Mori-Brown was elected. She served for eight years, and then Sheila beat her in the election twelve years ago.

"Everything was going great for the first three years, but then she started to change. She started paying closer attention to her poll numbers and wouldn't make a decision unless she knew it would bump up her numbers. She would announce programs that would raise her numbers and then issue executive decisions in secret if they would hurt her."

"How long have you been recording her?" asked Carmen.

"I used to be privy to all her decisions and her thought processes. She treated me like an advisor and an equal. But after Enrique Medina came into the picture, she appointed him deputy mayor and shut me out. So I put a bug in her ear about listening devices. Ooh, that's a good one!" Tiffani giggled and primped her bottle-blonde hair, checking herself out in the visor mirror.

"Anyway, I told her I would have the IT department make a bug detector so she could make sure no one was trying to bug her office. And I put a recording device inside it that would save all her conversations into a microchip inside it as well as upload all the files to my personal cloud storage. Each week, I downloaded the files and had the office AI transcribe them and save them to another online drive. I shared everything with you while you were driving up here."

Carmen double-tapped her left PDT temple. "Iris, what's the status of files from Tiffani Stoudemire?" she asked.

"All files mentioned in the past conversation are accounted for," said Iris.

"Cross-check voice print of Mayor Sheila Windsong against past *Mail-Journal* stories and interviews to confirm identity."

"You don't trust me?" said Tiffani.

"Trust but verify," said Carmen. "I don't want to get sued."

"Smart," said Tiffani.

There was a short delay as Iris processed all the voice files Tiffani had sent to Carmen. After ten seconds, Iris reported back. "All files confirmed with 99.8 percent accuracy that Mayor Windsong's voice was on received recordings."

"Is there any chance they were edited together or artificially created?"

"None. All voices have been confirmed with the *Mail-Journal* AI software," said Iris.

"Are there any recordings of conversations between Mayor Windsong and a representative of Braun McLaren Energy?"

"Yes, there is a recording of a conversation between Mayor Windsong and Roy Burkhart-Lanning of Braun McLaren Energy on Monday, August 11, 2053. And another on Friday, August 15, 2053."

"Excellent. Isolate both recordings and save them as separate audio files. Then I want you to transcribe it and summarize it into a 500-word story."

"Isn't technology wonderful?" said Tiffani. "I remember when people first started using AI, and we were all so scared of it. Now it can do almost anything."

"True, but we still can't let it write the actual news stories. Ever since President Ocasio Cortez passed the AOCAI Ban Act in 2029," she pronounced it 'A-OK', "humans must write more than seventy percent of any story, script, or online marketing material. So I'll have to rewrite it by hand once we get to where we're going."

There was a ten-second delay. "Operation complete. Will there be anything else, Carmen?" asked Iris.

"No, continue to record this conversation and provide a transcript once we arrive at Dexter's."

"Understood," said Iris.

As the two drove on, Tiffani told Carmen about Sheila's plan to profit off the Braun McLaren plasma gasification plant, about the $10 million consulting fee, and how she was going to put Appleseed's forty-three sanitation workers out of work.

She also explained how Sheila had written the executive order about Camp Breakthrough in August and had used it to intimidate some of her political opponents as well as a neighbor whose dog kept barking in the middle of the night.

As they drove, Carmen received a voice message from Sara, informing her about a press conference to be held on the Appleseed College campus. "We're not hiding from Will's incarceration. We're going on the offensive," Sara's message said.

Carmen responded with a dictated voice text: "Great. You do the press conference, and then we'll publish my big story right afterward. Be sure to mention it in the press conference in case I don't make it back in time."

Once they arrived in Cincinnati, Carmen parked three blocks away from Dexter's apartment, and the two hurried to his place, looking over their shoulders the entire way.

"Were you followed?" said Dexter once he closed the door behind them. Carmen gave him a disgusted look as if the suggestion was ludicrous.

"Are you Dexter?" asked Tiffani, immediately embracing him in a big grandmotherly hug. "Carmen talked about you non-stop the entire way down here. I feel like I know you already!"

Dexter melted into her arms and closed his eyes, smiling and remembering his own grandmother.

"OK, Dexter, please entertain Tiffani for an hour. I have to knock out this story and head back up to Appleseed." Dexter shrugged and the two left to get cinnamon rolls from Afternoon Delight.

Carmen sat down at her laptop and rewrote the story that Iris had churned out just thirty minutes before in full compliance with AOCAI. As she started to type, she double-tapped her left PDT temple and said, "Call Sid Santos-Gupta. Priority one."

After a few seconds, she said, "Sid, I've got the story of the year coming to you right now. Get the legal team and crisis editorial team to work on this. I'm putting it on the cloud, and you need to vet everything immediately. We need to go to press today."

She listened for a moment. "Yes, I know we don't have a press anymore. It's just an expression."

She listened further. "You'll just have to wait until you see it. Follow along in the doc. 'Bye." She tapped her temple again and began typing:

```
On August 11, Mayor Sheila
Windsong solicited and accepted
bribes from Braun McLaren Energy
Group of $10 million in con-
sulting fees and a $775,000 per
year lease agreement in exchange
for building a plasma gasifica-
tion plant on land owned by the
mayor's family.
```

According to AI-verified audio recordings, Mayor Windsong demanded these bribes in exchange for pushing through the plasma gasification plant she proposed at the Appleseed City Council meeting on Tuesday, August 12.

The plant is proposed to be built on a piece of property that Mayor Windsong's father purchased in 2017 in order to grow legalized marijuana.

Carmen double-tapped her temple again. "Call Mayor Sheila Windsong." She waited for a few seconds, but there was no answer.

She double-tapped again. "Call Enrique Medina." She waited a few seconds, and Enrique answered.

"Mr. Medina, Carmen Cowen from the *Appleseed Mail-Journal* on a recorded line."

"Good afternoon, Ms. Cowen. What can I do for you?"

"I'm working on a couple of different stories right now, and I wanted to get your comment before we go to print."

"OK, how can I help?" said Enrique warily.

"First, where is Will Gant?"

"Ah, Professor Gant was asked to voluntarily participate in a 96-hour inclusivity counseling and training session at Camp Breakthrough. He will be released on Monday morning after successful completion of his weekend."

"What kind of things will he be learning at this re-education camp?"

"Training session," corrected Enrique. "Mayor Windsong created these voluntary inclusivity and training sessions this past August to help Appleseedlings who might express undesirable or harmful viewpoints to the harmony and civility of our fair city's sense of community."

"Hmmm. OK, and he's free to leave any time he wants?"

"Yes, he's free to choose to leave," said Enrique.

Carmen decided to leave that one alone and went in for the kill. "OK, next question: I have a copy of your phone records that show you placed a call from an obsolete flip phone to your own phone call moments after you pulled the fire alarm at the mayoral debate this past Monday. Why did you make that call?"

"That's bullshit!" shouted Enrique. "You can't prove anything."

"I have a record of your call and a recording of your actual words. Plus, I have video footage of you making a call on a phone that is not your usual phone."

"That's an invasion of privacy! I'll sue you and your paper for every penny!"

"Yes, and then we'll need to share all the recordings and information with the court."

Enrique said nothing; Carmen could hear him breathing heavily.

"My second story is about how Mayor Windsong has solicited and accepted a $10 million consulting fee from Braun McLaren, plus $775,000 per year for leasing her property where the proposed plasma gasification plant will be built."

"Ten million? She told me four—" Enrique stopped talking. "Listen, goddammit, you don't have anything on me or her. You've got no proof. This is all fake news."

"Calling it fake news doesn't mean it didn't happen. In fact, it usually means the opposite. I have audio recordings of Mayor Windsong soliciting bribes from Braun McLaren. How do you respond?"

"Fuck you, that's how!" screamed Enrique.

"I'll be sure and quote you on that. Do you have anything else you would like to add?"

"Double-fuck you, you fucking delusional hack!"

"I haven't been able to find Mayor Windsong. Do you know where she is?"

"Eat shit, lady!" Enrique hung up, and Carmen tapped her right temple one time. "Iris, did you get all that?"

"Affirmative," said Iris.

"Good. Transcribe it and upload it into my own cloud account and to the paper's cloud. Share it with the editorial staff and legal team."

"Completed," said Iris, a few seconds later.

Carmen continued to write.

```
When reached for comment, Deputy
Mayor  Enrique  Medina  said,
"F--- you" and "Double-f--- you"
before questioning this report-
er's writing abilities. He then
invited her to perform a dis-
gusting culinary act.

After being informed of Mayor
Windsong's receipt of $10 million,
Medina said, "Ten million? She
told me four—" before stopping.

The  Mail-Journal  was  given
audio  recordings  of  Mayor
Windsong's  meeting  with  Roy
```

Burkhart-Lanning of Braun McLaren. Here is a brief excerpt of their conversation:

RBL: "Your family farm is nearly two miles as the crow flies to the Appleseed Power and Light generators, which we could reach with high-tension wire. We would pay a $650,000 per year leasing fee to turn the farm into our PG plant."

SW: "$900,000 per year. That farm has been in my family for generations."

RBL: "$775,000. Your father bought it in 2017 because he thought the government was going to legalize marijuana."

SW: "$775,000 plus an $8 million 'consulting fee' to be paid for each term I'm the mayor."

RBL: "$8 million? Your mayorship could end at any time. This year is an election year. Why wouldn't we just wait and see who the next mayor is?"

SW: "Because there's no one to run against me. Appleseed has always leaned left, but ever since The Takening and thanks to the Appleseed College Of The Arts, I can always rely on the artists' vote. No one has ever even considered running more than a token candidate in the last three elections—I mean as a political token, not a racial token, so don't 'at' me—and this year, the Reformed Democrats aren't even putting up a candidate. Even Cody f---ing Asher doesn't want to risk a run. So, my guess is you'll have me for at least twelve more years until I decide to retire. So, sure, you can wait and see who might be the mayor in four years, but oh look, it's still me, and now my fee is $10 million."

Readers can hear the audio recordings on our website.

Mayor Windsong proposed the plant as a way to provide electrical energy to Appleseed, reduce the city's landfills, and generate

revenue by accepting garbage
from outlying communities.

Professor Will Gant, the conservative candidate for mayor,
was recently taken into custody
by the Appleseed Counseling and
Enforcement Division and placed
at the Camp Breakthrough re-education camp because of his
opposition.

We will have more details as
they emerge.

Carmen's PDT rang, and she answered.

"You got it? OK, good. I'm heading back up to Appleseed right now. I should get there in about an hour. Will we be ready to run then?

"Excellent. I'll see you then."

CHAPTER 18

"*Political upstart and rabble-rouser Will Gant has finally been arrested and placed in a local inclusivity center, courtesy of the right honorable Mayor Sheila Windsong. The Mayor's office has reported that Gant was taken down after a brief scuffle and feeble resistance by Appleseed's brave Counseling and Enforcement Division. Her Honor, Mayor Windsong, has said Gant will be released on Monday after the voluntary 96-hour training session. She has been encouraged by several community leaders, including the ownership of this station, to extend Gant's detention, but she insists on following the letter of the law. We applaud Mayor Windsong's full support of law and order. We'll have more news for you tonight at 11:00 on WSED, Appleseed's best TV news station.*"

"*Mayoral candidate and unrepentant Nazi Will Gant has been arrested in the city of Appleseed, Ohio. Regular listeners will remember how Gant has groomed and indoctrinated many of Appleseed College's students, encouraging them to rebel against the school's safe and acceptable protest practices. Rumors are swirling around the west Ohio town that Gant's jack-booted thugs, the Students for a Conservative Future, have scattered to the four winds, presumably running home to the safe embrace of their parents' basements. We'll have an analysis by political historian Cheryl Clayton tomorrow morning about whether we have to worry about these Nazis expanding into our quiet, safe little community. That's tomorrow morning on Ann Arbor's Community Radio Station, WARB."*

"Good morning, Appleseed. It's a beautiful fall morning, and today kicks off the Johnny Appleseed Festival to celebrate our town's namesake. We're going to have apple bobbing, hay rides, a corn maze, and an apple pie contest. Come on out to Gordon Jump Park between 8 a.m. and 5 p.m. to visit the artists' tents, the merchant tents, and the classic car show. Speaking of which, Stanwick Richelieu-Shackleford promises to show off his fully-restored Chrysler PT Cruiser with faux wood paneling. Stay tuned to WAPPL for more local community news here on Appleseed's Golden Oldies with the hits of the 10s, 20s, and 30s. Next up is a little song to lift all our spirits: 'Dog Days Are Over' by Florence and the Machine."

"Good morning, my name is Sara Cooper-Wright, and I am the campaign manager for Will Gant for Mayor. Last night, Professor Will Gant was illegally detained by Mayor Sheila Windsong over his opposition candidacy in the upcoming mayoral election."

Sara was standing behind a lectern in the ballroom of the Bench Student Union with members of the campaign staff behind her. Katie Sartoris had joined them, standing shoulder to shoulder. The lectern was covered in microphones, and small camera drones floated in front of her, something that had been missing at Sheila's press conference. A large number of reporters, students, and staff members filled the ballroom.

After her call with Carmen yesterday, Sara gave a rousing speech in front of the library to the 457 members of Students for a Conservative Future that they were going on the offensive. She bellowed through her trusty megaphone that they "would not go quietly into that good night." Rather than hide the fact that Will had been arrested, they were going to announce it in a press conference in order to draw attention to the Mayor's illegal practices.

Sara glanced down at her prepared statement printed on paper, another practice she and her fellow campaign staffers had adopted while working with Will. They found using paper created less strain on their eyes than their PDTs, so they began printing out press releases, position statements, and speeches on paper. As she spoke, several members of the staff were handing out copies of the speech to everyone in the room. Many of the journalists were young enough that they hadn't seen a piece of paper in a long time. The staffers were also beaming links to prepared videos and written statements to everyone's PDTs as well.

Sara and her team of writers were very careful in the words they used the night before. Rather than toning everything down, she insisted they use incendiary language to put Sheila on her heels. They had even borrowed several books from Will's office about dictatorships and their practices of silencing opponents and dissidents and had peppered their statements with that language.

"Make her defend her actions rather than us trying to defend ours," she had said last night. "I want words that make it sound like she's in the wrong. We've done nothing wrong, so we don't need to defend ourselves!"

Sara continued her statement, "He was enjoying dinner with a friend and colleague, Professor Katie Sartoris," Katie raised her hand, "at Bottles and Cans Craft Brewery when he was illegally detained by members of the Appleseed Counseling and Enforcement Division, but they did not tell him why he was being taken. After repeated phone calls to the Appleseed Counseling and Enforcement Division, we learned he had been taken to Camp Breakthrough, the city's new re-education camp. Professor Sartoris was not abducted and was free to leave. She notified me of Professor Gant's abduction and illegal detention immediately afterward.

"This camp was established in secret by Mayor Sheila Windsong two months ago for the sole purpose of intimidating and bullying people who disagree with her or pose a threat to the stranglehold she has on this city. Fortunately for our democracy, incarceration in Camp Breakthrough can last no longer than ninety-six hours, so Professor Gant is expected to be released on Monday. Our legal team is working around the clock to get him out before then."

Their legal team was three law school students on fall break from Ohio State University who had traveled up to volunteer on the Gant campaign.

A young woman raised her hand. "Sara, Brooklyn Hazel-Stinebaugh of the *Celina Daily Standard*. Do you know what Professor Gant has supposedly done?"

"No one will give us a clear answer on that. He was having dinner when members of ACE abducted him without cause or justification. We are, of course, concerned for Will's safety. No one has been allowed to visit him at Camp Breakthrough, and we are not aware of his condition or health status. We're not even entirely sure if he is being kept at Camp Breakthrough, or if he has been taken to another undisclosed location."

This last point was a bit of a stretch and led to a shouting match between Kyle and Sara. He maintained that while it may have been true, it could be a little misleading.

"Do you know for sure if he's at Breakthrough?" Sara had asked. "Can you say with one hundred percent certainty that that's where he is?"

"Well, no. I guess not," Kyle admitted.

"Then it stays. Windsong's not against lying, so we'll use her tactics against her."

"But we're in danger of becoming her. I don't want to turn into the thing we hate," said Kyle.

"We won't," promised Sara. "We're not going to lie, but we're going to put her on the defensive for once. At the very least, she'll have to answer questions from the media about it, and she'll have to defend herself instead of making up her bullshit lies. Let her deny that she didn't move him instead of making up reasons why she took him."

Kyle decided he needed a pack of organic clove cigarettes and stormed out of the SCF headquarters, which at the moment was in Sara's kitchen. Volunteers streamed in and out, bringing news, supplies, coffee, and snacks for the writers. Grace and Trent were sending people out with tablets and a voter registration app, making sure that the election would go forward.

"The only way we can save Will is to beat Sheila in November!" Grace and Trent reminded their volunteers.

Back in the present moment, Shamma Etienne-Baptiste, a reporter from the *Pittsburgh Post-Gazette* media outlet, asked, "What are these re-education camps? How did they even start?"

"Mayor Windsong signed an executive order this past August that lets her round up her political opponents and disappear them for up to ninety-six hours," Sara said.

"'Disappear them'? That's pretty harsh language, isn't it?" asked the *Star Sentinel* reporter. "General Pinochet did that in the 1970s and '80s, didn't he?"

"Yes, and we believe the term fits," said Sara. "It was a practice of dictatorial regimes to 'disappear' people who spoke out against them, and this is what Mayor Windsong and ACE have done to Professor Gant. They have violated his civil rights and compromised the democratic process in Appleseed."

"Have you spoken with Will Gant?" asked Mitchell Day-Kroczek, a reporter with the *Muncie Star-Press-Journal-Times*.

"No, nobody from our staff has been able to contact Professor Gant. We tried to see him at Camp Breakthrough early this morning but were threatened with being tased and abducted ourselves if we did not leave. Even when we left, we were followed by members of ACE to this location. In fact, they are in the back of the room."

Everyone turned around, including the camera drones, and spotted two members of ACE, replete with navy blue golf shirts and white button-up sweaters. A few members of the press approached them and began to ask questions—"Is Will Gant in your custody?" "Is Professor Gant still at Camp Breakthrough?" "Are you mistreating Will Gant and the other prisoners?"—so the ACE members quickly left the building.

After they left, the media turned back to Sara, who answered their questions for another thirty minutes before finally ending the press conference.

"I would also advise you to look to the *Appleseed Mail-Journal* at 3:00 this afternoon. Carmen Cowen has a new story that will demonstrate why Mayor Sheila Windsong does not deserve to be the mayor of Appleseed, Ohio any longer."

If the ballroom had been louder when Sara had pointed out the ACE officers, it positively exploded with Sara's final statement. When asked for more details, she smiled, and she and her staff left the stage and exited through the kitchen entrance.

Deputy Mayor Enrique Medina Identified As Bomb Hoax Caller

The identity of the caller of the October 2 bomb threat at the Appleseed Mayoral Debate has been confirmed as Deputy Mayor Enrique Medina.

A recording of the bomb threat was obtained and confirmed of Medina calling his own phone from an old phone previously owned by his mother, Juliana Ramirez-Medina, who died in September 2048.

The Mail-Journal received a copy of the call from Ramirez-Medina's phone to Medina's city-provided phone. The Mail-Journal has also received video footage of Medina shutting off the house lights of the Nikki Giovanni Memorial Auditorium before pulling the fire alarm and then restoring the lights.

Medina then walked out on stage and informed Mayor Sheila Windsong and Dr. Caden Grogan, president of Appleseed College, of the bomb threat.

As Medina returned backstage, he then placed the bomb threat phone call from his mother's phone to his own phone.

"Blah blah blah, this is a bomb threat blah," Medina said during his phone call.

The time stamp on the video and the time of the phone call have been confirmed, and they show Medina making the bomb threat call after informing Windsong and Grogan about it.

The recorded audio has been confirmed to be an original. The Deep Fake Foundation (DFF) certified the audio to be Medina's voice by comparing it to several hours of public recordings of Medina at various Appleseed City Council meetings. The DFF's

AI detection software has also shown the recording to be 99.99% human in origin.

According to Appleseed Police Chief Colin Sipe-Lockwood, calling in a fake bomb threat is a second-degree felony that could lead to up to eight years in prison.

When reached for comment, Medina became verbally abusive and encouraged this reporter to commit anatomically impossible and scatological acts.

Both the Appleseed Police and the Ohio Department of Homeland Security and Well-Being are said to be investigating the bomb threat as well as possible financial crimes by Mayor Sheila Windsong, Medina, and the Braun McLaren Energy Corporation.

Click here or visit our website for more on that story.

A quick command to one's PDT or a tap of a mobile phone led to the next story.

Financial Crimes Swirl Around Mayor's Office

The Federal Bureau of Investigation today confirmed that they are investigating Appleseed Mayor Sheila Windsong, Enrique Medina, and executives of the Braun McLaren Energy Corporation for financial crimes. They are acting on information from audio recordings of conversations between Windsong, Medina, and Roy Burkhart-Lanning, the vice president for Community Relations for Braun McLaren.

According to these recordings, Mayor Windsong has solicited and accepted a $10 million consulting fee from Braun McLaren, plus $775,000 per year for leasing a rural farm property that Windsong's family has owned since 2017.

Appleseed College art professor and Windsong's ex-husband Bert Welch has also been named as a co-conspirator.

When reached for comment, Medina said, "Ten million? She told me four—" before he denied the story and said there was no proof.

The proof comes from hundreds of hours of audio recordings from a microphone hidden in the Mayor's office for the last ten years.

We have an excerpt of an audio recording on Monday, August 11, which shows the mayor solicited a bribe from Burkhart-Lanning. Visit the Appleseed website or click the link to hear the actual audio recording.

The audio of Windsong's and Burkhart-Lanning's voices has been confirmed to be original by the Deep Fake Foundation (DFF). They compared Windsong's voice to several hours of public recordings of Medina at various Appleseed City Council meetings; Burkhart-Lanning's voice was compared to dozens of hours of presentations at industry con-ferences. The DFF's AI detec-tion software has also shown the recording to be 99.99% human in origin.

The Appleseed Police Department is coordinating its efforts with the FBI to locate Mayor Windsong as well as Enrique Medina and Bert Welch.

A spokesperson for Braun McLaren said the company did not have a statement at this time but would conduct its own internal investigation into any wrongdoing.

This story comes at the same time that Enrique Medina is being investigated by the Ohio Department of Homeland Security for the bomb threat made at the October 2 Appleseed Mayoral Debates.

Click here or visit our website for more on that story.

Ten minutes after these stories were released, the FBI raided Sheila and Enrique's offices and houses. Fifteen minutes later, the FBI raided Camp Breakthrough and released all participants, who were then forced to walk five miles into town before they could find a phone.

"Sorry, the FBI is not a taxi service."

CHAPTER 19

IT WAS SATURDAY NIGHT AS WILL LAID BACK IN his bunk, reading and re-reading the graffiti left by YMWNBCA campers of summers past: *Bradley + Phoebe, 2009; Wherever you go, there you are;* and *Hawks rule, Eagles drool.* Apparently, this cabin name was the Hawks during the regular summer session. Either that, or someone really loved hawks. He wondered what happened to Bradley and Phoebe. Did they die in The Takening? Did they have a happily ever after? Or did they sneak a kiss behind the chapel, never to see each other again?

The night before, everyone participated in an encounter group session in the camp chapel and meditation retreat where they were asked to share stories about their pasts and times when they had experienced racism, sexism, homophobia, and ageism. A few stories were about events that had happened before The Takening, but those instances of overt occurrences had greatly diminished in the last twenty years.

But many more had stories of allies who were given to more subversive displays of overcompensation, gaslighting, whitesplaining, straightsplaining, mansplaining, or cisplaining. Several participants themselves were guilty of at least one or two of the offenses and felt attacked and responded with "Not all White people" or "Not all straight people." And the more they explained how they were one of the good ones, the worse things got.

Soon, the group broke down into fighting, shouting, and accusations of full-blown racism, sexism, homophobia, and ageism—all the isms. The group nearly came to blows, and Camp Breakthrough staffers—easily identified by their calming yellow sweater vests—were forced to restrain several participants with threats of tasing and loss of privileges. The worst offenders were placed in time-out corners and told to repeat "I will use my words, not my fists" one hundred times.

Will noticed that none of the staff members seemed to actually be armed or carry tasers or restraints of any kind. He wondered if it was possible to run out and make a break for it. One of the other participants had the same idea, bursting through the door to the chapel. Sixty seconds later, he was dragged back in by two other staff members wearing the same black protective gear the ACE members wore when Will was arrested, but they also wore the same yellow sweater vests.

The man was barely conscious with a burn mark on the front of his turquoise polo shirt and his hair was smoking, so he had clearly been tased. There was a large wet stain on the front of his pants as well. The staff members set the man in a chair and left. Several seconds later, he almost fell out of his chair, but Will and two others helped the man sit up as he mumbled, "Don't tase me, bro. Don't tase me, bro" over and over.

That answers that, Will thought.

This morning had been spent sitting in diversity training seminars where the presenter shared information that was at least twelve years out of date. Everyone was still a little salty after last night's blowup, so people scooted their chairs so they were away from the people who had upset them. The room was more or less divided into seven different clusters with several people who had scooted their chairs completely away from anyone so they were sitting by themselves.

Rather than addressing the issue, the presenter, Chelsea Woodfin-Levine, said she thought that today's presentation would "heal the rift caused by last night's unfortunate incidents."

Woodfin-Levine shared several slides that were crammed with eight or nine bullet points and two or three sentences per bullet point. They read every word of text, staring at the screen, and not actually looking out at her oh-so-bored audience.

It would have been easy to beam the information to everyone's PDT, but Will had left his off for his run with Katie the day before. That, and everyone else's PDT had been taken away so as to cut off all access to the outside world.

After the morning session, all participants were forced to run two miles as part of their therapy. "Fit body, fit mind," cheered the instructor, who was entirely too perky for her job. She smiled the entire time she ran alongside the other participants as they circled the camp's sports field. "Hustle for that muscle!"

Will rolled his eyes so hard he stumbled but recovered in time.

Lunch was vegan lasagna with unseasoned french fries, followed by another equally boring seminar with Chelsea Woodfin-Levine. Will said to the guy sitting next to him, "I don't know which is more bland: lunch or this."

The other guy snickered and covered his mouth. Woodfin-Levine whipped around and said, "What was that? I didn't hear that."

"Nothing," said Will, feeling like a kid getting caught passing notes in class.

"No, no, Participant Gant. You clearly find this whole thing amusing. You apparently don't take the idea of diversity and inclusion very seriously, so why don't you share what you said with the rest of us?"

Will shrugged and stood up. "I said I didn't know which was more bland: this or lunch."

The rest of the participants cracked up at this. It wasn't that funny, but everyone was punchy after last night's drama.

"That's not funny, Participant Gant," said Woodfin-Levine.

"I disagree, Pedagogue Woodfin-Levine," said Will. He was determined to be as much of a pain in the ass as he could without actually getting tased. It was actually kind of fun because he was sure they wouldn't actually punish him unless he tried to escape. In the meantime, he was enjoying just goofing off and being the class clown, something he never did when he was a kid because he didn't want to face his parents' wrath. This was fun!

"Pedagogue? You motherfu—sit down, CHiPdammit!" shouted Woodfin-Levine.

"Fine, but I'm doing it because I want to, not because you told me to," said Will. The rest of the group laughed.

After the session was another run, followed by more vegan lasagna and unseasoned fries. Afterward, the participants were granted some free time followed by another encounter group session. There were more staff members on hand this time, many of them carrying tasers and restraints. They were seated around the room and looked ready for action, even though they were bored out of their skulls.

Tonight, no one wanted to share any stories, so the session was wrapped up after thirty-seven awkward minutes, and everyone had a chance to return to their cabins. Will read one of the books left in the cabin, retired to his bunk, and waited for sleep to overtake him.

By the time "Taps" played on the camp PA system at 10:00—a tradition since the camp was first started in 1949—Will was wide awake and wondering what he could do to escape. But without a PDT, he was just going to have to wait until Monday, assuming they didn't find a reason to detain him any longer. He at least wanted to get word to Katie and Sara and let them know he was alright. Or get the legal team working on getting him released. If only he could—

Will froze as the front door squeaked open and then turned and eased closed without slamming. There were only two other participants in the cabin, and they were both snoring heavily, worn out by the running sessions. The moon was in its last quarter, so there was not much moonlight coming in through the windows. But the faint glow of a nightlight helped Will see the shape as it moved toward him. He closed his eyes partially so he could appear asleep but could still watch the stranger.

The figure crept over to one of Will's snoring bunkmates and then to the other, as if checking them out to make sure they were still asleep. Will could make out a shape of some unusual headgear over the figure's face and—He? She? They?—held something small and cylindrical in their right hand.

They continued to slink over to Will and brought the cylinder down, pointing it at Will. When the figure got close enough, Will snapped on his bunk lamp and twisted to grab the figure's right wrist with his left hand.

The figure cried out and clawed at the headgear with his other hand. "My eyes, you fuck!" cried Bert Welch.

Will saw that the cylinder was a hypodermic syringe. He twisted Bert's arm and slammed it up against the top bunk frame, forcing him to drop it. Bert cried out again, and Will felt oddly satisfied. He wasn't used to violence, but this felt good. He let go of Will's arm and punched him in the jaw. Bert slumped to the ground but didn't go down. Will shoved him back, sprang out of bed, and punched him two more times, knocking him out.

The two other men in the cabin barely broke their snoring.

Will grabbed the hypodermic from the floor and held it at Bert's neck while bunching his collar up in his other fist. "What's in this?" he hissed in Bert's ear. "And what will happen if I jam it in your neck?"

Bert snapped awake and tried to jerk his head away from the needle. "There's nothing in there!" he shouted.

"Shut up!" whispered Will. The two cabin mates continued snoring. "What were you going to inject me with?"

"Nothing!" Bert whispered.

"Bullshit. Let me inject you and see what kind of nothing there is." Will pressed the needle into Bert's neck, breaking the skin.

Bert mewled and squirmed, fighting to free himself from Will's grip.

"I mean there is literally nothing in there!"

"Then why were you going to inject me?"

Bert stopped struggling. "Air. It would put an air bubble in your bloodstream and give you a heart attack."

Will relaxed his grip but didn't let go. He jerked the needle back out of Bert's neck. "Who told you to do this?"

"No one," Bert whispered. "I'm here of my own volition."

"Bullshit. Your work is derivative and accidentalist, remember? You haven't had an independent thought in years. Now tell me, or I'll jab this in your neck and see what happens."

"Sheila!" he whispered, his voice cracking. "It was Sheila."

TWO DAYS EARLIER — THE OFFICE OF MAYOR SHEILA WINDSONG

"Bert, I need you." Bert played the voice message from Sheila for the tenth time, tapping his PDT temple over and over. "Bert, I need you. Bert, I need you." Finally, he let it play to its end.

"Bert, I need you. Come to my office as soon as you can."

It was 9:05 a.m. on Thursday morning, and Bert was at Sheila's office thirty minutes later, where Tiffani buzzed him in.

"I'm here for you, Sheila. I need you, too." He rushed to embrace her and squeezed her in his arms.

"Not like—let me go. Bert, you're smothering me. Let me go!"

Bert loosened his grip but didn't let go. "Sorry, sorry, I just got caught up in the moment. I've been waiting for this day."

"Oh, er, me too. Uh, darling," Sheila said, extricating herself from Bert's embrace. "I have something I need to ask you." She turned her head toward the open door. "Tiffani, close the door, please."

"Computer, close the door," Tiffani called.

"Don't worry. I've already broken up with Katie."

"You did? Why? Uh, that is, why did you wait so long to tell me?"

"I wasn't ready to talk about it. But now it doesn't matter. You and I can be together again." He went to embrace her again, but Sheila put her hand on his chest and held him off. "First, I need something from you."

"Anything, darling. I'll do anything to be with you again."

"I'm counting on it," Sheila said.

"What?"

"I mean, I knew I could count on you. Now, listen, here's what I—"

"Do you need to sweep the room for bugs?"

"No, I swept it this morning. But I can't be too careful. Sit down on the couch."

"I like where this is going," said Bert, fumbling with his belt.

"Eww, no! Er, I mean, not until this is done. If you do this for me, then we can finally be together again."

She sat down close to Bert and rested her hand on the inside of his thigh, near his knee. She swallowed hard and closed her eyes for a few seconds, as if saying a silent prayer. She leaned in and whispered in Bert's ear, "Will Gant is a serious threat to me in this mayor's race. If he wins the race, I won't be able to pursue this plasma gasification plant, and I won't make any money off of this. And if that happens, we can never be together."

"How does that work?"

"Because with my millions, I can retire once the plant is built, and we can go wherever in the world we want."

"I've always dreamed of living in Europe," said Bert. "Being surrounded by all those museums, all those artists."

"And we can have that," said Sheila, her hand creeping farther up Bert's thigh. She suppressed a shudder. "But we won't if Will becomes the mayor."

"How should I do it?"

Sheila stood up and retrieved her purse from her desk. "With this." She pulled out a hypodermic syringe and held it out in both hands as if she were offering a gift.

"What's in it?" Bert asked.

"Nothing."

"Er, what am I supposed to put in it?"

"Nothing, you id—I mean, you're not supposed to put anything in it. Just inject some air into his bloodstream, and it will look like he had a heart attack."

"Ah," said Bert, not really understanding.

"People will think he died of natural causes, and no one will question it. Just jab it in his leg and push down on the plunger. He'll have a heart attack, I'll continue to be mayor, I'll divorce Fallyn, and we can start over again." She crossed over to Bert and put her arms around him, resting her head on his shoulder. She grimaced and stuck her tongue out as if she were gagging.

"But how am I going to get into his place and actually do it?"

"Ah, that's the best part. You don't have to get into his place. In about six hours, Gant is about to become a four-day guest of Camp Breakthrough, our new Inclusivity Counseling Center for the next four days."

"Sheila? She sent you to kill me?"

"Yes, she said if I killed you, she would take me back."

"Fucking idiot," hissed Will. "Why would she want to do that?"

"Hey!" stage-whispered Bert. "I'm a fucking prize!"

"How did you get in here?" Will demanded. He tightened his grip on Bert's shirt collar, cutting into his windpipe and jugular, making him light-headed.

"Back fence," gasped Bert. "I climbed the back fence."

"There's no security?"

"No, there's only security out front. I can't breathe."

"Where'd you park?"

"What?"

"You didn't walk here, so where did you park your car?"

"I can't breathe," Bert wheezed. Will loosened his grip for a few seconds so Bert could catch his breath and then retightened it.

"It's on the county road behind here. Climb the fence and go through the woods. Please, you're killing me."

"Where's your PDT?"

"I left it in the car. Now, please. Let me go, and I'll leave."

"Sure thing," said Will. He released Bert's collar, and Bert took a deep breath, right before Will punched him in the jaw, knocking him out. He took off Bert's black sweatshirt and trundled Bert into his bed. Bert started to wake up again, so Will punched him one more time and shook his fist at the pain. He had to quit doing that!

Will covered Bert with his blanket and turned off the small lamp. He put on Bert's night vision goggles and realized they were cheap kids' goggles like a 10-year-old might get for his birthday. He took Bert's wallet and keys and crept out the door of the cabin, easing it closed behind him.

Bert had left the goggles on, so Will was able to see immediately. As long he didn't look at any light sources directly, he could see everything in green. He crouched down and looked around, removing the goggles again. Most of the cabins had front porch lights, so he couldn't use the goggles at the moment.

Will spotted a couple guards fifty yards away walking in front of another cabin, so he ducked quickly behind the cabin before they turned around and spotted him. He crouched down, trying to make himself look small.

The cabins were arranged in a ring, and Will was now outside the ring in the dark. Unless the guards had night vision goggles themselves, they wouldn't be able to see him The woods were directly behind him, so he crept forward, making sure not to step on any twigs or branches.

Will moved slowly away from the camp, trying to move in a straight line so he didn't accidentally wander in a large circle. That often happened to people crossing unfamiliar terrain—they would end up traveling in a very large circle—so Will turned and looked behind him once in a while to make sure he was still heading in the right direction.

He stopped and crouched down a few times, looking behind him to see if anyone had discovered his absence. No one had raised any alarms, there weren't any spotlights or raised voices, and no one seemed to be pursuing him.

After several minutes and nearly half a mile, Will came out of the other side of the woods to a country road. He looked left and right and spotted Bert's car just a couple hundred yards down the road. He walked toward the car, waiting to see if anyone would spring out and try to recapture him, but no one did.

Will climbed into the car, located Bert's PDT in the glove compartment, and put it on.

"Initializing," said the PDT. "New user detected."

"Guest mode," said Will. Guest mode was a security feature that would limit the use of a PDT but would also allow the police and the owner to locate it if it were ever stolen.

"Call Katie," Will said. The PDT screen lit up with Katie's name, and he could hear the ringing tones through the bone-conducting earpiece in the temple end.

"What the hell do you want, Bert?" Katie said when she answered.

"Katie! It's me, Will."

"What?"

"It's me, Will. I took Bert's PDT, and I escaped."

"Oh, my CHiP! Where are you?"

"I'm heading to town. Bert tried to kill me at the camp—"

"WHAT?"

"I can't tell you now. I have to get rid of these PDTs. But Sheila got him to try to kill me. I overpowered him and took his keys. I'm driving his car now, and I'm heading to town."

"Don't do that. They'll be looking for you. Which way are you heading?"

Will checked the car's dashboard. "East," he said.

"OK, you're about ten miles from a Super-Mart that's open twenty-four hours."

"I know that one."

"Ditch the car about a half mile away and then jog to the Super-Mart but try to stay off the streets. Go behind the building, and I'll drive there and pick you up. I'll be there in twenty minutes. I may even be there before you. I'll let Sara know what's going on."

"Great, thanks. I'll see you soon. 'Bye." Will disconnected the call and threw the PDTs out the window. He drove the speed limit so as not to attract any undue attention and reached the area in about fifteen minutes. He pulled into a residential neighborhood that butted up to the Super-Mart, parked Bert's car toward the very back of the neighborhood, and then jogged through the woods to reach the back of the Super-Mart.

Katie was sitting in her car, looking toward the front of the store, expecting Will to come from that way. He approached her car from the rear and waved his arms so she would notice him in her mirror and not pee her pants if he banged on the window.

She sprang out of the car, ran to Will, and threw herself into his arms, smothering him with kisses. Sara popped out of the passenger seat and hugged them both. Will put his arms around them both but made sure to only kiss Katie.

"Alright! Alright! I'm safe. It's OK," he said as much for his benefit as theirs. "We'd better get out of here."

"We'll get a hotel in Cincinnati and lay low there. Lie down in the backseat and get under the blanket, at least until we're out of town," ordered Katie. "We've got a lot to fill you in on." And they told him everything that had happened in the last thirty-six hours.

CHAPTER 20

"**M**a'am, is there anyone besides you and your children in the car?" asked the border agent at the Sault Ste. Marie border crossing from the United States into Canada.

"Uhh, no?" said Caitlyn Burkhart-Lanning. She was driving her family's Tesla Hologram SUV and was at the border waiting to be cleared by US customs officials.

"Is that a question or an answer, ma'am?" said Bella Sproles-Benevides, the US border agent.

"That sounded like an answer to me," said the Canadian border agent, Taylor Hayden-Drew, who shared the booth with Sproles-Benevides.

"What? She clearly used upspeak. You know? Where your voice rises at the end of a sentence? Like in a question? Moron?" said Sproles-Benevides, whose family had a long history of protecting US borders and transportation hubs.

"She sounded totally normal to me," said Hayden-Drew, a member of Canada's First Nations whose own family had a long history of dealing with interlopers and invaders. "And so did all of your statements."

"It was clearly a question," said Sproles-Benevides. "There was a rising inflection at the end of a declarative statement. Like this one?"

"Sorry, I'm not hearing it," said Hayden-Drew.

"Are you out of your mind? It was as clear as a bell!"

"It clearly wasn't clear if I didn't hear—hey, stop!"

"Ma'am, stop right there! Stop, or we will be forced to take action!"

"No, you won't. I will," said Hayden-Drew, reaching over and pressing a large red button without looking. "The subject is clearly on Canadian soil now, and so you will take no further action or else that could be construed as an invasion."

"Listen, you jumped-up little hoser. Just because you have a uniform and a little red button doesn't mean you're in charge in here. I've got half a mind to come over there and beat your—"

"Ah-ah!" interrupted Hayden-Drew. "Stay on your side of the line!" He pointed at the bright yellow line that ran straight through the middle of the guard shack. The shack sat right on the US-Canadian border and was split by the yellow line that kept all border guards in their respective countries.

Thirty feet away, a large steel pole shot up out of the tarmac in the middle of the road, and the Tesla Hologram smashed into it, completely crumpling the front end. The airbags deployed, and everyone was unhurt. The rear trunk popped open, Roy Burkhart-Lanning clambered out and began running farther into Canada, leaving his wife and children behind.

Taylor Hayden-Drew smacked another large red button without a glance, managing to look smug while doing so, which irritated Bella Sproles-Benevides to no end. Three seconds later, Roy was snared in a net and lifted twenty feet off the ground as several Canadian agents rushed to retrieve Roy, Caitlyn, and their two children.

"You're such an asshole," said Bella.

"Shrew," said Taylor.

"I hate you."

"I hate you more."

"I'm so hot for you right now," said Bella.

"Oh, fuck, me too," said Taylor. "Your place or mine tonight?"

"Yours. Mine is still a wreck from the last time you were over."

Two hours later, Roy Burkhart-Lanning was sitting in an interrogation room in the American Sault Ste. Marie. His wife was in a second interrogation room, and the two children were sitting with a patrol officer playing video games on the department's murder board, which hadn't been used for its original purpose in three years.

"Things will go a lot easier for you and your family if you'll just tell us what you know," said Agent David Cowper-Doyle with the FBI.

"You don't want to drag your family down with you, do you?" said Agent Mitchell Schenck-Doyle (no relation), also with the FBI.

Inspector Mikayla Mercer-Mercier from the Royal Canadian Mounted Police spoke up from her seat next to the table. "Right now, your wife is looking at charges of accessory to immigration fraud and conspiracy to commit immigration fraud by the Canadian government."

"Is she facing charges in the US?"

"Eh, not really?" said Agent Cowper-Doyle.

"What would we charge her with—wanting to flee to Canada?" asked Special Agent Schenck-Doyle. "I mean, I wouldn't flee there, but some people are clearly willing to settle in life."

"Hey!" protested Inspector Mercer-Mercier.

"Hey!" echoed Roy. "What could happen to her?" he asked after a few seconds.

Inspector Mercer-Mercier's shoulders slumped. "Well, uh, she'd, that is, she would—"

Agent Cowper-Doyle sighed. "They'd give her a ticket, and she would be banished from Canada for five years."

Roy snorted. "Oh, no! Not that! Anything but that! Whatever shall my family do? Where will we spend our winters?"

"Alright, alright, tough guy. Just because we're in your country doesn't mean you hold all the cards," said Inspector Mercer-Mercier.

"What are you gonna do—extradite me for a ticket?"

Inspector Mercer-Mercier leaped to her feet and sent her chair clattering backward. "Don't think we won't, buddy! We'll extradite her ass and make her pay that ticket."

"How much is the ticket actually for?"

"$1,000," said Inspector Mercer-Mercier, folding her arms triumphantly.

"Canadian or US?"

She slumped her shoulders again. "Canadian."

"So that's what, $800? I've got that much in my wallet. Tell you what: I'll pay it now, and we'll call it even."

"Deal!" said Inspector Mercer-Mercier.

Roy reached for his wallet and handed Inspector Mercer-Mercier eight $100 bills. She counted them twice, folded them, and tucked them into her suit pocket.

"Sucker! We'd have let you plead down to $500," she shouted. "Canadian!" She cackled and ran out the door, slamming it behind her.

"God, I hate her," said Agent Cowper-Doyle.

"Agreed," said Agent Schenck-Doyle.

"So is that it? Are we good here? Am I free to go?"

"Sure," said Agent Cowper-Doyle. "Pay a $500 fine, and we'll completely overlook all the counts of bribery, racketeering, price fixing, interfering with an election, corruption of a public official, and violating the Fugitive Felon Act. Plus, conspiracy to commit all of those crimes."

"When you say it like that, I don't think you're going to let me pay a fine."

"Really? What gave you that idea?" sneered Agent Cowper-Doyle.

"You're looking at spending decades of your life in prison," said Agent Schenck-Doyle.

"Many decades," said Agent Cowper-Doyle. "You're looking at a minimum of 250 years."

Roy gulped. "Is there anything I can do to reduce that?"

"Well, there's time off for good behavior," said Agent Cowper-Doyle.

"How much?"

"You could get 125 years knocked off your sentence." Roy did the math in his head. He'd be 167 when he got out. His grandchildren would be dead by then.

"What if I could give you Sheila Windsong?"

"We've already got her on audio soliciting a bribe and you agreeing to give it to her," said Agent Cowper-Doyle.

"And?" said Roy.

"What do you mean 'and'?" said Agent Cowper-Doyle.

"What do you mean 'what do I mean'?"

"What do you mean 'what do you mean "what do—"

"Goddammit, we're not doing that again!" said Agent Schenck-Doyle. "Last time you did that for five minutes."

"Fine," groused Agent Cowper-Doyle. He folded his hands together and held them in front of his chest as if he were about to sing. "Please share your thoughts with us, Mr. Burkhart-Lanning."

"I mean, is the only thing you have an audio recording? That's not going to get you a conviction. Hell, we could have been rehearsing a play or making a joke."

"Were you rehearsing a play?" asked Agent Schenck-Doyle.

"Umm, sure, yeah. That's what we were doing."

"We're not stupid," said Agent Cowper-Doyle. "You clearly weren't rehearsing a play."

"Well, you're stupider than you look if you think an audio recording is going to get you a conviction."

"Hey, fuck you, asshole!" shouted Agent Schenck-Doyle, lurching over the table toward Roy.

"I'll give you evidence!" shouted Roy, shoving his seat back out of Agent Schenck-Doyle's reach.

"What?" said Agent Schenck-Doyle.

"I'll give you evidence of the payoffs if you give me full immunity."

"Don't you want immunity for your family?" asked Agent Cowper-Doyle.

"You already said my wife wasn't in trouble."

"Fuck! You've got to quit giving away our bargaining chips," Agent Cowper-Doyle said to his partner.

"Sorry," said Agent Schenck-Doyle.

"If you grant me full immunity and a new identity with an overseas location of my choosing, I'll give you the names of the people who actually made the payoffs from Braun McLaren as well as all the financial records related to those transfers.”

“We can get that with a subpoena,” said Agent Cowper-Doyle.

“Not all of them. I’m thinking the south of France.”

“Bullshit, our forensic accountants will track them down.”

“Not the ones in the Swiss accounts. I’m thinking a nice chateau in the Bordeaux region.”

“The Swiss have never shared banking details,” Agent Schenck-Doyle muttered to Agent Cowper-Doyle.

“Plus, you’ll get all the other ‘financial agreements’ Braun McLaren has made in five other cities worth over three billion dollars,” said Burkhart-Lanning.

“*Vive la France!*,” said Agents Cowper-Doyle and Schenck-Doyle. The two shook his hand, grinning like idiots.

Sheila and Fallyn were huddled together in the storm shelter on Sheila’s dad’s old farm, lights out, not making a sound. They would occasionally whisper to one another, but they otherwise stayed quiet. They could see by the night-vision capabilities of their PDTs, and from what Sheila could see, Fallyn was pissed. More pissed than Sheila had ever seen her.

“I can’t believe you would do that,” Fallyn hissed for the seventeenth time. Sheila knew exactly how many times because she had been counting.

“I will tell you, for the seventeenth fucking time, I did it for us.”

“Bullshit! You did it for you.”

“How many times do I have to tell you? I wanted to make sure we could take care of ourselves in our old age.”

"More than fucking seventeen!"

"Shh!" shushed Sheila. She was sure she had heard a sharp shriek in the shrubbery near the shelter's shutters.[1]

"Don't shush me!" hissed Fallyn.

"I heard something outside," Sheila hissed back.

The doors were yanked open, and several members of the Ohio Department of Homeland Security and Well-Being tactical unit stormed the shelter, rifles aimed, laser sights converging over the hearts of both Sheila and Fallyn.

"Go, go, go!" the ODHSWB agents shouted. "Go, go, go!" They loved to shout "Go, go, go!" whenever they stormed a room or building.

The two women threw their hands in the air and froze.

"Clear!" called different agents. The room was only twelve feet by twelve feet, but when ODHSWB agents weren't shouting "Go, go, go!" they loved shouting "Clear!" Each officer made sure to shout "Clear!" at least twice, scoping out each corner and behind each paint can before standing down.

"All clear, sir!" one of the agents shouted back outside. The agents parted as if Moses himself was entering the room.

"Sirs, ma'ams, or preferred nonbinary designations, I'm Lieutenant Moses Somsri-Ferguson. Which one of you is Mayor Windsong?"

Sheila wiggled her fingers; neither she nor Fallyn had moved yet.

"Mayor Windsong, I am arresting you for bribery, racketeering, price fixing, interfering with an election, and corruption. There may be more charges forthcoming pending the final outcome of the investigation into these alleged crimes."

Another agent whispered into Lieutenant Somsri-Ferguson's ear.

---

[1] A little present for the audiobook reader.

"Oh, and conspiracy to violate the Fugitive Felon Act."

"Conspiracy to violate the what?" said Sheila.

"You were going to flee the country with your bribe money and the sale of your farm."

"No, we weren't," said Fallyn. "We were going to go to Oregon."

"Shh!" shushed Sheila.

"They can't charge us for attempting to flee the country if we were only going to Oregon," Fallyn continued.

"Oh. Er, yes, that's right, we were only going to Oregon to visit some friends," said Sheila. Her forehead was beaded with sweat, and she looked like she wanted to throw up.

"Then why did you purchase a one-way ticket from Seattle to Auckland, New Zealand?" asked Lieutenant Somsri-Ferguson.

"Aww, you were going to take me to New Zealand?" said Fallyn, getting a little misty-eyed.

"A single one-way ticket," clarified Lieutenant Somsri-Ferguson.

"What?" shouted Fallyn

"Wha-a-a-at? That's crazy. I would never do that," said Sheila.

"Plus a copy of the guidebook, *Emigrating to New Zealand for the Newly Single Woman.*"

"What the hell, Sheila?" yelled Fallyn.

"That's a lie!" Sheila said.

"Plus, you had spoken with a realtor about finding a one-bedroom condo in Auckland."

"You bitch!" Fallyn screamed, punching Sheila in the mouth and knocking her out.

Five hours after the ODHSWB arrested Sheila and Fallyn, the FBI escorted Braun McLaren's CEO, CFO, CMO, and the entire board of directors out of their offices with dozens of media outlets streaming the arrests. They were charged with a combined total of 387 counts of bribery, racketeering, price fixing, interfering with an election, corruption of a public official, and violating the Fugitive Felon Act. Plus, conspiracy to commit all of those crimes.

They settled the entire matter for a $500,000 fine and 400 hours of community service, which they served by hiring disadvantaged teenagers to caddy for them on weekends.

The following year, Braun McLaren had its most profitable year ever, and each of the previously arrested executives received a $20 million bonus.

Bert Welch had been caught trying to escape from Camp Breakthrough and was detained for a week until they realized he was not actually a participant. He was released on his own recognizance, only to discover that Sheila had been arrested and that no one was looking for him for attempted murder. Rather than risk facing any retaliation from Will or Katie, he resigned from ACOTA, cashed out his pension, and moved to Albuquerque, New Mexico where he found a job teaching art to elderly tourists and occasionally serving as a male escort for some of the wealthier tourists.

Enrique Medina avoided being taken into custody and escaped to Mexico before sneaking his way through Ecuador, Argentina, and Brazil, living in cheap hotels or on the street for the next six months before he finally found work on a freighter that landed in Portugal, which he believed did not have an extradition treaty with the United States.

It actually did, but since he only fled the country with his own savings, plus $2 million embezzled from the Inclusivity Counseling Department, no one really cared. He read back over old *Mail-Journal* stories to see that his name was barely mentioned. He cried when he realized he could have just caught a flight out of the Cincinnati/Northern Kentucky International Airport and been here in a matter of hours.

Enrique became an English teacher, married another teacher, and raised a family, never telling any of them about his past. His family found out when he died at age 82 and they found his journals and poetry books. They published his poetry, which every poetry critic agreed was the worst poetry of the 21st century, beating out the poetry slam wave of 2015 – 2020.

MONDAY, NOVEMBER 3, 2053 — CHAPMAN COUNTY COURTHOUSE

Sheila's trial started almost three weeks later, on October 28, for bribery, racketeering, interfering with an election, and corruption—the price-fixing charges were dropped in a badly negotiated plea bargain—and ended the day before the election. She had pulled out of the election, and no one could be found to run in her place, so Will was guaranteed to become Appleseed's newest mayor.

The US prosecutors agreed to drop the Fugitive Felon Act charges since she hadn't actually made any effort to leave the country, let alone Appleseed. The case was reviewed by a three-judge panel comprised of two humans and the TrialJudge3000™ artificial intelligence system.

The case took less than a week and was covered heavily by all the area media channels, as well as national media. The Chapman County Court system made over $1.5 million on its pay-per-view stream through the in-court cameras, as well as picking up a major sponsor, the New Zealand Department of Tourism. ("When you want to escape from it all, think New Zealand!")

Sheila's attorneys made a good case, but in the end, Tiffani's audio recordings did her in, as well as Roy Burkhart-Lanning's testimony, which he delivered via streaming from an unnamed location, although several acres of healthy grapevines could be seen outside his office window.

Fallyn, still feeling the sting of Sheila's near abandonment, gleefully testified against her now ex-wife, also via a video stream. She had taken Sheila's plane ticket and copy of *Emigrating to New Zealand for the Newly Single Woman* and put it to good use. She had also sold Sheila's farm to the city for $500,000, and the plasma gasification was still built by one of Braun McLaren's competitors without all the bribes and consulting fees.

Exactly two hours after both the prosecution and defense rested, and one day before the election, Sheila was called back into the courtroom.

"Sheila Windsong, also known as Sheila Jenkins," said the presiding judge. "After extensive deliberation and debate between the judges and TrialJudge3000™, we have reached a 2 – 1 verdict. In the counts of bribery, racketeering, interfering with an election, and corruption, we find you guilty on all counts and sentence you to eighty-seven years in the St. Louis Women's Correctional Institute."

Her KNCLD score dropped to 28, and she was forced to attend weekly training sessions for her entire prison sentence.

CHAPTER 21

"Following her arrest and resignation from office, disgraced mayor Sheila Windsong was soundly defeated in this year's mayoral election with 85% of the vote. Noted history professor and political newcomer Will Gant has become Appleseed's newest mayor, despite many, uhh, detractors and pitfalls along the way. Mayor-Elect Gant will take the oath of office on January 17, 2054, and city councilwoman Naomi Saito will serve as the interim mayor until that time. We, uhh, congratulate Mayor-Elect Gant on his, uhh, well-earned victory and look forward to covering his tenure for the next four years. We would also like to apologize for our past statements and, uhh, any insinuations we may have made in covering Mayor-Elect Gant's political stance. We have heard from Mr. Gant's attorneys and will have a statement to share as well as more news for you tonight at 11:00 on WSED, Appleseed's best TV news station."

"Little trouble in The Big Appleseed, Ohio. Mayor Sheila Windsong has been arrested and found guilty on several counts *related to corruption surrounding a proposed plasma gasification plant. She was found guilty on all counts and sentenced to 87 years in federal prison. It also seems that, uhh, Professor Will Gant has, uhh, been elected as the mayor of this fine town. In light of the stories about Sheila Windsong and her corruption charges, we, uhh, would like to apologize to Mayor Gant for our enthusiasm and possible misunderstanding of his political beliefs. We have heard from Mr. Gant's attorneys and will have a statement to share on our political call-in show this afternoon as well as further commentary by political analyst Cheryl Clayton. That's at 3:00 on Ann Arbor's Community Radio Station, WARB."*

"Good morning, Appleseed! It looks like there are some big goings-on at City Hall this week. There will be a mid-week farmer's market in front of City Hall as folks get ready for Thanksgiving. We'll also have artists' tents and face painting, although I'm afraid the classic car show has been canceled on account of the weather. Oh, and apparently we have a new mayor. Congratulations, Bill Grant. Stay tuned to WAPPL for more local community news here on Appleseed's Golden Oldies with the hits of the 10s, 20s, and 30s. Next up is a personal favorite, 'WAP' by Cardi B and Megan Thee Stallion."

"Congratulations, Mr. Mayor," said Sara Cooper-Wright. The election for Appleseed's mayor came off without a hitch. The electronic voting system tabulated all of the votes and spit out the results five minutes after the polls closed. Will Gant had won the election, garnering 850 votes out of the 1,000 eligible voters. Even in 2053, people just didn't care about city elections.

Despite being arrested and charged with numerous crimes, Sheila still had some supporters who refused to accept what the mainstream media showed them, even when presented with audio and video evidence showing that she had, in fact, attempted to defraud the citizens of Appleseed and committed numerous crimes.

"Thank you, Councilperson Cooper-Wright," said Will. The two clicked the champagne glasses they had just been handed.

Sara, without wanting to, had received 457 write-in votes from Will, his friends, and members of the Students for a Conservative Future. She beat out Zack Windless, who decided to exit the race after news of his receipt of a "campaign donation" from Braun McLaren made front-page news a week after Sheila's arrest. It was a nugget she threw to the FBI in exchange for some of her charges to be dropped. The FBI dropped the price-fixing charges, which would have, at most, added six months to her total sentence.

Will, Sara, and the rest of the SCF were holding a victory party in the Appleseed Grand Hotel's ballroom, along with nearly five hundred of their supporters and friends. They had just received the news and were standing together back in the green room before they went out on stage to make their victory speeches and do their media interviews.

"I'm looking forward to working with you," Sara said. "We make a pretty good team."

"Ah, about that," said Will. "I'm not actually going to be the mayor."

"What?!" Sara shouted. "You can't do that! The only reason I agreed to be on the City Council was because you were going to be the mayor."

"But I never wanted to be mayor. Remember our lunch with Cody and Naomi?"

"God, that seems like years ago."

"They told me they wanted me to run, but they didn't expect me to win. The only reason I ran was because I wasn't going to win. It was my civic duty, but it was never my dream or desire."

Sara stared into her glass without saying anything.

"I don't want to do this without you," she said, sniffing. A tear trickled down her cheek and a second one threatened to follow.

"But you can," urged Will. "I'm not going anywhere. I'm staying right here in Appleseed, and I'm staying at the college. I just won't be the mayor."

"Then who's going to do it?"

"Cody Asher. He wanted to be mayor eight years ago, but he lost to Sheila, so he never ran again. I've already appointed him as the deputy mayor and signed all the forms with the city clerk's office. Then, I'm going to step down, and he'll step in to fill the position. Don't tell anybody just yet. You and Cody are the only ones who know. Oh, and Katie."

The other tear rolled down Sara's cheek and then another. She threw her arms around Will and squeezed. "I feel like we're going our separate ways," she choked. "Like when Frodo left with the elves to go to the Undying Land."

"I promise you we're not going anywhere. I'm staying in Appleseed, and you are, too. We'll have lunch at The Three Fives or the Bottle and Can, and you can fill me in on what's going on."

Kyle burst into the room, his suit fitting like he was on the cover of a men's fashion magazine. Sara raised an eyebrow, and her face flushed a bit. Kyle caught the look and smiled at her.

"Hey, are you ready to go onstage, Mr. Mayor?" Kyle asked, turning back to Will. "The crowd is getting restless."

The two followed Kyle and made their way to the stage where the lectern had been placed front and center.

"My fellow Appleseedlings!" Will shouted into the microphones. "Thank you very much for this great honor. When I ran for mayor, I never actually expected to be elected."

The crowd cheered wildly.

"But we showed them that honesty and integrity will win over graft and corruption!"

The crowd cheered once more.

"We showed that the people of Appleseed deserve a mayor who is eager to guide them and has the experience, knowledge, and willingness to serve the people of this wonderful city."

The crowd screamed, whistled, and thundered their applause.

"People of Appleseed, thank you for this fine honor and for making me the mayor. I can promise you that you will be well served by a man of integrity, a man who wants only the very best for the city, and a man who has been a pillar of strength for so many of us for the last several months."

The crowd exploded and shouted themselves raw.

Will smiled at Katie and gave her a wink. The two were married six months later.

BOOK CLUB QUESTIONS

1. There are several characters from *Mackinac Island Nation* who make an in-person appearance in the book, their name appears, or in one case, their daughter makes an appearance. Did you catch any of these?

2. I also used several notable people who lived in or came from Ohio—Gordon Jump, Johnny Bench, Nikki Giovanni, etc. Who would you have included in this roster?

3. If you had the power to give funding to any government or social program, what would you give it to? What does the ideal situation look like?

4. What could happen if you gave them too much money? How could things go badly?

5. Who was your favorite character? If you were to place them in another story, what would it be about? What situation would they be in?

6. Who did you love to hate? What was irritating about them?

7. I wrote the introduction to this book in early 2020. When
    I finished the book in 2023, I saw that I was not far off;
    it was not as much of an exaggeration as it was when
    I first started. What would have made it more of an
    exaggeration?

8. In Chapter 5, Will says, "I sometimes think maybe the
    dead got the better end of the deal." Given the state of
    society in 2053, and everything that he described during
    The Takening, what do you think?

9. When there is no one to "push against," no loyal oppo-
    sition, power can run unchecked, and you get people
    like Sheila Windsong in positions of authority. Agree
    or disagree?

10. In 2053, there are no more "newspapers" and very few "TV
    news" stations, just multimedia outlets—newspapers
    with TV news shows; TV stations that run like newspapers.
    What do you think the media will look like in 30 years?

11. For the classic cars mentioned in every WAPPL news
    broadcast, I tried to pick some of the worst cars from
    those decades. What would you have picked?

AUTHOR BIO

Erik Deckers is a professional writer and the author of *Mackinac Island Nation*. He is also the co-author of four social media marketing books. Erik has been blogging since 1997 and a newspaper humor columnist since 1994. He was the Spring 2016 writer-in-residence at the Jack Kerouac House in Orlando, FL, and is now president of their board of directors.

Discover more at
4HorsemenPublications.com

10% off using HORSEMEN10